THE
SLEEPERS

THE
SLEEPERS

A NOVEL

MATTHEW GASDA

Arcade Publishing • New York

Arcade Publishing books may be purchased in bulk at special discounts for sales promotion, corporate gifts, fund-raising, or educational purposes. Special editions can also be created to specifications. For details, contact the Special Sales Department, Arcade Publishing, 307 West 36th Street, 11th Floor, New York, NY 10018 or arcade@skyhorsepublishing.com.

Arcade Publishing® is a registered trademark of Skyhorse Publishing, Inc.®, a Delaware corporation.

Visit our website at www.arcadepub.com.

10 9 8 7 6 5 4 3 2 1

First Edition

Library of Congress Cataloging-in-Publication Data is available on file.

Jacket design by David Ter-Avanesyan
Cover painting by August Lamm

Print ISBN: 978-1-64821-125-6
Ebook ISBN: 978-1-64821-126-3

Printed in the United States of America

To my friend David Yaffe, the first and best reader of this novel. Rest in peace.

I

Yet somehow Ulrich could not help thinking: if mankind could dream collectively, it would dream Moosbrugger.

—Robert Musil

1

Akari decided to walk north along Bedford Avenue instead of switching to the G train. The fresh air felt good, and it was a beautiful day, so why not? In LA, she had to drive everywhere.

Akari was a cinematographer and traveled frequently, usually for commercial work, which was why she was in New York for the week. She made more money than she ever imagined she would make (and in a predominantly male field). The cinematographer partied, slept around, was always on the move; charm and talent carried her wherever she wanted to go, and allowed her to eschew commitments that would gum up the machinery of experience and pleasure.

For this reason, Akari dreaded visiting her sister: the general tenor of the apartment Mariko and Dan, Mariko's boyfriend, shared was claustrophobic and repressed; there was a pervasive atmosphere of rot, or if not rot, ferment.

There was so much the sisters never talked about. Mariko was so stubborn: she stage-managed all her relationships (insisted on it)—planning pointless activities, the purpose of which was to indefinitely forestall the possibility of meaningful conversation. For their entire adult lives, the sisters had sustained a cordial, functional relationship, which indefinitely forestalled any deeper engagement with long-gestating resentments. They would end phone calls with "I love you"—but the love they referred to was a kind of perfunctory, false love and not the real, almost primitive feeling of kinship that they both understood was supposed to be there. Love was a signifier that they both used to shore up the insecurity around the issue of their estrangement from each other.

Or the issue of Dan himself, with whom Akari got along really well, eliciting Mariko's intense jealousy. It wasn't like Akari was particularly attracted to Dan; she was just nicer to him than Mariko, and he was nicer to her than Mariko was too; they were situational allies.

Akari read his think-pieces, appreciated their strategic and clever blandness, sent him curt but complimentary emails, and took his ideas seriously when they spoke in person; that was the extent of things.

Dan had dopey charm—it had to be admitted—and there was even a moment, while Mariko was at the grocery store two years before, where Akari thought Dan might try to kiss her in the middle of an episode of *Arrested Development*. He hadn't done more than inched closer to her, but she could feel the physical craving.

It had been strange, definitely uncomfortable, but not, fundamentally, unwanted: the giving and receiving of attention. They went just far enough not to feel guilty, and to maintain plausible deniability; in the end, they both came away with a respect for the other person's pragmatic sense of tact.

As time passed, and Mariko and Dan seemed increasingly permanent, Akari sensed that these little games could no longer be permissible; Dan no longer had any emotional collateral to spend.

Dan and Mariko were either going to get married or never speak to each other again (put up or shut up).

Walking parallel to McCarren Park, Akari noticed that the leaves were not really changing colors. Rather, they were simply dying: falling off the branch, half-green, in unusual late September heat.

A text from her sister: *"Hey, what time are you getting in?"*

Pointless nagging: there was no need to respond.

Akari felt like she was punishing the couple with her arrival, just as she felt that they were punishing her with the invitation.

On the browser of her phone was an article that Dan had written in the latest issue of *n+1* called "The Death of the Interface," which she had been reading on the plane. The piece was a sociological analysis of the effect of digital communication on personal communication (a predictable topic). Dan's article was too deft; it found new ways of talking about an over-analyzed subject, and more importantly, it was funny and self-effacing. But maybe that was the trap: the piece was cool, inventive, witty, but ultimately, destined to become part of the internet culture that the piece itself claimed to abhor.

Akari people-watched: cyclists, power-walkers, bums, bros, basic bitches out for brunch, stroller dads (taking a call while pushing their kid through McCarren Park).

There was no theory for watching people stream by into emptiness, for watching a face materialize through a car window and then disappear forever.

She'd had too much to drink on the red-eye, but she enjoyed the feeling of being slightly delirious in New York: it enhanced the sense of cinematic blur.

Her consciousness opened, almost like a pupil: birds, scampering children, rustling brown-green leaves—a beautiful confusion. It was an incredible thing to be alive in New York; it was amazing that no one noticed how impossible it should be for all these pieces to add up to something like consciousness—to produce feelings like love, to produce civilization, cities, or the images of cinema. And yet they did.

While waiting for the signal to cross the street, Akari bit the nail of her ring finger on her right hand, a nervous habit.

She was aware that, on some level, she was avoiding going to her sister's too early, that she was meandering on purpose to kill time.

It was ridiculous to expect that at this point, when they were both set in their ways and their opinions, the visit could be at all productive. Mariko would inevitably talk about herself, depending on her sister to affirm whatever choices she was in the middle of making. She inevitably would have a new workout, a new acting class, a new wardrobe, and, if she didn't, it would be even more depressing, because then, Akari would have to find herself praising—having to praise—the old wardrobe, the old acting class, the old workout or diet. And Akari would have to perform the same ritual in return: she would have to share her own bullshit, fish for compliments about her own lifestyle, and so on.

They used to be so much more honest with each other—used to push each other, challenge each other, confide in and confront each other; they used to be best friends. They used to have a sense that they were in this together, whatever this was. And it was exciting to have this ally, this person you could count on, this person who never needed much context to *get it.*

But somehow, gradually, that sense, that overlapping zone of subjectivities, had disintegrated, and they had become two very different, very separate, very adversarial siblings—members of the same tribe: no more, no less.

Akari missed that magic bond, that naive, uncritical closeness.

The sense of subtle antagonism between the sisters had grown to the point where Akari could admit to herself that she had come to New York to feel better about her own life in Los Angeles, to juxtapose her own life with Mariko's out of spite.

Still, Akari felt guilty about how much pure pleasure she got from the contrast. It was fascinating how much she could discern about the real nature of her feelings towards Mariko without understanding their source, or being able to give them a precise name.

She was now walking parallel with McCarren Park, which had a ragged, unmanicured charm: softball games, picnickers, frisbee, a single football, poorly thrown, some Mexican guys playing soccer. Brooklynites in their late twenties and early thirties (plus a few forty-somethings determined to remain young) ran around grinning and sweating and showing-off, self-consciously having fun.

Akari thought about a film producer she had talked to on the plane; he'd been such an asshole—talked about himself for four hours.

What was his name again?

All this guy wanted to do was name-drop. He hadn't even figured out that she worked in film, that they knew many of the same people. He just thought she was attractive. He'd invited her to a party that night in Tribeca; she probably wouldn't go.

Men secreted these little poisonous gestures that gradually spread out and enveloped everything, sludge-like. There was nothing more abominable and disturbing than having to endure the pretensions of the middle-aged members of the species in particular.

Akari was fond of Dan because he was *so* acutely aware of the limitations of masculinity—because he was so self-consciously a feminist, so self-consciously tolerant, sensitive, *concerned*—even if he was still *essentially* a mansplainer. Awareness was worth slightly more than nothing.

Men her age, Millennial men, had grown up with a value system that didn't leave room for any real sensitivity, cleverness, or kindness. Most of the dudes Akari worked with, conversely, still played video games, jacked off to porn three or more times a week, and congratulated themselves on the size of their paychecks. Tech bros, finance bros, art bros, preppy bros, blue collar bros all shared the same rudimentary social-emotional habits.

Interesting men were increasingly hard to find.

Akari's stomach rumbled; she hadn't eaten since lunch the previous evening, when she'd made a smoothie before taking a car to the airport: bananas, blueberries, almond milk, greens, raw honey. She was starving.

New York was a system that (seemed to) resist entropy, but the individuals who made up the system, the cells, died off; in a century everyone in this park would be dead, even if the park itself, the city block, the structure of the neighborhood, would be the same. Different forms of life passed through the same space of life. If New York City could still enchant, it was because of this synthesis—this sense that all these different smaller parts added up to something bigger.

Her stomach gurgled; she had a headache; she felt almost like she would pass out. She was about to get her period.

Fuck.

Akari kept thinking about Suzanne and the breakup and the awkward weekend when she'd brought Suzanne home to meet her parents (not having told them that she dated girls more than she dated boys). It was so awkward. Akari had caught her Mom crying in the bathroom—as if she'd lost a daughter in a car accident or something. Her parents were too polite and California fake progressive to *say anything*, but there was a palpable sense of disappointment, like their worst suspicions of her had come true.

Suzanne had been good about it though, powering through the awkwardness and unprocessed discomfort.

The one thing that Akari couldn't bring herself to do that weekend was fuck in her childhood bedroom; they'd slept side by side like good, platonic friends. It was kind of hot to want to touch, but not touch.

Why was she thinking about Suzanne again? Why couldn't she stop thinking about Suzanne? It had been almost two years.

They'd even started emailing again, which was stupid.

Suzanne still needed her, emotionally and financially. She was so fucking unstable.

Having graduated from college in the middle of The Great Recession, Akari still felt that her income, her stability, her tangible, proper adultness, was a magical accident, something that could go away or dissolve any day—but she was also proud of it; she was proud of being a working artist. She liked taking care of Suzanne, and the fact that Suzanne was there to be taken care of served as proof that Akari's success was not a fluke.

She spent a lot on Suzanne when they were together—the spring-break trip to Thailand for example. That had been an incredibly erotic trip.

The memory was so vivid that the cinematographer could almost still feel Suzanne's gummy skin against her own, as if their bodies were entangled subatomically—as if there were no way, and no hope, of ever disentangling those particles, of freeing up the present *for* the present, and the gradual unfolding of the future.

Suzanne had a slight build, wavy brown hair, a few pimples, a bird nose—an incredible sense of style (incredible in the sense that it was preternatural). Akari was shorter and a little more butch (she kept her hair short). They made an attractive couple, which was something that Akari was proud of. She missed being seen with Suzanne; she missed the feeling of having what other people wanted.

Was there a difference between sensuality and narcissism? Was there a way to revel in the sensual presence of another person without giving the ego too much of what it wanted? Was it possible to lust after Suzanne without seeing her as a good to be consumed?

There was a part of Akari that was so damn competitive (was it younger sister syndrome?). She was ashamed of how much pride she took in her success—as if it (success) really meant anything in the grand scheme of things.

Her clean, tidy, cactus-filled two-bedroom; her sexual conquests; Suzanne's beauty in general; her awesome gigs (and she was getting lucrative offers to direct music videos too)—what did all that add up to other than some kind of baseline level of attainment you had to keep working hard to maintain? There was no holiness, nothing sacred, in all those little fragments of comfort and pleasure.

Crossing into the park for a moment, through a gate at the north end, she found a little patch of grass fully in the sunlight and laid down. Akari took a deep breath, so that both her chest and belly temporarily distended, and she closed her eyes. The tenuous connection with the earth felt right.

She took one breath after another, trying to find a sweet spot that she could consider meditation. She could fall asleep, but part of her was too anxious. Her pulse, against her will, ticked faster rather than slower.

In a way, she felt insanely happy that she was here, despite her anxious thoughts, or because of them—happy that her body had an intelligence all its own, that it could bypass or set aside the problems her brain set up. The grass felt good; the sun on her face felt good. She was nobody, and there was a sweetness to that—just melting into everything.

So much lived in the body. Her nervous system was responding; all sorts of sense memories were dimly called up: playing tag in the backyard, playing soccer, having sex in the cemetery near their house as a teenager, random picnics and meetups since college, the little bit of grass outside her place in LA that she kept watered. . . .

She was relieved to be off the plane, off the subway, just out in the fresh air. Air travel always kind of fucked her up, even though she flew a lot; she could never *not* think of the plane crashing, or a terrorist being onboard. Flying meant several hours of simulating your own death over and over.

There was some kind of relationship between the casual, off-hand nature of her lifestyle and the underlying morbidity of her thoughts.

For instance: Was it possible that Suzanne's suicide threats were real? Akari couldn't help but think about it.

How would she do it? With pills or with what? Would she hang herself or get hit by a bus or go swimming in the Pacific at night—wash ashore days later, eaten by fishes?

Love for Suzanne and concern for Suzanne were all mixed up. Tenderness was mixed up with resentment, desire with a hard sense of boundaries—of wanting things to be finished, done.

Akari took a last belly breath and sat up, blinking in the direct sun. She took an Evian she bought in the airport out of her book bag (the only luggage she brought). Finishing off the bottle, she found a trash can, over-flowing with plastic junk, and stuffed the bottle in.

She was starting to want a bite to eat.

There was a bar across the street from the northwest corner of the park, at the border of Williamsburg and Greenpoint (one of those generic American food gastropubs that served expensive burgers with aioli). Why not though? That was the only option in the neighborhood, and these places were usually pretty good quality. If she didn't eat now, she'd end up eating greasy Polish food at the place by her sister's late at night.

Inside the restaurant, Akari felt a little overwhelmed. Everybody seemed to be having an amazing time—*just the best time ever*—and she was out of place. It almost reminded her of LA (as Dan always said Williamsburg represented the LA-ification of New York).

After a brief conversation with the hostess, who seemed annoyed that Akari was alone, and not with one of these incredibly buoyant groups of corporate Millennials, Akari got a seat in the corner, which felt something like punishment.

She couldn't really tell if she was hungry or what. Maybe she would just get a coffee, except the wait staff would probably flip passive aggressive shit. She didn't want to deal with more body language.

Waiting for someone to take her order, Akari opened her phone and opened *Tinder*, which she had avoided since she'd landed, but now couldn't resist. The app had become something of a crutch, an automatic response to having too much free time, a way of structuring her time and space without much effort; she had been trying to wean herself off it. She wanted to make a real effort to meet people again. She missed glances, fertile moments, desperately wanting someone to break the ice. She missed the enchantment of a number written on a scrap of paper, of someone buying her a drink. She missed trying and she missed other people trying. Effort was important in erotic life; it told you important things about yourself; it tested and challenged the ego, helped you determine boundaries.

Swipe.

She couldn't help herself: the game-layer of life was more interesting than life itself.

Swipe.

The bus boy brought her a napkin, fork, water, and a menu.

"Thanks," Akari mumbled.

Did she really want to waste a whole hour on a meal? It was such an ordeal sitting down; she could have just gone to a bodega.

She needed a cigarette and a nap.

She had stopped trying to buy packs though.

She could just go out and ask someone for a loosie . . . would that be embarrassing?

The waiter was attractive, but in a generic way that told you he was probably an actor, or former actor, or model, who was just waiting for aging to destroy his pointless ambition and allow him to settle into an ordinary life. He clearly was accustomed to attention.

Akari opened *Tinder* again, and then closed it immediately, annoyed at herself.

However, the second she put the phone down, she picked it up again and reopened the app.

It wasn't like anyone was watching her. She could sit in the corner of this bland restaurant all day, swiping, and no one would say anything; she was anonymous and would remain anonymous, there was very little anyone could do to stop her from being anonymous; people were too busy to arrest the motion of busyness; she could just flow through the city like this, consumed by private anxieties, indifferent to the individuals and events around her. That was how everyone else did it, right?

Swipe.

She had, in fact, met Suzanne IRL, which maybe explained why it was an order of magnitude better than her other relationships over the past few years.

Akari yawned loudly.

Her exhaustion, she was beginning to realize, was not just the product of the red-eye. She stayed out every night, drank too much, chilled at people's apartments, was always hungover on set. And she could *never* sleep in: her body naturally woke up after first light; the more she drank, the earlier she woke up, actually. She was slowing down physically, ever so slightly, and she knew she couldn't keep this up forever (whatever *this* was).

All around her, in contrast to her diminished state, was an explosion of organic vitality: the clatter of dishes, the squawking of traffic and birds, the crying of babies, the vibration of phones, idle brunch chatter—the wave function of life.

Swipe.

Akari made eyes at the waiter across the room. He *was* super hot, and he seemed into her too. She could write her number on the receipt; she'd had success doing that before.

Swipe.

Akari thought of her eyes as camera lenses: adjusting, noticing, framing, panning, weaving.

She scanned the restaurant: no sign of the waiter. No sign of anyone else interesting.

She closed her eyes.

The whole world was exhausted along with her, like everyone was running on some alternate energy source that did not burn as cleanly or as efficiently as sleep.

Akari opened her eyes.

She saw human animals eating pink, grass-fed burgers. She was in the forest, the jungle, of modern man.

Her stomach growled. She rubbed her eyes, trying to stay awake. No, she had not been treating her body very well at all. It was only genetic luck that her lifestyle hadn't shown up on her face yet.

Her sister, as Akari had noticed on her last trip east, was beginning to get crow's feet. The change was small, but permanent. A wrinkle was like waking up looking tired, but forever—a scar without a wound to valorize it.

The waiter returned, smiling coyly.

"Hi, what wouldya—"

"Can I have the mushroom and arugula omelet . . . and a coffee?"

"Would you like your coffee black?"

"Do you have almond milk?"

"Yes."

"I'll take that."

Fragments of conversation coalesced out of the ambient noise: someone was talking about their start-up, about the angel investors they'd recently been out to dinner with in "SF."

The waiter came back with the coffee, thick swirls of chalky almond milk floating on the surface.

"Do you have any agave?"

"Agave?" This request was not quite routine enough for the waiter: he had to pause very briefly to think about it. "Sure. Yeah. Be right back."

The effect of agave on her body was basically the same as sugar; agave was a fake health food, but she didn't care: it still felt like the best option (a weird thing to put in coffee though). It was better than sugar or Splenda; she hated black coffee and wouldn't drink it under any circumstances.

The door swung open, a new party entered the restaurant: loudass college bitches.

Billions of people watched as billions of other people gradually disappeared and the whole thing unfolded without anyone's protest: that was life.

The waiter came over with the strange agave-almond-coffee confection. Akari thanked him (she wondered what his name was) and took the first sip: stupidly, pointlessly sweet.

How many of the people in this restaurant wanted to be there? Maybe ten or twenty percent? Or maybe zero? Or was everyone, with the possible exception of herself, completely content, happy to be enjambed between Williamsburg and Greenpoint, at the edge of the park, on a warm morning of no particular significance?

Could it be both? Could contentment and discontent exist simultaneously?

She felt vulnerable to what the people around her might be thinking. New Yorkers made so much aggressive eye-contact. People pretended like they weren't watching, like they'd seen it all, like nothing fazed them, or even caught their attention, but it was a pose: the indifference New Yorkers showed towards each other highlighted their obsession with one another.

Akari worried about running into friends from Chapman here; there were a lot of film people in Greenpoint—there was always something shooting around here. She hated running into old friends; the term "old friend" told you everything you needed to know. Truth be told, she had a lot of contempt for all the fake somebodies, the

Hollywood kids with connections and no drive, who she'd gone to college with—who'd she'd seen make half-hearted at best attempts to make it, to make something. She worked too hard to pretend to be friends with that kind of person.

She could see her face reflected in the glass storefront, hazily.

If someone started talking to her, then her stupid loquaciousness would take over and she would be trapped; the key was to avoid catching anyone's gaze, to not seem like one of those people eating alone who wanted to be spoken to. One of those women, in particular, who wanted to be spoken to.

Akari jumped to another mental association: He Who Shall Not Be Named. Her ex before Suzanne.

He lived in Portland now, but Portland and Brooklyn were transposable; he could be in Brooklyn at any time. He could walk through the door of the restaurant right now.

He wouldn't, but he could.

He wouldn't, but she wouldn't be upset if he did.

Swipe.

A few days of being alone, physically alone, with no one to fuck or snuggle with or provide basic baseline comfort, quickly made her exes seem more appealing. In some ways, it was like dating was just a way of keeping the memory of old heartbreaks at bay; dating was a cope.

Akari watched a few *Tinder* faces go by; she looked around the restaurant; looked at the blur of pedestrians outside. One day all of these people would be corpses. They would smell and rot, grow putrid, disappear, melt into the earth. Why didn't anyone else realize that they were *actively* dying, that they were hastening the decay process with each mouthful, with the mastication of the food? Was she the only one who obsessed over this shit?

Swipe.

She took another sip of the sweet coffee. It tasted better; she was getting used to it; it was waking her up. And she liked that feeling.

She thought about texting Suzanne instead of swiping. It wasn't so unusual; they usually exchanged a few texts every day now (now that the ice had been broken).

The post-break up state, in that way, was ideal: you could retain the halo of togetherness without the responsibility of maintaining the actual physical and emotional relationship. It was comforting.

Swipe.

Akari shifted in her seat. Her ass was uncomfortable.

She took another sip of coffee, blinked, yawned, took another sip between yawns. What was this place? It had no character whatsoever. The people here had no distinguishing characteristic except that they could spend money without thinking about it (or successfully hide that they were thinking about it).

In LA, once you created a glamorous aura, you could do whatever you wanted inside its protective shell. In New York, you were supposed to show that the aura was cracked; you cultivated the aura of *not having an aura*, of being tough and authentic—worn-down, work-weary, street-smart.

hey i landed i'm safe how r u? she texted Suzanne.

Suzanne started typing immediately. *I'M GREAT . . . lies i'm OK. Or. or what?*

just chillin. Netflix and homework.

sounds like fun.

it's not. missing you.

u r?

yeah a little.

Akari was tempted to switch to *Snap*, because that was where Suzanne usually sent her nudes. Akari really got off to images of Suzanne touching herself.

that's interesting.

why? Suzanne replied immediately.

because i miss u too . . . definitely a little.

. . .

stop this is just teasing me . . . not fair

yeah i get it . . .

do you?

yes i do

ok still you know i like talking to you

This was already confusing.

i know that's our thing: talking

i miss the physical things

torture

yeah so?

fuckkkk

Akari put her phone face down on the table. This was pathetic.

Her phone buzzed again immediately.

let's try again

Images traveled up to consciousness from the back of Akari's skull: Suzanne straddling her, twisting the stiff nipples of her small breasts; Suzanne's ass, sauntering to the bathroom after sex.

Animal images.

Reveries: broken, chopped up, frozen for reheating later.

maybe

please

you don't have to beg . . . just like

what?

define "try" Suzanne

like be in the same room. i wanna kiss u

possibly . . .

can i call you later . . . ?

maybe. just chill for now ok? this is a LOT

ok . . .

Another buzz: Ana. 5'2". Queer. Into French cinema.

Swipe right.

You've matched with Ana!

The phone is a serotonin dispenser, Akari thought, that was its most basic function, not communication.

Hey!! Ana wrote.

Hey what's up?!

Not Muhc! just got into town

There was a pause in which Akari found herself refreshing the *Tinder* chat.

from where?

LA

cute

Akari, ashamed, put her phone facedown on the table. This isn't what she wanted at all, even if it felt superficially good.

Picking her phone back up, she closed *Tinder* without looking at her notifications and opened up *iMessage* again.

i'm serious about wanting try again i just want u to know ☺

I know youre serious

you don't think i'm old enough to be

serious?

ja

that's not true!!

explain

explain what?

Akari was still just so into Suzanne. Suzanne had access to Akari's brain 24/7—whenever she wanted to fuck Akari's shit up, the message would always be delivered and opened. Akari could block Suzanne, but that was so drastic, and there were always ways around it.

I dunno. just like what your thiniing

I'm not thiniing anything

lol, but seriously

I'm just doing my thing.

How's New York?

I just got here, so

Ok . . . if you want me to go away, i'll go away
i dunno
please . . .
please stop . . .
ok u hate me
no . . .
i'll just stop
ok.
The waiter arrived with her omelet.

"Thanks," Akari mumbled, half-looking at her phone.

The waiter nodded and vanished again.

It wasn't hard to imagine why Suzanne was so needy: she emancipated herself from her meth-addict parents at fifteen, living with her rich, Christian grandparents for two years before graduating from high school. She needed Akari to be an older sister as much as she needed her as a lover; the two roles had fused (it was unclear if Suzanne was even completely attracted to women, or if she just felt safer around them).

Suzanne constantly oscillated between destructive behavior and seeking security. She unconsciously undermined the relationships she built, even if she craved or needed those relationships. She recreated the chaos of her childhood in her adult life.

Akari felt her phone buzz on the table twice—momentarily ignoring it.

She picked at her plate. The omelet was bland.

hi . . .
i'm still here.
talk to me
i'm eating
sorry agian
When Akari was Suzanne's age, she'd had an eating disorder; Suzanne would probably develop one sooner or later, because that's what everyone did.

There were a group of college girls across the restaurant, laughing and drinking coffee together. One of them noticed Akari staring at them; there was a brief exchange of eye-contact which made Akari feel slightly embarrassed.

Akari was alone at the table and was very conscious of it—that she was the only person in the restaurant dining alone. In LA, she never went out alone, except maybe to coffee shops, but even then, she largely went with friends, or for meetings.

One of the college girls was *really* attractive—dark features, heavy breasts, a mini-skirt.

"I have a crush on you," Suzanne, who was an intern on set at the time, said on what became their first date. "I've had a crush on you for weeks."

God—it was torture to think about, especially in the context of how much had gone wrong, in the context of how poorly Suzanne had acted, how immature she'd turned out to be. It felt like so long ago now. Suzanne had once been real, flesh and blood; now she was a phone-phantom. "Suzanne" wasn't a single thing, a single form or body; she was distributed across platforms: *Instagram, Facebook, Tinder, Gmail, Snap*—a hive of Suzannes. And it was for this reason that a clean break-up was semi-impossible: there were too many versions to break up with.

Suzanne's dream was to direct a film after college and have Akari shoot it; this was something they discussed often, and Akari, maybe against her better instincts, had offered to use her own connections to help her lover's career. She wondered, now, if this was why Suzanne kept contacting her: because Suzanne felt like she'd lost a patron, because she wanted to rope Akari back into supporting her. This was a reasonable, albeit extremely embarrassing, assumption.

Akari played with her napkin. When she was traveling or tired, or in this case, both, Akari's unwanted thoughts found a way into her conscious mind.

Was she being used? The cinematographer wanted to reject the possibility, push it across the table like the scraps of napkin, but she couldn't.

The potential truth just lay there, inert, but threatening, like an old attack dog. It wasn't the case, it couldn't be the case, it wasn't possible for it to be the case, that the *entirety* of Suzanne's affections was an attempt to gain connections—right? Of course she wanted help, but. . . .

Akari started to arrange the bits of torn-up napkin into geometric patterns.

Nothing was simple. Suzanne's neediness—her vulnerability to need—was what made her appealing; Suzanne would never stop needing her, and Akari liked that. Akari just needed Suzanne to not need her *that* much, to not be *so* dependent on her. They hadn't gotten the recipe right the first time . . . but if they got back together—? A part of Akari wanted to believe that Version II of the relationship would fix all the problems that had emerged in Version I.

should i just stop texting you? be honesttt Suzanne asked.

yes Akari texted back immediately before adding, *or i dunno . . . maybe fuck*

It was easy to imagine Suzanne saying "fuck" under her breath as she typed; she did things like that; she was charmingly uncensored. This is what made Suzanne so lovely: her personality seemed to flow out of this much deeper, much more physical *thing*. Suzanne was basically an innocent, silly person; she only pretended to be serious—so it was hard to admit that Suzanne was fundamentally manipulative, that Suzanne had become extremely adept at getting what she wanted, like a house cat.

There was really no way of escaping the fact that human beings were animals, programmed to survive. Young people needed older people for this reason: support from an older person assured survival.

OK . . . Let's meet up when I get back

Akari couldn't believe she was offering.

when's that?

couple days

i feel like you never come back when you say you will

i'm free to do as i like

i know

ok then

so . . .

Or was Suzanne *just* hurt? Was she *just* an unhappy person who felt abandoned or alone or unloveable?

Akari wanted to smell Suzanne, slip into the odorous casing of her flesh, be with her again.

Akari realized her own body was lonely—pure and simple.

God.

She kept making eyes with the voluptuous young woman across the restaurant. There was no chance she'd talk to this person, who was definitely straight, but was perhaps subconsciously picking up on Akari's desire for attention, desire for desire. Akari was aware that she had her own, special charisma.

What made cinematography interesting to Akari was that the body could take over from the mind; there was no anxiety about what to do or to say; you could capture life; you didn't have to be responsible for it—for life.

In LA the day before, she'd gone to see a photo exhibit of portraits taken of people on their last day of college and then again, fifteen years later; the difference between the age of twenty-two and the age of thirty-seven was simply astounding. Faces changed; they slipped away like someone was tugging at the skin. Faces dried up, caved in. And it wasn't just aesthetic: there was an inner caving-in too, a resignation. Your cells turned over completely in seven-year cycles; every seven years you were a different person, had a different brain. Who was even to say that in a way, you didn't die in the process of evolving? That *you* didn't gradually supplant *yourself* over time, the way a weed takes over a garden?

Why did her mind do this?

Akari stuffed a forkful of arugula in her mouth. Eating arugula was supposed to increase your libido, Akari had read recently—but did that apply only to men who needed help getting it up? Probably.

Limp dicks were one of the main reasons to date women. How often had she plowed through a date with a hot guy only to discover that nothing was happening below? Seemingly healthy men were increasingly unable to get it up. Her idea of the male form had been disfigured; men were manifestly and extravagantly disappointing.

She had no compassion for men who melted into sticky sentimentality and weakness and self-hatred after a few drinks—who unthinkingly adored her, worshiped her. It was lame and boring.

But that's how Dan was with her sister, or used to be.

The fact remained that Akari was avoiding going to her sister's place. She was avoiding both of them and they were avoiding her, too, in a way, by not really checking in very much, by not making any definite plans for lunch or dinner or a movie or a show. It was really embarrassing; it drove home the fact of the sisters' increasing estrangement and spiritual distance. Akari missed that implicit sense of shared secrets, shared ideas, shared visions, shared memories; the satisfaction of knowing that you were never alone in the world because there was this person whose experience matched and merged with yours. She missed having a sibling in the platonic sense.

Akari opened her phone. No texts from anyone.

Akari signaled for the check; there was no point in pretending to finish this omelet. She should have just ordered a beer, because beer, in a weird way, tended to wake her up. Beer would have given her the energy and the courage to complete the trip to her sister's. The coffee just made her feel anxious, like the world was about to fucking *end*. The check couldn't come soon enough; she already had her credit card out.

The college girls were gone. She hadn't even noticed them leave.

She started to think about her favorite Kurosawa movie, *Ikiru*, a film about mortality and regret. Mr. Watanabe, the protagonist, who is dying of cancer, seeks to give meaning to his life—and succeeds . . . realizing, after a series of mishaps and embarrassments, how deeply miraculous it is just to exist at all, even for a few minutes, a day, on earth, as a human being. *Ikiru* was one of the first art films she'd ever seen. Her mother had taken her to a screening as a senior in high school. Akari had been thrilled to understand enough Japanese not to have to read the subtitles. For whatever reason, she'd associated herself with Mr. Watanabe. She'd had the sense, even then, that it was easy to waste your life, to give it away, to sleep through it. *Ikiru* had captured this incredible sense of fleetingness, preciousness, fragility. It, *life*, would all be gone one day—and what would you have to show for it? Or better yet: *who?* Who would be there to hold your hand, wash your corpse, dress it, bury it? Who would remember you?

When the waiter arrived, she stuck the card out like she was paying a highway toll.

"Thanks . . ."

She waited impatiently for the waiter to return, tapping her foot against the floor and swiping through *Tinder* again without finding anyone interesting.

The waiter returned; Akari signed the check, tipping too much to compensate for not flirting with him more, as she sensed he wanted (after all, she was the only solitary woman there).

She stepped outside.

A gust of fresh air, the sound of street traffic, a bike bell ringing, a child crying . . . shouts from across the park, birds, an airplane on its way to LaGuardia, rolling, billowing, cumulus clouds . . .

A text from Dan: *on your way?*

yeah couple blocks

cool I'm waiting to let you in . . .

He was so passive-aggressive.

Akari started walking north, away from the park.

She was on Manhattan Avenue now.

Still no text from Suzanne.

Suzanne did this: ran hot and cold, which was addicting about her. You could never really stop checking your phone because there might be something exciting or dramatic that you didn't expect; or you might be the one to send that dramatic/exciting/surprising message. You couldn't even predict your own behavior. It was like the phone was in charge of communication.

Akari remembered a friend in the psychology program at UCLA telling her about an experiment with rats who could press a lever to get a food pellet reward. Rats would stop pressing levers that didn't offer rewards, use levers that always offered rewards as needed, but would literally press the levers that *might* offer a reward over and over until they died.

Akari couldn't conceive of how she had gotten to this point, having grown up basically without excess technology. She remembered getting a Motorola Razr as a senior in high school. That was it. Yet, now, it was like she'd been born with her phone. It extended through her: linked up with her nervous system.

Akari needed to sleep.

She passed by corner market after corner market, each stand presenting some variation of the same display: flowers and fruit. The cinematographer was tempted to buy an avocado or some watermelon slices. The omelet hadn't really been satisfying and Dan and Mariko never kept any real food at home; Mariko just drank green juice and kelp or whatever.

Something really sick started to happen to actresses after they turned thirty; they started to slip away, and only the strongest kept working after that cut-off date. Akari watched it happen all the time.

She pitied her sister. She pitied her whole family. Happiness and togetherness had never really worked out. Both their parents had a quiet drinking problem; getting older wasn't easy, they had no support, no friends, they were really isolated people. Her father didn't adjust well to retirement; he wasn't adjusting . . . and her mother wasn't adjusting to her father not adjusting.

Akari imagined their funerals: she flashed to two coffins, side by side, lowered into the ground.

As she passed into Greenpoint, the whole flavor of street life changed. Polish shop owners, chatting amiably in the sun.

i'm sorry

Akari sent the text before she had time to reflect on what she was doing. It was too easy. The impulse had been too strong.

She really hated herself now.

i'm sorry for keeping you at arm's length for so long and for continuing to do it . . .

thanks I appreciate that Akari

do you?

a lot yeah

i'm glad . . .

The feelings that surged up in Akari now were very powerful. She had to keep walking to stop herself from crying or calling Suzanne—which would have been one step too far.

They both had manufactured this conversation; they both knew that it was basically artificial, that nothing would change. The depressing thing was just realizing that the drama, the cries of loss and longing, were by and large manufactured, half-hearted attempts at feeling more alive; the depressing thing was that the breakup, or breakdown, or blowup, or whatever it was, was the most interesting thing that had happened to either of them in a long time.

so . . .

i'm so sad.

ok . . .

and I'm super horny . . .

A sexual relationship was painfully imprecise.

you're not with anyone else?

no Akari. I'm not. I haven't touched anyone.

Are you lying? Akari wrote, feeling guilty (she had been with several people).

no not lying

hmm

what?

nothing

you have been?

yeah.

I don't blame you.

r u sure??

ja

it's making me wet just thinking about u, Akari texted impulsively. She was on Mariko's street. *what r u wearing right now?*

underwear

that's it?

yeah?

There was a note from Dan on the door:

Akari: had to run. Long story. Use your intuition to get in. You know? D

Akari reached under the mat: there was the keyring. She opened the door. The apartment was on the third floor.

Walkup.

She waited until she was in the apartment before she looked at her phone:

yeah . . . Suzanne had typed.

I want u to touch urself

I am.

good . . .

r u getting wet?

i told you I'm already wet . . .

Akari laid down on the couch and thrust her hand down her shorts and began to massage her clit.

good

2

Across what was left of the waterfront, Manhattan leapt and licked at the sky, like a Van Gogh cypress, or a city in the Bible: hallucinatory and raw.

Mariko turned away from the window.

Her legs were cold, and she wished she had put on leggings. She didn't like the look of her thighs, which were increasingly, incrementally flabby. She felt self-conscious, as if someone were watching. In fact, Mariko was watching herself. She had just turned thirty-two.

The direction that the world was going in was not helping things; she spent her free time reading the news, fretting.

Dan, her boyfriend, was asleep. He was a good listener: intelligent, thoughtful, able to put things in perspective—so it was beyond frustrating that he had passed out early.

On the table of the small, circular kitchen table was a week-old, out of order Sunday *Times*, as well as a mug of cold coffee, which she now found herself sipping from. The coffee tasted good, better than it had tasted when she'd made it that morning, and the late-hour caffeine mitigated a low-level depression, which she could feel setting in.

She scanned, or rather re-scanned, the headlines of the Arts & Leisure section and put the paper back down: the paper was boring; she'd already read it; she didn't know what she had been expecting (maybe a little bit of distraction to pair with the little dose of serotonin provided by the coffee).

Anything was better than lying in bed and trying to fall asleep; irrelevant details would clutter the air around her head like motes of dust: family, work, theater, the man who slept outside their building (she never learned his name; was there anyone who called him by one?). She would pick apart the things she said to people; she couldn't shake the feeling that she sounded stupid, or inarticulate, or insensitive, or self-involved.

Akari, her sister, was arriving the next day from LA, which added to Mariko's anxiety. It didn't help that Akari was more successful and younger, if not more traditionally beautiful.

While Mariko had nearly given up on acting, Akari had flourished as a director of photography; her name had already appeared in the credits of several well-received independent films, which Mariko pretended to have seen. The images Akari made were ingenious, provocative, original.

It went without saying that the sisters bickered constantly, agreed on almost nothing, tolerated each other out of a sense of duty and the intuition that later in life they would need each other more than they did in the present. In this sense, they were like their parents. Akari resembled their mother, who was from Japan; Mariko resembled their father, an American of German descent. Akari always had a clear sense of who she was. She spoke Japanese in the house, did a year-long exchange program in Tokyo during high-school, watched Japanese films, generally refused to give a fuck about life in their suburban California town.

Mariko picked up the Business section. An article about Tesla was on the front cover. Dan had bought Tesla stock a few years ago and was proud of his foresight, although he never told anyone about his stocks, because he was publicly known as a leftist. Privately, he justified owning shares of Tesla—not that Mariko cared—because their success was generally good for the world, relatively speaking. Dan liked to assuage his guilt by suggesting that he could sell his Tesla stocks one day to buy an eco-friendly cottage upstate (as if selling the stocks would purge their evil aura).

Mariko wasn't worried about the ethics of stock trading, only the financial risk, and she was concerned that Dan was deeper into the market than he was letting on. Having graduated into a recession, she was financially risk-averse.

Her sister, of course, was not. Akari told Mariko to invest in *Snapchat* when it went public; some of her friends worked there (Akari lived in

Venice Beach, near the *Snapchat* offices). Akari herself had invested a little bit and stood to earn real money down the line, or so she claimed. In essence, Akari, like their mother, who lost a few thousand dollars a year at Indian casinos, liked to gamble; Mariko, like their father, who still clipped coupons, refused to.

And it was getting harder and harder for Mariko to feel that her own tendencies were the more productive; her own trajectory was flat while Akari's tumbled upward.

Mariko didn't want to let her sister see what her life had become: fastidious, repetitive, essentially suburban; Mariko didn't want to admit that she'd stopped auditioning, that she'd grown comfortable working at a wine bar.

As deliberate as Mariko had been in her life, Akari was reckless, converting hookups into relationships without foundation or future. What both sisters shared, however, was an ability to rationalize their choices, to convince themselves that arbitrary choices were necessary choices, differing only on the choices themselves. They each saw in the other what they denied in themselves: the awareness that things didn't have to be a certain way, that different kinds of choices could be made.

The actress opened the fridge and looked around. There was nothing good. A carton of eggs, coconut milk, cashew yogurt, kale, some cheese, white wine.

She closed the fridge, then immediately opened it again: the contents were exactly the same as they had been a second before, having failed to transform themselves by magic.

Mariko sat back down at the little table, that spiritual desert.

It annoyed her that Akari and Dan got along well; that was another thing. It was so easy for her sister to show up in New York and play the free spirit on the stage that she, Mariko, had built. Akari and Dan would watch TV, giggle, gossip, talk about interests that neither of them particularly shared; the whole project of the pseudo-friendship between her boyfriend and her sister seemed to Mariko like a form of revenge against herself. The thought made her wince.

Mariko picked at her cuticles, which were always in a raw, mashed-up state.

Her relationship had produced an abiding, almost cosmological sense of loneliness: loneliness as the constituent property of existence.

More than anything, she didn't want to find herself admitting to her sister that she often went days at a time without touching Dan, that they often slept side by side like siblings (and never talked about it, never acknowledged it).

The reality of the situation was shameful. And yet, the shame was derived from the decay of the good—years of tenderness, and mutual support, Dan's general good-guyness and patience with her—into the bad, or present state.

There was a strong sense of "could have been" and "could be" between them . . . of "almost" and "nearly."

Minor self-deceptions fed into a cascade of larger anxieties.

There had been other men—in coffeeshops and on the train and in parks and on the street—who had wanted her and whom, on occasion, she had wanted back. But she'd pretended not to hear them or see them, had denied any link between her body and the bodies of others.

She had fantasies about strangers who would tie her up, eat her out, pump her full of their semen, but these were fantasies for a reason.

Mariko had never really learned how to fuck: how to abandon all the higher, critical, self-aware functions of consciousness. She'd only ever had the kind of sex that was about other people feeling good about themselves, the kind of sex that people had out of secret contempt. Some part of her clung to control, to pseudo-rationality, to convention, and structure. Her relationship was designed to keep chaos out—and, in that sense, it served its function very well.

It was around this time of night that she often practiced conversations with Dan in her head—conversations that she never had. And not just

Dan: her parents, her sister, her acting teacher, certain friends, her boss at the restaurant. She conducted a whole shadow life between the hours of 11 p.m. and 2 a.m.

Ironically, given the fertility of her mental performances, she was never on stage anymore. She'd stopped auditioning, stopped really making an effort to have a career. It was much easier to ignore her ambitions, to pretend that her desires had never existed, than to commit to them, and to the possibility of failure.

Acting classes were preferable to actual acting because they remained in the soft realm of the ideal rather than the hard, brightness of the real. In an acting class you could theoretically play any role you wanted; in auditions, you were either rejected or typecast, marginalized in one way or another.

So Mariko remained in class; she remained in therapy; she remained a person in progress. To stay creative, she did little one-acts, workshops, and half-heartedly auditioned for Netflix pilots. She went for projects that were either too big to happen or too small to be noticed.

The actress closed her eyes, which were green, and rubbed them, her thumb on her left eye, her pointer finger on her right. They hurt. She'd been on her phone too much. Her long, taut body shook slightly.

She looked over at the bedroom door and wondered again if Dan was awake.

She began to tap her foot on the floor, as if the surplus of energy in her body could be safely released through the working of a single muscle.

Tap tap tap.

She reached for her phone, which was on the toaster: no messages, only notifications from apps she didn't use.

Tap tap tap.

She looked at the Sunday Review section of the *Times*: climate change, rising temperatures, drought in Africa, melting icecaps. She didn't like being reminded that her life took place inside a thing called History; she didn't like to be reminded that there were events going on that surpassed the relevance of the things going on in her head by several orders of magnitude. The notion that the world was ending produced devastating melancholia. She imagined droughts, wars, mass migrations, rising seas, incredible heat, dried up sea-beds, exhausted species slouching towards extinction. Dan dead, sister dead, parents dead, everyone dead; dead pets, dead planets, dead, blue planet: serene and empty.

And yet, all of this, all of *that,* seemed impossible from her perch in gentrified Greenpoint. There was no ecological crisis, no existential crisis, here. There was just this little table and the little light above it and Dan asleep in the other room. There was something spiritual about it: the sense of extreme intimacy, of being totally alone with another person, of the shared space being theirs, *utterly theirs.*

She remembered the first night they'd spent there. They'd gotten kebabs from a Turkish restaurant on Franklin Street and walked along the water, before coming back and falling asleep on the couch, exhausted and wine drunk and happy (before waking up in the morning and having sex).

"You're so fucking insanely beautiful," Dan had said when they woke up. "Just like–insanely wildly beautiful."

And she was, or used to be, Mariko knew that. *She used to be beautiful.* Now she was merely good looking. The glow had faded, just like that. But she was still proud of the fact that there was that flowering, that moment where one other person on Earth had looked at her and found her completely perfect, a kind of miracle. Not everyone could say that, very few in fact.

She stared at a perfume ad, went back to the election. There was speculation about the first presidential debate, which would be next week.

The actress wiggled her long, irregular toes; her legs were falling asleep. She stretched and yawned. Her brain was so awake.

And what was that—her brain? The shuttling of ions, the flow of blood, the communication of neuron to neuron . . . the web of interactions that produced this niggling little "I" of anxiety and disappointment. A brain was a failed piece of evolutionary technology; it had all sorts of features that were completely unnecessary. It questioned, picked-apart, worried, analyzed; it talked to itself. So much of what the brain did was ancillary to survival.

She sighed, brushed her hair back, massaged the bones on either side of her sinus, half-consciously trying to increase airflow to that brain.

She was feeling increasingly hungry, but the fridge was almost barren. Why hadn't anyone gotten groceries? They both had been home all day.

She was craving steak—really craving it. Blood and flesh.

Mariko was conscious of the fact that she was warding off depression, almost like it was bad luck. She was totally vulnerable to everything, or she felt herself to be. There was nothing solid to tether herself to except Dan, who increasingly resented her for depending on him emotionally, insisting on his own brand of aloof, elitist independence. He judged her for everything that she considered totally hers: her life in the performing arts, her emotionality, her friends who didn't read.

She looked over at the door again: the beige paint was peeling off slowly; the apartment was a classic New York shithole (despite how much work they'd done to make it feel like a home). The space affected her psychologically, fed into her already-complicated loop of obsessions and emotions—into the feeling that she was trapped.

Her hatred of the apartment had a lot to do with the house she'd been raised in. Her mother was an incredibly fastidious, neat person; her father was basically a slob, whose slob-like tendencies were governed only by a mild fear of his wife's wrath. Every room, every object, every guest, every holiday was wrapped up in this eternal struggle—each child too.

It made sense, then, that she would choose to cohabitate with someone like Dan, who was an artful slob. It wasn't that he couldn't clean up after himself—he did the dishes, took out the trash, did his laundry—it was that he couldn't function unless there was a certain amount of sprawl: books, papers, records, sweaters he might put on, shoes he might need to hitch to his feet at a moment's notice. He needed a certain vibe; his persona was tied up in a certain vibe. Her style of minimalism, he claimed, was soul-sucking; he couldn't produce deep thoughts in the kind of apartment she wished they lived in.

Mariko stared at the fridge, contemplating whether she should open the last Forager cashew yogurt, add chia seeds and banana.

The act of eating was calming, even if she didn't particularly enjoy what she was eating.

There was some other internal force compelling her to stay put and to not get up and open the fridge, however. Was there something to feel guilty about?

There was.

No matter how healthy the snack was, it wasn't a good idea to eat at night. You should resist the urge; eating late could disrupt your metabolism.

She got up and went to the fridge and took out the cashew yogurt. There were just two clean spoons in the drawer, which meant that Dan had forgotten to unload the dishwasher. *Fuck him*, she thought, seriously.

The cashew yogurt tasted like shit, but it was better than straight-up carbs.

Was there honey in the cabinet?

Yes.

She found the honey (raw honey) and took a knife from the drawer. She dipped the knife in the honey and added a dollop to the cashew yogurt.

Chia seeds?

Yes.

She took them from the cupboard and sprinkled them in.

It still tasted terrible.

The banana!

She reached for the bowl of fruit next to the sink, under the window, peeled it swiftly, and began to slice the banana into the plastic yogurt cup, which was really not big enough to fit all the slices of banana, meaning that half the banana was left unsliced, and thus potentially destined to go to waste, which made her feel bad.

The cashew yogurt still tasted like cardboard, but the banana was enough to make it palatable.

So much extra sugar though. Bad habit.

She reached for her phone on top of the toaster and opened *Facebook*; she scrolled through her news feed, which was dominated by election commentary.

So obnoxious.

Mariko's acting teacher, Yanna, told her that she acted too much with her head, as if she'd planned out each micro-gesture, every subtlety (which was true). Class after class, Mariko was told the same thing, had the same flaw pointed out, and resolved only to hide it rather than eliminate it. She couldn't act unless she had complete control over what was going on. Intentions were important, they needed to be clear; was she really doing something wrong?

Mariko never understood how to balance freedom with her own need for control.

This problem had become a part of her narrative. She was someone with neurotic tendencies. It was like she had a weak heart or clubfoot. There was no way of separating who she *was* from the accomplished, secure artist *she'd failed to become.*

Her work was always praised, well-liked, even admired and talked about—but it never led to anything, never secured her the professional attention that some, if not all, of her peers from Tisch had received in the decade since they'd graduated together.

Her life narrative had become fractured, put out of joint. She actively compartmentalized the different parts of her life: art, relationship, family, survival job. Each compartment was neatly sealed off, functioning independently of the other. Maybe work frustration would bleed into her relationship, or acting frustration bleed into her relationship with her sister— but, by and large, these critical boundaries were maintained. They *had* to be maintained.

The side-effect was that she couldn't sleep, couldn't get her brain to turn off, couldn't turn her phone off. The compartments were watertight, but great force was required to maintain the seals, especially in the unde-fined minutes between waking and dreaming. Late at night, her subconscious would pound on the hatches that separated the different parts of her mind, and she would sink a little deeper into the depths, like a ship that had begun to leak.

She was halfway done with the cashew yogurt.

Mariko looked around the little living room-kitchenette, as if some activity or idea would present itself. She licked her gums, to clear them of yogurt residue, making an audible sucking sound.

Ugh.

The apartment wasn't big enough to properly pace in. All you could do was sit in place and think and pull your hair out.

Her book was on the windowsill: Janet Malcom's *Reading Chekhov*. Even though it was a short book, she still wasn't done after three weeks. Nevertheless, the subtle way Malcom brought Chekhov and his work to life thrilled Mariko. There was a humility and gentleness to everything in both Chekhov's life and work, a touch of deep humanism that had faded from the world. Why was she not allowed to work on the plays that interested her the most? Why was a life in art, to borrow Stanislavski's phrase, impossible now?

She wondered what Dan was thinking, if he was enduring the same confused, shiftless thoughts, if he was awake in the other room. If he was, and that was a big if, then maybe they could sit up and talk about things—slowly, patiently, in a roundabout way that would gently release the pressure. It had been so long since they had done that.

She had no idea who he was anymore, really; she'd stopped paying attention to the physical details that mattered so much to people who were in love. She never remembered what color his eyes were (brown). Her boy-friend had become shapeless: a mass, a thing, which emitted radiant heat, someone who kept the bed warm in the winter, but too warm in summer.

She had never been in a relationship where this didn't happen at some point; Dan had lasted the longest, but the result was the same: he lapsed into thingness.

All her previous exes had at some point resisted becoming or being objects, space-occupiers. They had ended things before they became things.

But Dan didn't fight. The paper-thin structure of their relationship was never tested, and therefore seemed incredibly resilient. Their relationship was like a city built on a fault line, which, through random luck, had yet to experience a major earthquake. What remained, what was left over, the absence of panic or crisis, was dull, persistent anxiety: the underlying awareness that someday, the natural cycle would reassert itself, and the city would fall into ruin.

Mariko looked at the bedroom door again, anxious that he might come out at any moment to take a piss, or get a glass of water, and interrupt her peace and quiet.

Half-bald and paunchy—his body embarrassed her. Mariko had been trained from a young age to care about how people presented themselves, but she concealed this training behind a veneer of naturalness. She appeared thrifty, conservative, plain to others. She bought nice clothes, but only when they were on sale.

Dan, conversely, didn't care about beauty; he was a Marxist (or claimed he was): appearance, in his opinion, was the fetish of a consumerist society. He couldn't realistically be expected to put much care into his appearance, but his posture, his choice of glasses, reflected subtle cultivation. He was an ethically concerned intellectual, someone exquisitely sensitive to the contradictions inherent to contemporary capitalism, to the warping effect a for-profit society had on the individual soul. The problem was that, in being so exquisitely sensitive, so refined in his awareness of the system he was a part of, and prisoner to, Dan had begun to believe that he was immune to many of capitalism's worse warp-effects.

He was more of a Calvinist than a Marxist: he believed that he was among the elect. He couldn't see that his intellectual posture was not, as he believed, a product of his ideological purity, but rather a behavior that he had acquired in order to flourish in the academic marketplace.

Mariko imagined her boyfriend combing what was left of his hair in the faculty bathroom before the seminars he led; she knew the real hours he spent crafting long posts about the election, as well as his think-pieces. The serious intellectual work, his early scholarship, had merely served to qualify him for the role of bullshitter. Dan had drifted from thinking to performing the act of thought for others, divesting himself of his own unique qualities, one by one, so that what remained was an indistinct, composite humanoid substance: skin, hair, blood, bone, muscle, organs.

No.

She needed to stop thinking this way: it wasn't right or fair. Dan was a person: vivid, changeable, and changing. He wasn't a thing, a prop. He was struggling to make sense of life like everyone else, wasn't he?

She looked at the bedroom door again, as if the door was about to be blown off its hinges.

Just come out here Dan.

Relationships were lashed together with false or inflated hopes; there were no exceptions; this was a law of psycho-physics. At the end of the day, one person produced new needs, new fantasies, conditioned you to imagine everything that you didn't have or had never experienced. A relationship produced an explosion of desire for life outside of the relationship.

Mariko found herself at the stove. She turned on the blue gas flame. She filled up the kettle quickly at the sink and added it to the raw flame.

Mint.

She took the bags down from the cupboard to the right of the stove. There was coconut milk in the fridge that she could add. She took an extra-large mug out of the cabinet to the left of the stove, ripped the lips of the paper packets that had sheathed the tea, dangling the two bags above the empty mug for a split second before dropping them in.

Mariko picked up her phone from the table.

yoooooooooo

What the fuck am I saying?

She saw that her sister was typing.

yo wat up??

cannnnottt sleep!

neither can I?

but it's only like ten there.

still I'm tryna go to bed early cuz of my flight

lol the way you type

I knowww I'm high

lol

The minute of chatter gave her mind a chance to rest and break the rhythm of its own relentless chain of logic.

She held the phone up to her face, snapped a selfie, and sent it to her sister. She had no idea why: it seemed fun on some amorphous level.

She did not like looking at herself. It was awful to see how crow's feet, which Akari had mercilessly commented on during her last visit, had begun to spread across her face like tributaries on a map.

Mariko saw her life as tragi-comedy like in Chekhov, her idol. Masha in *The Three Sisters* was the last serious role she'd done (that was 2012). Since then: toothpaste commercials and bad festival one-acts, workshops, staged-readings, and student films. There had been nothing to justify the faith she had placed in herself: the faith with which she'd come to acting, the faith with which she had been received by her first teachers and directors. There was nothing to show for the potential she had once shown. Failure—or rather, the absence of success—had done immense spiritual damage to her. She resented Dan for his success, for the way he'd climbed the ladder of his chosen profession; she could barely bring herself to congratulate him the day he'd gotten tenure; it was too much; she couldn't look him in the eye, couldn't respond, just said in a small voice, "that's wonderful."

With each article he published, each interview he gave, his status rose, while hers remained where it had always been, which was nowhere.

He had begun to receive emails from young women who wanted to meet him, who admired him, who wanted to audit his classes, be taken out for coffee, courted, fucked. She knew because she read his emails.

Bennington girls who'd just moved to the city. Bard girls. Cute, alternative girls. Kids who wore Che T-shirts and listened to Pavement in seventh grade and wanted to call someone "Daddy." He didn't respond now, but one day, soon, he would—he would give in, and then everything would change.

There was no other explanation why he over-published, why he worked so hard to say the same thing in different ways in different forums, why he had made himself a ubiquitous presence among internet leftists: he was trying to make himself hot through prestige. He didn't want to work out, didn't want to do skincare, or change his wardrobe: he wanted to have a brilliant reputation. He wanted eroticism by other means.

Thus, her boyfriend had developed an erotic relationship with his readership and his *Twitter* followers rather than her. He no longer asked for her opinion, no longer developed his ideas in dialogue with her, no longer pretended to take the theater seriously; he discounted any influence that wasn't a part of his own intellectual worldview.

Should she be jealous? The thought often occurred to her. Was she jealous? This was something she couldn't fully admit to herself, or admit the possibility of. She had so much power—there was no doubt about that—within the emotional dynamic of the relationship that it seemed absurd to envy him, the person she essentially dominated. She didn't want to be Dan, didn't want his life, but he possessed certain concrete *things* which she wanted. If she had those concrete things, well, then she might be a little happier.

There was so much she and Dan needed to say to each other: so much that demanded examination, interpretation, illumination. If they could reach each other on that level, if they could bypass all the damage on the road, find an alternate route, then there would be something resembling hope, or just hope, and the time-costs of the past few years would not be completely sunk (which was her greatest fear).

Mariko now became aware of the fullness of her bladder. The bathroom door was a few steps away; it was open.

She sat down on the toilet, pulled down her panties, felt warm piss shoot from between her legs into the toilet bowl—wiped, flushed, pushing the lever down with her toes. She didn't wash her hands, didn't care.

The kitchen was saturated with light: street lights, bodega lights, moonlight; she imagined that her life was a movie: she could see herself come in from the bathroom, take a step into the kitchen, stand still, look at the electronic clock on the microwave (12:12).

It felt good to have urinated; she could relax now; the tension had been released. It was time for her period too, but her cycle was inconsistent, so it could be days, maybe even another week. There was no fear of pregnancy. He had eaten her out a few times this month; she had sucked his cock one night. He still had his foreskin, and she liked men with foreskin; there was a sensuality, an art, to caressing it, folding it over carefully. It was weird, but she liked his cock more than she liked the rest of him.

12:13.

There was no going back to sleep now: she was fully awake: mind, body, cunt.

She thought about masturbating at the kitchen table; she did that sometimes; the apartment was so small that it was either there or the bedroom.

She was so fucking horny.

What had Dan had for dinner? He'd just been writing all day. Maybe he hadn't eaten at all. He always seemed to be going out to dinner or ordering food at his office. There seemed to be endless department meetings, visiting speakers—either that, or he stayed late at his office to write.

He was avoiding her obviously; they both knew it; it had been a part of their daily ritual for a year.

She worked late most nights at the wine bar, so it didn't matter what he did; they were more like roommates than lovers.

She put her nose to her left armpit. She smelled a little ripe; she always smelled worse when she shaved her armpits; the hair was probably a natural defense against unpleasant smells, and yet laws of femininity still forbade keeping them.

She still shaved them, she supposed, because a serious audition could come any time.

She bit her thumbnail, tearing away the thick off-white keratin disk, and thus, imperceptibly wearing down her front teeth.

The brain couldn't dissolve itself into the body it was attached to, the brain couldn't sever itself, and float free. There was constant tension between body and mind, she thought. The mind kept trying to jettison the body, transform itself into spirit.

The night they met at Abbie's party, they couldn't stop talking, she and Dan. He was funny, intelligent, warm, spontaneous; he seemed to know a little bit about everything; the way he kissed her outside the party was perfect, perfectly timed, perfectly tempered (the velocity with which his neck craned towards her, his use of the tongue, his intuitive awareness of the sensitivity of her neck).

She started on the thumbnail on her left hand.

The first year of their relationship all they did was talk and fuck. She worked nights; he taught mostly in the mornings; it didn't matter; the few hours of overlapping free time that they shared became charged with anticipation and carnal intensity—discovering, unconcealing, pushing, tugging, demanding.

She found him insightful, caring, ambitious; in many fundamental ways she felt that he completed her, that he filled in the parts of her own personality that were lacking. And, of course, he never dated anyone nearly as dashing as her, anyone who could light up a room the way she could. She loved that he loved her looks, that he admired her, was obsessed with her, could never replace her.

Thus, she gave up her apartment in Williamsburg; they signed a lease together. She was happy; he was happy, and they talked about getting a dog, or getting married, or having a kid.

And it was at that point that Dan lost interest in fucking her.

And it was at that point that she became obsessed with fucking him, in direct, inverse relation to his gradual withdrawal from her.

If he didn't want her, who would?

Sex, perversely, became more interesting the longer a relationship went on, because it was almost impossible; the discoveries took more time, revealed more, came from a deeper place . . . or were supposed to. She wanted that—had expected that to happen, was still trying to manipulate her relationship so that it produced that deepening, vivifying effect. She imagined that some kind of cathartic fuck might be in store for them: a healing, transformative fuck that would bring them back to the start.

It might still be possible. He might start going to the gym. She might get a little work done. Or they might just start getting that bodyfeel back even if nothing changed about their bodies physically.

The chemical-level was ultimately what really mattered, and that was tied to the mind-level, obviously.

Women assumed men were as interesting as they were, but they weren't: *they were men.* His desire would swing back. It had to swing back. He wasn't complicated enough to do anything else than be completely hers again.

It occurred to her that white men, academics, who had rejected patriarchy in their published work, often courted Asian women in order to regain access to the very object they had theoretically rejected: a submissive female body.

Her sister had subverted this stereotype, but Mariko hadn't; she had cultivated it precisely because it granted her a secure basis for erotic power. The actress was enmeshed in a gauzy web of expectations, representations, habits; everything had become automatic except falling asleep.

She heard a noise.

Footsteps.

So he *was* up!

This is what she had wanted: to project an aura, an awareness, deep into the tissue of the apartment, to arouse him indirectly through the projection of her own physical and mental anxiety.

She wanted to bind his body back to hers: to taste his dry, sleepy, rancid mouth, to smell his rancid armpits, the shampoo from his shower the previous morning. She wanted contact, transmission, sensual envelopment. She wanted to be pushed against the stove, slapped on the ass. She wanted to be played with; she wanted to feel his fingernails dig into her sides; she wanted to moan, *release*, beg for more and more.

Mariko turned around and Dan was there, wavering in the doorway.

She studied him: he was still lean in some places, paunchy in others; he was aging unevenly: towards boyishness, towards middle-age, towards old-age, simultaneously. Parts of him hadn't changed, parts of him were changed beyond recognition.

Her boyfriend slouched carelessly, carefully in the doorway; he was posing, presumably trying to make an impression, like a toreador or simply an actor in front of a camera, trying to find the right angle to dazzle her, and win her instant submission and admiration.

It was too mental, too much a game.

He was probably awake thinking about how to make his entrance; she knew that he couldn't stop calculating, adjusting, rationalizing; he needed to maintain power and self-esteem at all times (but then again she was the same way).

During the trip they had taken to Greece in August, they only had sex twice: the first and last nights. Strangely, however, Dan had always been careful to appear affectionate in public, at hotels, on the street, at museums, at restaurants—as if they were experiencing new love. Death by decorum.

"Am I bothering you?"

She followed his eyes as they scanned the room: hungry and analytical. He was using her as a mirror, searching himself out in her. It made her feel used and all she could think about was how pissed she was at him, how much he fucking pissed her off.

"No."

"Are you sure?"

Mariko exhaled. "Yeah."

"What's wrong?"

In his own way, Dan was good at creating the appearance of caring; she used to fall for it, but now she spotted it right away. A part of her wanted to fall for it even now, to make things easier.

He was so close to her now, a few feet and she could smell his breath, or thought she could. The kitchen was so small; his face was stubbled; his shirt was creased; his cock stood out slightly in his briefs.

They were both sweating; it was hot in the kitchen. She was sweating on her forehead, under her heavy breasts, between her thighs, between her ass-crack.

She could blow him again; they would both feel better; they needed to exchange heat and fluids. When was the last time that had happened?

"I was having a nightmare, so I forced myself to wake up."

"What was your nightmare about?"

Again the false concern, the false interest, the automatic response. Was it real? Did he really want to know? Was he interested in the contents of her dream-life? Did he want to learn from them? Learn about her?

"I was walking through the woods of somewhere very foreign, like eastern Europe or something, and I didn't know why. I was just walking. And as I went along, strange, ghost-y figures would come and talk to me, tell me stories, offer me food, suggest paths I should take in the forest. And for a while I trusted the ghost creatures, and took their advice, but as I went along I lost all sense of where I was . . . as if I had it anyway . . . and suddenly the ghost-creatures stopped talking to me and I realized that I was all alone, in total silence, and I just began to get scared, like hysterical, and I thought I'd never make it out, and that's when I woke up."

"Shit."

"Yeah."

Dan ran a hand through his thinning hair. Mariko bit her thumbnail, staring at the kitchen walls.

"Dan, can we talk?"

"About what?"

There was so much defensiveness, even potential violence, in his rhetorical question; he, in fact, *didn't* want to go there, didn't want to know "about what." He didn't want to have *this* conversation, that was apparent. He wanted her to feel naive for asking, for proposing a dialogue at this time of night. He wanted her to feel like a fucking child.

The best defense was offense.

Mariko sighed again, bowed her head, exasperated, planting her forehead into the center of the palm of her right hand, massaging the spot between her breasts with her left hand. She wouldn't answer him. She couldn't. It was better to let silence reign . . . which was what he wanted anyway: dense, beautiful waves of non-sound.

He wanted an emptiness in the world to mirror the emptiness he felt inside.

Was that too cruel? Or even right?

Maybe.

She was exhausted.

It was time to start going to yoga again; she could make it to a Yoga For The People class in the morning. It would feel good. She badly wanted to feel good.

"I'm going to bed," Dan said softly.

"Come over here and sit with me."

The desire for closeness was stronger than any rationalization or strategy. She didn't care what either of them said to each other, all of that was ephemeral, neither of them ever meant what they said. Relationships exhausted language over time, so other resources had to be deployed in the effort to cross over into the other's consciousness, inhabit it, and see from the other person's perspective for a second.

He had been avoiding her since they got back from Greece.

There was a moment on a boat off the Dalmatian coast when she was tanning in the sun, feeling sexy, and he wasn't even looking at her—he was reading news on his phone—and he realized that he should be ashamed of how disconnected he was. That indifference wasn't neutral, but very violent and cruel, almost like striking someone hard across the face.

But, the problem was that he didn't *feel* ashamed, not then, for being on his phone, and not now, for not knowing what to do or say. He only knew shame theoretically, externally, as a behavior that he was expected to exhibit. He could only perform it, not mean it.

She could see that he was pleased with himself, having assumed that the whole routine would be a success—because, practically speaking, it always was. He always retained his routine and his comfort and always mollified her. The relationship had never been seriously disturbed. He was amazingly impervious to whatever kind of crises she created. And his strategy worked because she wouldn't acknowledge what was happening, because she wouldn't force him to acknowledge that his interest in her feelings was a ruse, because she'd let him off the hook countless times, and as she would again.

"Okay."

Dan took the second—the only available—seat at the table, fiddling, as soon as he sat down, with the saltshaker, and then, immediately bored of the saltshaker, the newspapers, the proper order of which Mariko had already ruined.

"Can you believe this shit?" Dan said, looking at the front cover of "The Sunday Review," which was divided into two sections, with two headlines, and two graphics, neither of which drew Mariko's attention.

"What shit?"

"This newspaper! The paper of record! It's so fucking stupid! Honestly it makes me furious—everything's dumbed down—I don't know why we subscribe!"

The pathos felt hollow.

"Because you like to complain about it and because you like to pretend that you don't read news on your phone."

This was said with distinct hostility, as a purposeful affront, a warning shot; for a second Mariko believed that, in fact, she was prepared to confront him, hurt him, break things, smash things open.

"Oh yeah. You're right."

Was this an attempt at self-awareness? A sly smile played across his lips; he opened his eyes wider, leaned across the table, kissed her on the forehead, and drew back: "I know it's an easy target—"

"The *Times?*"

"Yeah."

"Why? What do you mean?"

He wanted to talk about himself, examine himself before her: his ideas, politics, habits, his soul. This was part of the ruse: he would inquire into her inner-life, really, her moral life, only so that he could feel justified in talking about his own. He wanted to turn the kitchen-table into a two-way confession booth—in truth, an impossibility.

"I mean, like . . . you know, true story, Noam Chomsky had to see a dentist because he was grinding his teeth every morning reading the papers. Like there's no . . . there's no . . . we've talked about this—there's no real Left; there's no Left left . . . and it's frustrating; liberalism is just kitsch-socialism . . . and I dunno."

Brown undergrad, Harvard for his doctorate. He'd made *sure* she heard his qualifications the night they met, and she'd heard him repeat it, in different ways, with different emphasis, hundreds of times over in social situations. And now this was the best he could do.

"I do feel . . ." he continued, "I do feel this kinda like empathy with *Times* reporters, or folks at *The Washington Post*, or whatever, because journalism is so, so important, but the situation we're in now, like the really dire economic situation honestly requires some kind of revolutionary response . . . shit can't keep going the direction it's going. Right?"

Her boyfriend talked like someone ashamed that his father was a Republican (Dan and his father, a wealthy cardiologist, almost never spoke).

"I mean like, the frame—the essential framing device—used by liberal mainstream papers," he continued, working up a head of steam, "is always extremely misleading, utopian, saturated in the kind of cozy progress perpetuated by the now-dissolving Obama years—"

"I've heard all this before."

"I know, I'm sorry."

"Are you?"

"Should I be?"

"You just said you were. Weren't you being sincere?"

"I dunno."

"I'm serious."

"I'm sorry if I'm boring you; I'm not sorry I have certain intellectual pre-occupations."

This made Mariko laugh aloud: the pretension of such a statement was enormous.

In Greece she had watched him silently, for hours, in the shifting, transitory light of the islands they had toured. She was looking—as she supposed she had always been looking, but with greater urgency, and less illusion—for the moral core that would justify the time she had invested in him, that would bind their relationship together.

Politics was not moral-*ness* (which was to be further distinguished from morality or moralism). Politics had nothing to do with a luminous heart.

"Why are you laughing?" His question was flat, toneless, replete with suppressed anger.

"Why aren't you?"

"Because I don't find myself funny."

"Which is exactly why I'm laughing."

Had she thought, just a second ago, that he was willing to show a little ironic self-awareness? Perhaps he had been, but only on his own terms; he hadn't expected her slashing attacks.

"Mariko . . ."

He reached across the table, took her hands into his.

"What?"

The clasp was like an umbilical cord.

"I'm thinking."

Somehow, she sensed that he was growing hard; she didn't have to look under the table; there was a pressure, perhaps just blood-pressure, which indicated to her that he was undergoing a physiological change. Encouraged, she squeezed his hands as if he were a hospital patient. She felt a slight wetness between her thighs too.

What was happening?

Probably nothing, a false signal amidst the noise of rage. She'd made him feel defensive so that he would use arousal, sex, offensively, to fight back, reclaim the ground he'd lost. She was good at manipulating him.

"I have to wake up early tomorrow; I have to teach."

No, that couldn't be right: he taught at ten, which wasn't that early, and he was an early-riser and never needed much sleep (which is what had gotten him through grad-school with relative ease). He was evading her.

"How early?"

He understood her suggestion: "Earlier than usual, I have some papers left to grade."

"I don't want you to go back to sleep, not yet—"

"Why, Mariko?" His question was tender, pleading, like he was talking to a stubborn child. He could be infuriating.

"What am I supposed to do?"

"What do you mean?"

"What am I supposed to do with myself? Right now."

"Right now? You have the option of sleeping too, you know—"

"No that's not what I mean."

"Oh."

"I mean in general. All of it. Right now. Tomorrow. I don't know. What am I supposed to do? What am I supposed to do about you?"

"You tell me."

He was giving her an out. He'd never given her an out before, though she had never positioned herself to receive one before—not like she was doing now.

"You tell me."

He repeated the question, as if underscoring its importance; he was telling her that he would never act, never propose a real break, that he had accepted their *detente* as a permanent condition of existence. Above all, she knew, he did not want to be responsible for any overtly negative feelings—or, in general, for any feelings.

He wanted her to reclaim responsibility for the hurt they had both endured. It was like he was asking her to clean up after him.

Fuck him.

"I don't know what you expect me to say."

This was the opposite of what she meant: she knew what he expected her to say, what he was longing, begging to hear—that they had reached the end. That this was it.

Dan closed his eyes and rubbed them with his right thumb and forefinger. "I feel like such a turd."

"Because you're being one."

"Okay?"

Mariko watched Dan's mouth grow small, pursed, like the last of opportunity for defiance, for independence, had just escaped through his lips.

"Fuck off," she said.

"Hey—"

"*What?*"

Mariko looked down at her breasts: her robe was open. She looked at her thighs, the unshaven pubic hair poking through her panties, and stared at her stomach, which had just, imperceptibly, begun to bulge, and she felt ashamed, as if someone had opened a valve in her abdomen, her chest, her brain, the backs of her eyes.

She had lost the definition and tan of Greece, where she had eaten mostly fish and goat cheese, drunk only white wine. Her body had begun to take on the qualities of a city-body again: paleness, flabbiness, shapelessness. Yoga in the morning was a must.

Dan leaned forward in his chair and kissed Mariko on the neck. She craned her neck away from him, towards the table, as he continued to kiss her. She put her hand over his face, like a muzzle.

"Stop."

"Let's have sex."

"Stop."

"I want to though."

Mariko saw that his cock was pointing straight up, making a tent out of his briefs. She wasn't used to this, not anymore—

"Please."

"Where is this coming from?"

"Does it matter?"

It had been almost a week, or maybe even two, since they'd even kissed with tongue. She'd lost track. Had it been a month?

Above all, she wanted to stop feeling so alone, so maybe it would be alright. She could just give in.

God—she wanted to.

Mariko, standing up, sat on Dan's lap, and their mouths met again immediately, softly; they were trembling. Awkwardly, he tugged at her shoulders, and all at once, they fell together onto the floor.

For a moment, she felt incredibly good, pure, unadulterated joy— chaotic, and basically primal. Here they were, two little creatures, exchanging the last of their love. She was experiencing her own charisma, her physical power to *draw*—and the refracted, muffled, transfigured expression of their original desire for each other.

"We need a condom."

Her boyfriend stood up, pulling his briefs up from his ankles.

"Where are they?" he asked.

"In the medicine cabinet."

"Really?"

"Yes, doofus."

Dan went to the bathroom, closed the door; Mariko rolled her eyes.

"Are you taking a shit?"

"Yes," he muttered loudly through the door.

"Remember to wipe."

Mariko stood up, went to the cabinet where they kept their alcohol (it couldn't properly be called a liquor cabinet), and took down a bottle of expensive vodka they kept for special occasions.

Why not?

She poured herself a shot, in a little shot-glass she'd bought in a set from Ikea the year they'd moved in together. Vodka never got her drunk for some reason; it made her feel a little bit warmer and looser, almost like she'd been exercising.

Mariko associated the smell of Dan's shit with her father's; those were the only two bathroom smells she'd ever known, besides, she supposed, her own. Women had a way of concealing their smells: it was semi-mystical, totally illogical, probably a function of repression. Nevertheless, the myth had power: she didn't know what her sister's shit smelled like, or her mother's, or any woman's.

Mariko didn't use public restrooms, didn't go at restaurants, only at home, only when Dan wasn't home, unless it was an absolute emergency (and sometimes even then).

Women were expected to envelop their bodies in shame. They were expected to simultaneously represent the dual ideals of dewy fuckability and maternal stability. Implicit in her upbringing was the notion that she should be well-groomed, clean, a machine for sexual-pleasure and childbearing.

Was he stalling for time?

She heard the water running: a flush, then the faucet.

The door opened.

There he was: a Quixotic figure with soapy red hands, a flaccid cock, red hairs curling over his slightly pudgy abdomen, a crooked, ambivalent grin on his face.

"So where were we?"

Mariko closed her robe, from left to right and right to left, with each hand, as if she were cold, which she wasn't.

"I find this upsetting—"

"Why?"

"Because I don't know why you want to sleep with me now, as opposed to all the other nights—"

Dan shook his head vigorously: "Don't think of it like that—"

"Why not?" she said. "Did you really poop?"

Dan laughed: "Yeah. I did. It was great."

What a fucking child.

Mariko scrunched up her face. "Do you ever try to see things from my perspective?"

"Sure."

"Really?"

"Yes."

"You have to know what my perspective is to see things from my perspective," Mariko added sharply.

"True."

"So do you know what my perspective is?"

"I'm trying to learn—"

"No, you're not."

Mariko looked at her phone on the table. It occurred to her that it would make her feel better, even for perverse reasons. She felt little tremors of pleasure just thinking about it.

Her phone leached away her attention, trivializing her thoughts, her values, her desires; she felt herself growing less intentional by the day: she was more and more willing to give into passing impulses, as if she were being conditioned (as if she were a lab mouse).

Her creature-brain was too weak for her phone: it stripped it of all its soul-like qualities. Sight: screen: pleasure.

The loss of something precious.

Me.

Massive flows of anxiety, concern, love, hatred, anger, hope, were produced by her phone, which acted like a toxin in a sensitive ecosystem.

"Mariko—"

"What?"

"Are you even listening to me?"

"No."

"Great . . ." Dan grimaced.

Mariko retreated back to the table, where her phone was. She picked it up and began to scroll.

"Mariko—"

She felt like laughing at herself—at both of them. He probably wanted to be on his phone, too.

"Understanding another person takes work," Mariko said in a flat voice, "and we don't put in the work anymore."

"Are you bored of me?"

"I wanna ask the same question."

"I'm not bored of you . . ." Dan started to say.

"But— "

"I'm bored of certain things. Tired of certain things."

"Well duh."

"I know, it's not a blindingly original insight—that things get stale or typical or whatever."

"It doesn't have to be blindingly original, Dan. It just needs to be accurate."

"I know. And we're talking about it. So."

"Are we talking about it?"

"What do you call this?"

"A negotiation to decide whether or not we're gonna talk about it."

"That's comical."

They were both aware that his hard-on was going to waste.

"Have you been drinking?"

What a question.

"I had a shot."

"Wow."

"What?"

"Vodka shots are a little trashy, don't you think?" He glanced at the bottle on the counter.

"Then I'm trashy. Next question."

"Why don't you just come back to bed . . .?"

"I'm curious to see where this conversation is going . . ." Mariko looked down at Dan's rapidly deflating cock.

"We can talk, but also be lying down . . ."

"You'll fall asleep."

"No I won't."

"You're so gonna fall asleep."

"It's two in the morning—"

"It's twelve thirty-three."

Dan raised his eyebrows, then looked away, past Mariko, towards the dimness in the window. She wondered what he was thinking, and wondered if she was going too far, if she was being too hard on him, if she was threatening breakup and breakdown and loneliness.

It was like they couldn't exist without the tension of possible catastrophe.

This was why she loved theater—or rather, the few great plays in existence—so much: because you play with the obscene darkness of the human soul without really risking permanent damage. Engaging in *real* emotional and psychological warfare like this was a waste of her talents.

Dan pirouetted on the parquet floor. There was a significant and growing patch of skin on the crown of his head. His baldness was an indication, a trace, of a more significant and less visible loss. But what was it? His mouth was open, but he couldn't speak.

"Didn't you hear me?"

"I heard you," Dan said in a toneless voice.

Mariko, avoiding eye-contact, slumped to the floor.

"It's something I've been thinking about—"

"That's clear enough."

"Don't pout." She waved dismissively in her boyfriend's direction.

"I don't think this is deserved."

"I'm not blaming you."

"Sure ya are." Dan looked around the room, as if they were being watched. "You don't take responsibility for anything that happens in your own life. It's always someone . . . a co-worker, a director, another actor, *your sister—*"

"What does my sister have to do with us?" There was a hint of deeper suspicion in Mariko's voice.

"You resent her."

"Tell me something I don't know—"

Dan, almost as if approaching a wild animal, crouched down on the floor.

"You resent her in a way that's really dangerous for you, because it's your way of narrativizing this feeling of martyrdom that you have; you use me for the same purpose, I mean . . ."

"What the fuck?"

"I'm telling you how I see things."

Dan's lips were pursed. She could tell that he was already tired of this line of argument, which wasn't an argument so much as an ambush, the ritual slaughter that he had unintendedly become the victim of. And she was aware that this was her tendency: to pick on the way he spoke, on the little slips of academic jargon that entered into ordinary speech, as if they were betrayals of some deeper authenticity.

This was their ritual: she spilled his blood, drank it to restore her strength. It could have easily been the other way around, and maybe it would be soon.

They were still on the kitchen floor. They both laid on their backs, fingertips brushing. Mariko felt a little thrill run down her spine.

"Why don't we have a real conversation? A real dialogue."

"Okay then let's do it. Put some coffee on."

He was hard again. His cock was pointing right at the ceiling.

Dan closed his eyes. "I think I've forgotten how to talk. Words curdle on my tongue." He licked his lips and front teeth, like he had just finished a greasy meal.

"Interesting metaphor."

"Soured milk?"

"Yeah."

"Well that's what it feels like."

"What a sexy night we're having."

"I'm embarrassed that I don't want to sleep with you more, Mariko."

"I'm embarrassed for you too."

"I know it hurts you."

"It doesn't hurt me," she said, angrily. "It confuses me."

"It hurts—"

"I'm hot, so you should want to."

"I know I should."

"But you can see why I worry that I'm not hot enough or that I'm losing my hotness."

"Absurd."

"Is it?"

"That's not how I think . . ." Dan whined.

"Okay."

When they had first met, Dan had promised to maintain, implicitly, an aesthetic partnership; he had promised to nourish her: mind, body, and spirit. Instead, she was starving. He rationed whatever soulfulness he had for himself and his own needs.

She understood that the same accusation could be leveled at her: that she'd fail to enliven his dry, academic existence with the frivolity and spontaneity of her dramatic life. He'd needed her, intuitively, that's why he'd sought her out, because he was seeking balance: a compensatory warmth and vividness. It was a highly traditional arrangement and highly gendered one.

This embarrassed them both. For Dan, a relationship of the kind they practiced meant violating in practice certain cherished theories about identity, gender, sexuality, and, improbably enough, economics, too. It was simply too traditional.

Movies, dinner, the expensive health food she sometimes insisted on eating—it all added up.

They never talked about it, never agreed that this was the way they wanted to live; they never had an honest conversation about their economic lives. New York was expensive; they didn't live extravagantly; they both worked hard, and therefore, there didn't seem to be an issue.

Dan's relatively higher (though still pathetic) associate professor's salary had totemic power, however: it underwrote, guaranteed, their continued life together; he imagined that he would have it for the rest of his life and counted on having it for the rest of his life. It was what he had worked so hard for; it was the fruit of more than fifteen years of apprenticeship: first as an undergraduate, then as a graduate, then as a fellow, then as an assistant professor.

To gain that modicum of security had cost him much of what was otherwise known as youth, the youth that Mariko, herself, had not been willing to sacrifice, and was, in her own fragile way, still clinging to.

She knew that he thought of her as a kind of freeloader (and assumed that when they got married, and he became a full professor, she wouldn't work at all).

She remained a server at a restaurant, moreover, simply because she hadn't developed herself, hadn't learned anything new. Dan, on the other hand, had embraced practical, boring, *real* adulthood. On a deeper level, he had accepted getting older and she hadn't.

But, for a man, it was easier (from Mariko's perspective). A man's self-esteem wasn't necessarily tied to the smoothness of his skin, the tautness of his body. Men got vaguely better-looking even while they got worse looking: grey hairs, weight, wrinkles—all seemed to add to their sex appeal (from Dan's perspective).

"Let's see a movie tomorrow night. Like a date night. We haven't done that in ages."

"I don't really like movies," Dan said, before adding, after a long pause, "I only like Lars Von Trier films."

Mariko rolled her eyes.

Only Lars Von Trier films. What the fuck did that mean? She'd never heard him say something like that before.

This was surely an affectation he'd picked up from a colleague, or an article. He was a sail turning to catch the wind.

Dan was unable to admit that there were gaps in his knowledge. He was a pseudo-humanist, a pseudo-generalist; he pretended that the scope of his expertise was large, when in fact, it was miniscule. He knew a few things about Marx and nineteenth-century literature, and beyond that, he was basically a philistine—not that he would ever admit it.

He covered his eyes with the palms of his hands and sucked air into his lungs, as if he was having trouble breathing.

"My eyes hurt," he offered.

"Okay . . . Dan–"

"What?"

"We never talk about it."

"Because I don't want to," he said gruffly.

It was coming up on the two-year anniversary and he still hadn't acknowledged that he was consumed by thoughts about his mother.

Was he even conscious of the pain he was in?

Did it matter?

Mariko refused to absorb that pain into her body and let him transform. That wouldn't be fair. It was better to just let him crumble.

Her mouth was dry.

"Can you get me water from the fridge?" Mariko asked. "I'm too tired to get up."

"Okay," Dan said, walking at most two steps from the table to the fridge to the Brita filter.

It was so hot in the kitchen. September had begun to feel like August; there was no autumn, autumn was shrinking into a few weeks between October and November. The leaves changed later, and the humidity of the summer lingered in the air for months longer than it had when she'd first moved to the city in 2006.

If Dan got a job outside of the city, she would insist that he take it. The more she thought about it, the more she was ready to leave (and had been for a long time). Mariko could not afford to live comfortably in the city; she was sick of this small, shitty apartment (even if her partner wasn't).

As part of his assiduous Marx-ish nonchalance, he never really thought about the conditions in which he lived. Dan wanted to be seen as someone who was willing to live in an undesirable place.

"You're so pretentious, you know that?"

"Because of the Lars Von Trier thing?"

"Yeah. Like, why did you feel the need to say that?"

"Because, it's, like, true."

"There's no audience here. You realize that right? No one's listening to us. No one's judging your judgement."

"I didn't say there was."

"You talk like it though—like someone's keeping a record of everything you say."

"I try to be self-aware, that's all."

"Fuck off."

"You really don't like me." His voice was low and chastened with a hint of anger.

"You're . . . I don't have words for what you are, what I think of you . . . right now . . ."

"Yes, you do." Dan reached across the table, stroking the top of her hands with the tips of his fingers.

"What are you feeling right now?"

"Dunno."

"You talk like a teenage boy sometimes."

"Habits are habits," Dan responded curtly.

Mariko withdrew her hand. "Are you fucking somebody else?"

"No—like, you always ask—"

"Dan, because something is clearly up —"

"We used to talk about how we didn't want to become this."

"And what's this?"

"Boring," he said, after a short pause.

"I see."

The thought couldn't be completed, and Dan had nothing to complete it with. There was no rejoinder, no dialectical maneuver. Boredom was a basic, constituent element of their relationship.

They had gradually, brick by brick, stone by stone, built this enclosure around themselves: an enclosure so complete, so airless, with walls so high, that neither of them could see what was on the other side of the wall (though they sometimes imagined it).

"Tell me how to get the passion back, Mariko."

"I hate when you use that tone of voice."

"What tone of voice?"

"Fake compassion."

"It's how I talk . . ."

"I hate how you talk then."

Dan, who had stood up again, tapped his middle-finger on the stove-top, as if he could drum out an answer.

Mariko got up and returned to the table.

What she had passed over, overlooked, for years, was his averageness, which now, to her, seemed incredibly significant. Her task, as his lover, his partner, was to recognize who he was, so that she could recognize who she became by choosing him. She had absorbed his averageness into her skin—now, she was sweating it out.

"Hey . . ."

"Don't be fake-sweet with me . . ."

"I'm not being . . ."

"Come on . . ."

"I just want to . . ."

"Shut up, just let me think for a second . . ."

He was physically closed off, or even afraid of her; his body language was closed down, closed away, like he was hiding a physical object from her—as if he were a prisoner and she was the guard.

"I don't even like Lars Von Trier—" Mariko said. "Such sloppy work."

"Why are you bringing that up? Like—"

"Because you think he's so great, so incisive or true or whatever bullshit, and he's not; he's an asshole; his camera, his actors—all lazy—he's dumb; I don't like his films. He has nothing to say except the world sucks—"

"No, but that's the fucking point, Mariko: it's raw . . . also—the world *does* suck—"

To Mariko, this sudden outburst of anger was comical precisely because it was so tragically out of place.

She laughed. Then he laughed, realizing what she was laughing at.

"I want you to let me see you, Dan. Like really *see* you."

"How do I *do* that?" he asked, with the emphasis on the *do*, implying that vulnerability was an action, a physical decision (which it probably was).

"You just do—like—look at me; look me in the eyes—"

"I am."

Dan stared at her, pleading.

They both wanted a great thing from a little moment: to bury time-past beneath the horizon of the future, to start over.

They could feel the slow century moving over them like water.

The professor, guiding Mariko back to the table, began to pry open her short, delicate fingers, petal by petal.

"So now: I'm looking you in the eyes," he said, almost confidently.

"What happens next?" Mariko said, sounding like a little girl.

"I kiss you."

"And then?"

"You kiss me back."

Dan leaned across the table, pushed his lips against hers, just like he had earlier, perhaps trying to, but this time, they both half-fell across the table towards each other, magnetized. They grabbed, groped, scratched—sliding to the floor again: Dan going first, bracing his body with his arm, so that he could half-catch Mariko, who landed on top of him, working her way into a position where she could straddle him.

It was like they were rehearsing a scene, starting and stopping the same maneuvers over and over again.

She bit his lower lip, his neck, his ear; he pulled her bosom towards his face, pressing himself to it.

Then: she drew back, rolled away, stood up, suddenly.

"What's wrong?"

"Everything, go away."

Dan raised his eyebrows and sat up a little.

His cock had been hard, then got soft, now it was hard again, maybe harder than ever. Mariko eyed it, suspiciously, as if it was a counterfeit.

"I live here."

"I wish you didn't."

"This is *my* apartment."

"It *was* yours," she pouted, "now it's mine too—I pay the rent too—and anyway, I just wish you weren't here; at least right now. I think I want to cry."

"Then cry."

"I can't—"

"In front of me?"

"No. Not right now I can't."

He was still on the floor, his hand lingering just above his groin as if he couldn't or wouldn't accept that Eros had fled.

Mariko leaned against the wall. She wasn't sure either. It would be easy to kneel back down, pull his cock gently from the soft folds of his pajamas, suck it clean, and go to bed. It would not be the first time she used sex, a specific kind of sex, to stop a conflict, or to neutralize it.

"Come here."

"No."

He motioned, smiling.

"No no no no no: gross."

Dan slipped his hand under his pajamas, began to pump.

"Stop."

"No, I'm turned on."

Fucking was how they discovered each other and how they lost each other.

"Why is it so hot in the kitchen? *It's horrible.*" Mariko complained.

"I'm turned on—" Dan repeated, ignoring her.

"Wish I could say the same."

"I know you're turned on too—"

"Get a life."

"I know you are—" he reiterated, almost as if he were drunk.

"I want nothing to do with you right now." Mariko's voice was soft and grainy—almost meditative, or maybe just numb.

"Thanks."

"You're so thin-skinned. I'm just speaking to you rationally about how I feel—"

"You really think you're being rational?"

"Yes, I do."

"How so?"

"How so? Dan, I mean—like—what? I'm being self-aware, or trying to . . . noticing patterns . . . trying to stop the same thing from happening over and over again . . . I um—"

"You um, what?"

"Rational. Using your head. Being logical. Logically speaking, we make, we're making, each other unhappy."

"I don't care about being happy."

"Very noble of you."

"I give up," Dan said, throwing his arms in the air.

Mariko rolled her eyes toward the ceiling, her fingers curled back towards the palms of her hands like she was trying to use her nails to pierce the skin and draw blood.

"I'm going to bed . . ." Dan continued.

Mariko didn't answer.

"Ah, but you don't want me to do that . . . actually you want me to sit here like I'm convicted of some emotional crime . . . to sit here and wait for you to pass a final judgment—"

"What judgment do you think I'm going to pass, Dan?"

"You've already said it."

"Because I'm angry with you—"

"Does that justify—?"

"Yes. It does. People should feel angry. People should be angry. If they're angry." Mariko asserted.

"Why?"

"Because then they're not mummified inside their own lives."

"Gross."

"You know what I mean."

"No, I don't think I do."

"For a smart person . . ."

"I know: for a smart person I'm really, really dumb."

"Yeah. You are."

She could tell that he was aware of the smell of her armpits; there was an odor, too, emanating from the area around her groin, slightly sickly-sweet.

He kissed the top of her wrist, caressed, rubbing fingers in hard, small oscillations against her wrist-joints. She responded, moaning again, almost giving in.

They each attempted to move closer together and further away simultaneously.

They were aroused, frustrated. They were losing consciousness of their own actions. They felt the heat from each other's bodies; they felt how tired they were—maybe they could just fall asleep, cozy and comfortable.

Yet intimacy had become so political that it was impossible to know what the implications of physical surrender would be. They both said that they wanted intimacy while simultaneously remaining uncertain of what intimacy was, what it meant, or why it was important.

When Dan moved forward, Mariko, even without shifting her position, would find a way to move away, shift backwards; it was a matter of energy and balance: the axis of her head on her neck, the plane of her shoulders, the balance of her body weight on her ass or on her feet—each muscle and joint—worked to keep him at bay, to maintain equilibrium.

Dan too, without being aware of it, kept recoiling from Mariko: if she began to bring herself forward, accepting him, he, terrified of her sensual presence, slipped back, or, rather, slumped back, his posture becoming more and more convex.

"I'm pissed off, honestly, this is just . . ." Dan trailed off before he could find the words to match what was going on in his brain. "This is just like fucking making me want to scream or . . . I dunno, Mariko; I'm seriously willing to like walk out and leave you here and get a hotel . . . I hate who I am right now . . . or who you make me feel like I am."

There were several seconds of silence.

"I don't like myself like this either," Mariko said.

"You need to start acting again."

"Duh, dude, duh."

"So do it."

Mariko folded her hands, carefully, right on top of left. Then, she began to squeeze her left hand in her right, as if she was trying to squeeze paint from the tube.

"So . . . what is it gonna be?"

"Leave me alone."

"I thought you wanted to communicate."

"I do, but my point is that I can't."

"Sure ya can: it's just a matter of trying."

"No, there's structural damage."

"And you expect to go on like this indefinitely."

"I have no expectations. I have no plans. I have no dreams or ideals. I'm blocked."

"Which brings me back to your acting career . . ."

"You're one of those people who find the arts ennobling without having any idea what it means to actually be an artist."

"See: that didn't sound passive-aggressive, it just sounded aggressive to me."

"Qualify it however you like. What matters is the content. Did you hear the content of what I just said?"

"I heard it, but I'm not sure I agree with it."

"What's there not to agree with?"

"The idea that I don't understand what it means to be an artist."

"Have you ever made anything, written anything, performed anything?"

"Not really. But."

"But what?"

"I've spent most of my adult life living inside the brains of geniuses."

"Which does not mean in any way whatsoever that you've understood them. It means that you've generated theories to compensate for your lack of understanding."

"And do you think that *you* understand, Mariko?" The emphasis on *you* was meant to wound.

"I understand what it feels like to try and fail, to be the object under examination; to be on the inside. But let's face it, you don't consider acting a real art, you think of it as entertainment, so—"

"You keep attributing things to me that I never said."

"I'm saying the things that you don't say out loud."

"You're boxing me in."

"You like it."

"You know, I just find it so pretentious . . ." he mumbled, looking away from her, "the whole notion of 'being an artist.' It's just crap."

"Okay, now you're proving my point for me."

"What point?"

"That you hold what I do in contempt."

"Sometimes, yeah. I can't help it."

Mariko's diaphragm contracted, the airflow cut off. She closed her eyes, smiled. "What about what you do? Well, indulgent is a good place to begin. You indulge the tendency people have to feel masterful or even, simply, intelligent. It's a low-stakes game played like a high-stakes game."

"Everything people do is a low-stakes game played as if it's a high-stakes game."

"So nothing matters and we're all pretending as if everything or at least some things mattered?"

Dan nodded gravely. "Yup."

Mariko analyzed her lover like she would analyze a character in a play. Dan was circumscribed, bound by certain rules: fixed into place. A dying sun in a Ptolemaic universe.

"There are moments where my brain is just like pulsating—like I hate you. Like I just hear the words 'I hate you' over and over in my head—"

"It's really infuriating the way you flip between extremes, Mariko. And disturbing."

"Cool."

Dan bit his knuckle, grimacing.

"What?" Mariko asked. "*What?*"

"I want and need us to work out."

"Same, I think."

"Really?"

She could see the genuine, almost childish fear in his eyes—and she felt immensely guilty, and as a result, resigned herself to not pushing things further than this. He just couldn't take it. Every time she contrived to trap him, hurt him, she regretted it; he was too easy to hurt, too naive and defenseless—that was his defense. Was he aware of this?

She thought about the suburb he grew up in (a new development outside of Cincinnati)—the house that his father, the cardiologist, had built from scratch in the late eighties: comfortable, sterile, unnecessarily large (the house his mother died in). The environment he grew up in was totally regulated, predictable, safe; according to Dan, his parents never fought openly. So, even as he approached forty, her boyfriend had no real capacity or tolerance for conflict.

Mariko went to go pee, leaving the bathroom door open, which she normally never did.

When she had emptied her bladder, Mariko used her right foot to flush, balancing on her left foot, leaning slightly against the wall adjacent to the toilet.

When she returned to the kitchen, Dan was deep in thought.

They sat in silence for a few awkward seconds.

"Well?" she asked.

"I have nothing to say."

She guessed what he was thinking about (his mother had committed suicide last Christmas), but didn't say anything.

Men poeticized their mothers because they couldn't poeticize anything else. Men revered and needed their mothers; only through their mothers could they access what was left of their emotional lives. And that was why Dan was struggling and suffering so much: because that link between mother and son had been severed, and Mariko wasn't game to play the role of replacement-mother. To stand in for that symbol, to absorb it into her skin, would mean nothing less than chaos.

Mariko moved close to the table, where Dan was resting his head in his hands; instinctively, she peeled his hands away from his face and kissed him. "You look tired."

"Yeah, duh."

Her instinct was to console him, draw him close, vivify his fading existence with what remained of her own ashy light. It would feel good to make him feel good. She played the role of sympathetic partner naturally; naturalness was an essential, the essential, part of acting.

A domestic relationship was no different to her than childhood in that respect: you had to manipulate your environment to survive.

It was so strange, she thought, that people entered into romantic relationships with others, when what they wanted was to be left alone! Being "with" someone meant keeping them at a distance: under control, pacified.

"Am I making you miserable?" Mariko asked, quietly, in her chest-voice, signaling her willingness to cooperate.

"Am I making you miserable?" Dan asked.

"We're making each other miserable. But."

"But what?"

"I don't want it to end . . ." Mariko said, to her own surprise.

"I don't either."

"So what are we going to do?"

"Who the hell knows?" Dan asked rhetorically, before slumping to the kitchen table, pushing his head into the crook of his elbows.

"Now can you leave me alone?" Mariko said, drumming her fingers on the countertop.

"I'll stay out here, you can have the bedroom."

"Oh, what an offer—"

"Please?" Dan pleaded.

"You're really desperate aren't you? Like, this is too much for you; you can't deal with it. I'm asking you to think too much about your own feelings, or feel them too much, and you can't . . . you can't do anything with them."

"Hmm . . . well . . ." he bit his thumbnail automatically . . . "Sure, yeah. I have issues. What do you want me to say? I have issues. Of course it's not easy for me to talk about certain things a certain way. I was brought up not to talk about my feelings. It's so ingrained in me, that um, I dunno. You can't shame me into talking the way you want me to talk."

"That's not what I'm trying to do."

"That's exactly what you're trying to do."

This gave Mariko pause. It was hard to deny. "I'm trying to provoke you, but not through shame."

"Then through what?"

"Truth."

Dan snorted at the word "truth."

"I'm serious . . ."

"Truth's such a weighty thing to invoke."

"Not eternal truth, Dan, just the truth of the way we are."

"There's no way to sum up our problems. They're complex. They're shifting. They're gonna keep changing. You can't rely on shitty, pop psychology . . ."

"What the fuck are you—?"

"'I think about my own feelings too much.' Wow. Amazing insight."

"It doesn't have to be surprising to be important."

"I don't think about my feelings too much, I feel them too little."

"There ya go."

A long silence.

"Don't you think that I'm upset too? That I want more too? Don't you think that I feel trapped? Trapped in my own head? In this relationship? Trapped in so many senses . . . this city . . . this livelihood? Don't you think I feel terrifyingly trapped? Like, of course I do . . . of course I do . . . I've never felt anything other than trapped . . . which is why I don't want to blame you . . . and which is why I wish you found a way to not blame me . . . because there are so many other things at play . . . It's too hard to have to constantly check in with yourself and analyze . . . I mean, you said I think too much about . . . but I'm not . . . I'm thinking about way more important things, honestly—things way more important than you or I . . . so much emotional life gets neglected. My sex life gets neglected. I'll admit. You get neglected."

"I'm not a child, I'm not asking you to take care of me."

"That's not what I mean by neglect."

"I know."

"Okay then. So what was my point? My point is that you need to be patient with me. My point is that I'm trying to get a little breathing space, but that I'm . . . um . . . cripplingly busy . . . cripplingly paralyzed by wanting to write, but needing to teach and research—"

"I'm so tired of that excuse."

"The excuse that I support us?"

"You don't—"

"You pay about twenty percent of the bills. It's basically a token contribution—"

"Bullshit."

"Let's do the math."

He was serious; Mariko looked at the ceiling. It probably *was* twenty percent—but that wasn't the point! She had savings. She could support herself if she wanted to. It's not like she was sponging off him. Was she?

Hell no.

"I'm going to bed. You can sleep on the futon."

Dan didn't move and neither did Mariko, for a moment. Neither party could tell if the other was bluffing. So they remained frozen, temporarily, like two animals staring across a clearing in the woods. They remained like this for at least thirty seconds. They were each afraid of the predatoriness of the world. Fear, hatred, distrust, deceit, irrational desire: they had closed the doors of their relationship on all of these things, or tried to—but suffering had found its way in. Indecision only preserved the feeling of fear, of disappointed love, emotional solitude, spiritual yearning.

Absurdly, Mariko was aware that she was still wet, and that Dan was *just* hard enough to fuck. She could just take two steps, hold out her hands, lift him out of the kitchen chair, draw him into the bedroom.

But instead she was frozen.

"Do you mean that?"

"Mean what—that you should sleep out here? Absolutely."

"Mari . . ."

"Does that scare you, Dan—does that make you feel naughty? Like you've done something wrong." Her tone was biting.

"It's just bleak. Very, very bleak."

"Because that's what things are."

"Mari . . ." he repeated again, almost whispering.

The space between them was tissue thin.

Reaching across the table, he stroked her forearms with his fingertips, kissed her neck. She shivered and went over to hug him.

"I do love you—" she said.

"I love you too, Mari, so much. Like holy fuck."

"Then what are we doing?"

"I don't know! It's so sad . . ." Dan said, continuing to kiss her neck.

"I don't think it has to be," she said, without any real conviction.

"I'm in so much pain."

"I know you are. I am too," she asserted, almost as if competing with him.

He stopped kissing her, and returned fully to his chair, taking a deep breath. Mariko studied him, feeling exhausted all of a sudden. Anger was energizing, vulnerability draining. They both really were terrified of being alone: she had to acknowledge it. They were both terrified of being separate people with separate problems: little atoms on the map of reality. Relationship problems were tolerable in the sense that the problems themselves were a source of meaning. A relationship was a cult of two.

"I'm in a lot of trouble," he said, surprising her with his choice of language.

"Trouble how?"

"Nothing real. Just internal. I feel like something in me has been collapsing for a long time, like a building implosion played in slow motion."

What do you do, she wondered, when the sincerity that binds you to yourself and the world disappears? Should you proceed as if nothing has changed? Propelled forward by one's own considerable self-deception and commodification, should you, and can you, hit the brakes? She had no idea.

"Damn, Dan."

"I'm being hyperbolic, but—"

"No you're not; you're saying something significant. It's okay. Just let it out. Talk about it . . ."

"I mean—you know, you know—I'm *grieving*."

"And what else—?

"What else? What else would there be? I mean my Mom fucking offed herself. *My fucking Mom*—"

She reached across the table for his hand. "What else?"

"Well, just like so much pressure with teaching, writing, being here for you . . ."

"You don't have to 'be here for me,' Dan. I'm fine. I'm doing fine."

"I'm not sure I really believe that."

This hurt her. "You don't have to."

He gave her a cold look: "I often feel like I do."

"Why?" She girded herself for his answer, but none was forthcoming. Dan bit at his thumbnail. "Yo—"

"It's the way you are, Mari."

"What does that mean?"

"It means you're kinda needy."

"'Kinda needy . . .'"

"That's what I said."

He'd never been that direct before. Was it really hard to tell her what she already knew? No, but it had taken years anyway. She felt a mixture of frustration and relief.

"It's okay to tell me things like that, Dan."

"Is it?"

"Why, have I reacted poorly in the past? At attempts to . . . ?"

"Yes, you have."

Mariko thought about this. She had, she had to admit, used her capacity for passion, for big emotions—stage effects essentially—to overwhelm him at key moments. She implicitly had always understood that his de facto reasonableness could never match the force of her sheer personality, and she had taken advantage of it. There was no hidden motive: it was just easier to dominate the relationship than be dominated by it. Ironically, in his own reasonable, timid way, he was letting her know this.

"Sorry about that," she said, a little sullenly.

"I forgive you."

"Do you?"

"I hope so."

"You really don't even like me, Dan, do you?"

"Maybe not, but I still love you."

"I guess those things are compatible, huh—"

"Amazingly, yes, they are."

"God damn."

"Isn't that kinda like—logical for people who have been together for a while? Certain things deepen while other things die."

"I'd like for you not to hate me actually."

"Mariko, I don't hate you. I just get frustrated."

"Okay, but it sounded like you were saying—"

"I just feel kinda browbeaten sometimes."

"*Jesus.*"

"I'm sorry, Mariko . . ."

"No—see I'm doing it again—right now—" Mariko admitted, catching herself.

"Yeah, you are."

"Can we get back to what you were saying about your Mom?"

"There's nothing to say . . ." he insisted, exasperated. "I mean—I said it—you know the basic state of affairs—"

"Why can't you just be emotional for more than ten seconds before clamming up?"

"Culture. Society. I dunno. My dad. Repression. Pick one."

"All of the above."

"I am the way I am."

"Same."

"So maybe we just don't get along," Dan suggested, rubbing his bald spot.

"Maybe we don't."

Had she ever "gotten along with" someone she'd been with? Did high school relationships count? Nothing had ever really been easy. The periods of flow state were always very brief, going back to when she was eighteen or nineteen.

"That sucks."

"Life sucks," Mariko said flatly.

She wanted to believe that relationships were about compatibility, about two people who just got each other, but there was no evidence that there was anyone who got her, and that there was anyone she got. The only evidence was for struggle, trench warfare, incremental gains of understanding and sympathy.

"I'm trying to think of something affirmative to say," Dan said after a moment.

"Oh, great, great."

"Can we go to the bedroom?"

"Why?"

"It's just a more comfortable place to talk."

"Okay."

Dan took Mariko's hands and led her to their room. The bed sheets were a mess, the window open; there was a pleasant breeze and a little light from the street and the moon. They collapsed onto the mattress, Dan first, Mariko second. She put her head on his chest.

"I can hear your heart beating."

"How's it doing?"

"A little gimpy."

"Gimpy?"

"Like it has a limp."

"Sounds bad."

"I'm joking."

"I know.

Dan kissed the top of his girlfriend's head. She wondered if her hair smelled good. She hadn't washed it in a few days (to preserve the natural oils, she rarely shampooed).

"I just want to feel loved and give love . . ." she said, closing her eyes.

He stroked her head. "That's all there is . . . all there is . . ."

"I'm so sleepy, Dan."

"Same . . ."

"But I don't wanna stop talking . . ."

"Me neither . . ."

"I love you . . ."

"I love you too . . ."

Mariko listened to a car drive by, zoning out on the situation at hand, and melting into her somatic awareness of the realm beyond the apartment: the street, the city, the earth itself. A part of her wouldn't mind if she never woke up, if this was the final sleep. She felt strangely at peace with the thought.

3

He could hear her snoring.

The mechanism that made communication possible was broken and there was, seemingly, no way of repairing it. They could no longer process the emotional data they provided one another; they both moved about in a strange lostness. The language they used with one another, their gestures, their touch, all had remained more or less the same; only the meaning, or meaningfulness, had been lost.

The professor's knees and back felt stiff; his eyes still hurt from staring at his Macbook all day. He desperately didn't want to have to wake up and teach; he felt an incredible longing to remain at home all day. It had been so long since he just relaxed and read a book for pleasure.

The array of messages and platforms assaulted and confused the brain, which already had its own inborn voices and perspectives—its own warring hemispheres. Modern people could only strive to retroactively make meanings out of scatterings, to fuse hurried improvisations into music, he thought. It was sad.

Dan resented the working conditions of cognitive labor, of content creation: 24/7 focus, one hundred percent response-rate; omnipresence was the expectation on social media (which was torture). He wanted a place for order, solitude, contemplation, self-effacement; he used to go to The Cloisters on the weekends, but he'd stopped doing that several years ago.

It had become impossible for an English professor to find time to think or read deeply: the irony did not escape him.

A dumbness rose through his brainstem like sap. When was the last time he felt truly awake? When was the last time he felt like he inhabited the body that carried him from place to place, day to day?

The kitchen was stubbornly warm. He hated how September nights no longer cooled down like they had in his youth.

What the body could sense the brain denied. Human cognition wouldn't act on the sense-data of climate change. That was asking too much. All connection to the mytho-poetic parts of consciousness had been severed. Equinox, solstice: these vitally important days passed by without anyone noticing.

If the sea rose, the place he was living right now would be under water.

He concentrated on the white spots on his fingernails, bit his knuckle, looked down at the table, at his feet, the floor, as if he were trying to push his eyeballs out of his skull, into the pit of the earth.

He started to think about the $250 check he'd get for whatever he came up with; at worst, he could write something for The Chronicle of Higher Education blog about solitude (or something like that)—the tragedy of distraction and wasted mental energy.

Yet another voice told him that the important thing, now, after midnight, was to be productive: to use these hours of forced awakeness, to convert sleep into verbiage, to be a machine. Dan began to type:

There is one political question which cuts across class, race, epoch: what to do with unemployed young men? There is no part of the country—really, no place on earth—where male youths are not alienated and disaffected, and therefore dangerous. There is no place where there is any clear answer to the question about what it means to 'be a man'—and no place where there is any agreement about whether that question is even worth asking.

He trailed off, bored by the sound of his own "voice."

There was a dog-eared copy of Henry James's *The Ambassadors* on top of the toaster; he reached for it, but then stopped himself.

He'd written about James in his first book (which had been based on his thesis). It had been blurbed by three of his mentors, received perfunctory reviews in two minor journals, and that was it.

University of Chicago Press. The name still gave him pleasure, even if the press hadn't really met his expectations. His next book would be with Verso and there was already a contract. Verso understood what he was about. A radical writer deserved a radical press.

Dan spent a lot of time reading comments on his old articles. He was completely invested in the world, the world of argument and counterargument, the thinking that surrounded the think piece, the chatter that grew, centrifugally, around the dim signal of his ideas. Chatter was better than silence: it told him that he was relevant.

He considered topics. Capital? Equality? Bernie? These were generalities, but they seemed incredibly fertile, charged with potential. The cognitive effect of the word "capital" was profound: he could feel his brain activate, neurons start to swim.

Dan wanted to write about hypertrophied, steroidal digital capitalism: the glossy, muscular, unstoppable flows of capital that coursed through smartphones.

The irony was that Dan wanted to sell books and academic publishers wanted leftists who could sell books. He wanted to turn his thinking into information and sell it just like everyone else. He dreamed about quitting teaching, or getting more money for teaching less (a bigger apartment too) and getting a Tesla.

Dan imagined driving to a house in the Hudson Valley with Mariko on Friday evenings; he imagined weekends with vintage wines, farm foods, little gatherings of intellectuals around a fireplace to talk about ideas and events. It was within reach.

Why has America self-fashioned as a Christian nation, when it is, in fact, an anti-Christian nation: conditioned to hate the poor, the meek, the powerless? The American right is simply Americanism taken to its *logical extreme: the hatred of those who symbolize the ignominy of the $ sign—those who lack it. What unites the Trump and Ryan (the usual alliance of emperors and opportunists) factions is this, this instinctual hate-lust of the poverty-Other. Christian love pulled inside out.*

His ideas, organically expressed, were gnomic and aphoristic. He'd fought this tendency his entire academic career, going back to his first undergraduate English paper. He'd been at his most original then, freshman year, when he didn't know how to write, and really didn't know how to do anything except argue with himself, with his own instincts. He wrote by hand on yellow legal pads that he'd stolen from his father's office.

He was a virgin then, too.

Those were his two dominant memories of the first year at Brown: his crazy, aphoristic papers and his determination to lose his virginity without revealing that he was, indeed, a virgin.

Had he always been trying to deceive other people about who he was? And if so, why? Why couldn't he let himself be seen? What was he afraid of?

This higher-level thought, or self-criticism, never really went away: it was the shadow cast by the quarter-truths with which he constructed his persona. It was so easy to continue as if there was no shadow, as if the quarter-truths were whole-truths.

He'd been in therapy for years—since graduate school. He needed to talk: for hours and hours, for years and years.

The basic position of psychoanalysis was a deeply empowering one. It provided Dan with the space to map his inner-landscape. Therapy gave him the courage to explore the shame which had compacted and crystallized within himself (which he located just below his sternum and slightly above his pubic bone—the node in which all his lived experience was stored like fat).

He slipped his left hand under his shirt and rubbed this area, the skin beneath his navel, with his thumb, stroking, directly above his bladder, with his fore- and middle-fingers. He did this unconsciously, finding in three-dimensional space that area that he had located mentally, in two-dimensional space.

He kept typing, as if in a trance.

We need to get rid of the idea that we have a life just because we're alive. Nothing could be less true. Nothing could be more antithetical to the spirit of life, in fact, medieval peasants only labored about five hours a day . . . and that much of the calendar was taken up with holidays. Culturally, we have created the narrative of progress, in order to justify a decreasing average quality of life—in order to justify the horror of monotonous office work. We have longer, richer lives than ever before—according to the measurements invented by economists and politicians. But how much time do we spend in celebration? In the sun? In the fields and trees? How much time do we spend together?

He stopped, briefly touching his cock in an homage to Balzac (who never wrote flaccid) and continued:

American fascism: the restoration of the pride of the American male via association with Donald Trump's outrageous phallus. The devotion of the laborer to the capitalist.

The professor flicked over to *Facebook*, interrupting his writing, as if his brain had said, in effect, "enough for now." Even late into the night, there was an almost audible hum of activity on *Twitter* and *Facebook*: likes, comments, news.

The whole world was being funneled through social media—refracted. Dan's mind melded with the hive-mind; the hive-mind melded with Dan.

Sputterings of melancholy and nostalgia.

The faces of people he would never meet or never meet again.

Time escaped in strange ways, excusing itself like a guest at a party, never really saying goodbye, shutting the door before he could say goodnight; in the hyper-fragmented time of the screen, time was itself a kind of ghost: a hallucination in which you sense that your material, embodied life has continued on without you.

He looked at one of the "stickies" on his desktop:

Marx compares bourgeois society to a sorcerer who can no longer control the powers of the underworld.

Possible book topic.

But somebody must be writing that book: the book about the transformation of mind into digital-matter.

The collectivization of opinion.

The algorithmization of consensus.

Someone a lot smarter than me.

The ultimate (and yet banal) taboo of digital capitalism: that it forces us to exploit each other.

Suddenly: a *Facebook* message, announced by a waterdrop sound.
hey what's what up?
What the fuck.

The message was from Eliza, a student from the previous fall, who was a junior now. He had received a friend request from her a few weeks before, but that had seemed entirely benign at the time. He probably should have ignored the request, theoretically, but he also didn't imagine that *Facebook* friendships had any specific meaning at all; *Facebook* was too lame to have causal power.

um hi?

He had no idea why he responded, except for the fact that she could see he was online.

Eliza was attractive, however. He had to admit.

He looked through her pictures to confirm his memory wasn't deceiving him. She was Latina, or half-light-brown skin and hair, discrete curves. She was from New Jersey, he remembered that too; Mom was an economics professor at Princeton. Lazy student though, despite the pedigree.

hey! I've been thinking about your class

o? what exactly?

lots of stuff lol

ok . . . you know it's late right now right?

i know. i didn't expect you to respond right away though, sorry. i stay up late.

so do I

Dan was answering mechanically, and he liked it—liked giving into the very technological mediation he was just decrying. The badness of it felt good; the stupidity of it felt like a release from being smart.

that's fun.

yeah so fun Eliza

I just like the way your mind works, and have been meaning to follow up with you.

that's flattering

can you tell that i'm flirting with u?

yes i can tell

is that bad? should I stop?

probably but

but what?

i haven't said stop yet

hahaha OK BUT i did i'm sorry BUT do you even remember me??

frankly, i only vaguely remember you.

liar

no really

but why are you talking to me then

because i'm clearly very very stupid

i'm not going to turn you in don't worry

o what a relief

Now that he had allowed himself to recall her, Dan realized that he remembered Eliza very well; he had sometimes made lingering, knowing eye-contact. He remembered why he had tried to forget her. It was simply necessary that she be repressed.

He had to admit it: the highest form of the student-teacher bond was erotic. Eros was the basis of his whole experience in the classroom, both as a teacher and a student. It had been the basis of his one homosexual relationship, the first year of graduate school, with Phil Grey, who lead a seminar on Thomas Hardy. This was something Dan never talked about. His gay experiences, outside of Phil, amounted to a few drunk makeouts at Brown LGBT parties . . . basically nothing.

He still had never admitted to Mariko that he'd been penetrated (a fact which he never discussed with anyone, including his therapist). He had hated it; it wasn't what he wanted: the odors, the sensation, the general roughness.

can i be honest? your class meant a lot to me

i'm still flattered

you inspired me! just like the way you talked about the world

what about it?

you seem passionate about changing stuff

i am passionate about changing stuff

well that's hot

uh

Had he really not noticed this chick was into him all last spring? Had he really gone through the semester ignorant of the vibes? It seemed so.

sorry . . .

it's ok

is it?

who knows

so i was thinking maybe we could meet and you could tell me more about your time in Occupy

lol, you're trolling me. i was only in the tents for a week ok just a little bit. but i do want to learn more about your life

i'm boring

no you're smart

frankly i'm not sure if i'm comfortable with this conversation

sorry i can stop

uhhhh

i'll go away now

hold up

what?

i'm hooked now, so

meaning your into it

Dan noted that she used "your" instead of "you're"—the tiniest reminder that this was not a conversation he should be having.

i'm sorry

you don't have have to be sorry

i'm genuinely interested in the things you have to say

that's nice Eliza but

but what?

i'm just not sure why you're messaging me at 2 in the morning

neither am i

well . . .

well what?

He waited anxiously for her to type. It was taking too long.

i hope I'm not making you uncomfortable but I really want to get to know you better

i've not heard that one before, from a student

fair

but it's ok . . .

is it?

yeah . . .

wow i'm so turned on rn

are you?

very

He had to gather himself. Was this really how younger people on the internet were? Was this normal for people under twenty-five? To just like log onto an app and hack into someone's brain? What startled him was how little control he had once she had a pathway to his consciousness. It almost wasn't fair. She was hot; he was lonely and underfucked; what outcome could there be other than what she wanted?

i guess i wanted to see if you wanted to get coffee or a drink sometime, she wrote.

Dan's brain was on fire. He folded his laptop screen down so that the power stayed on, but his line of sight to the screen was broken. He waited for about five heartbeats before opening up the screen again.

It immediately occurred to him that, if it was going to be effective, he would have to take a Cialis now.

ok

ok? so you're down?

in theory

yes or no babe

did you just call me babe?

i did hahah

oh my god

deal with it babe!

He laughed under his breath. Eliza was funny. How had he not noticed this during class time. Had he been doing all the talking?

so anyway, i would be interested in meeting up but i'm definitely wary

chill it's fine

i'm really not sure it is . . .

i'm cute and i'm into you it's not that complicated

you ARE cute.

if you weren't up for it you wouldnt have responded

true

so . . .

what's on your mind?

I think we should get a drink if you're over 21

I am.

haha what a relief, Dan wrote, not a little disgusted with himself.

how about right now?

holy shit. um.

um what? i'm wide awakeeeee

ummm

just say yes

yes

hahaha so what's your number i'll text you

Dan couldn't believe he was being this bold, but he was being encouraged, so he messaged his number, and shut his laptop.

He considered masturbating, but that seemed absurd.

The Cialis pills were in an unlabeled bottle in his briefcase; given the anti-depressants he had started taking, also secretly (the bottle was in his office), they were necessary. Much of his physical aloofness, his astonishing remoteness from Mariko, was a result of the carelessness and inconsistency with which he self-administered this chemical cocktail.

The briefcase was under the kitchen chair by his ankles. He reached down, fished around, came up with the bottle.

If the girl ghosted, he would just fuck Mariko.

He waited nervously for her text.

He opened the Cialis bottle.

Twenty seconds later: *hey there! what's up?!*

He smiled, typing his response. *just killing time until you texted me muahahahah*

Dan turned the bottle into his left palm, three pills fell out, he put two on the table (to be transferred to his pocket before he left), screwed the cap back on, and returned the bottle to his briefcase.

He had to remind himself she was not his student anymore; she was talking to him as an adult.

His thoughts broke off. He stood up, stretched, looked at the clock on the stove. 1:53 a.m.

are you there?

She was persistent.

yeah i'm there/here

where should we meet? are you getting cold feet?

tbd

From across the room, Dan scanned his bookshelves in the common area: a nostalgic, haunting procession of spines. They were of almost no use to him now. They were relics of his intellectual life.

Was this a set-up or trap? No. This girl was not deft enough; there was something clumsy in the directness of her approach.

what neighborhood are you

i live in greenpoint

i live in the EV

He paused.

Fuck it.

i could come to your area; we could meet at a diner

ok . . .

Dan enjoyed each step along the way towards compromising his integrity; it felt good, like stripping off sweaty clothes after coming back from the gym; he felt progressively lighter talking to this young woman. He was excited and hoped he hadn't taken the Cialis too soon.

ok I'll call a car

really?

yeah really why not I'm game. howabout Veselka's?

sure why not?

Dan opened *Uber* on his phone, feeling ridiculous.

be there in 30 . . .lol

There was a practical problem: he had to put on pants and a clean shirt without waking Mariko up.

The door to the bedroom was already open a crack, so he nudged it open wider with his toe and entered.

His girlfriend was asleep; she'd exhausted herself, he thought.

He could be home in four hours and not wake her up. Mariko woke up at 7 a.m. or 8 a.m. usually, but it would be a little later tomorrow (technically this morning) because they had been up fighting. He hoped so at least. He was willing to gamble on the possibility. He could always just say he went for a walk because he couldn't sleep. That was plausible.

The professor crept over to his dresser, opened the second drawer from the top, took out a black sweater, crouched down to the bottom drawer and pulled out a pair of jeans.

Were they too small? He hadn't worn them in about a year.

As quietly as possible, carrying the sweater and jeans, Dan crept back to the door. Mariko turned over in bed, mumbling something, apparently still asleep.

Safe!

He was still a little bit excited, so he had to wait a moment before zippering his jeans, which just barely fit.

The *Uber* was one minute away.

Ahmed. Black Toyota.

Dan closed the door to the apartment, not locking it for fear of making too much noise.

He hurried down the stairs, going faster and faster, making more noise than he should have, as if he wanted to get caught.

No matter. He had reclaimed unilateral decision making.

Suddenly, the night air felt wildly pleasant and not too warm at all.

The *Uber* pulled up.

"Dan?"

"Yup."

The car raced down Manhattan Avenue, hanging a right, encouraged by the lack of traffic.

Dan felt unutterably free, though he was afraid to check his phone and discover that Mariko was awake. But what did it matter?

What time was his class? Two. That was enough time to sleep. That was enough time for anything. The reasons why people worked so hard for tenure were obvious enough once you had it: teaching two seminars was easy work, coasting. It was nothing like the year he spent teaching high-school English in between college and graduate school. Then he woke up at 5 a.m. and often didn't get home until 7 or 8.

That had been the worst year of his life, the reason why he'd gone to graduate school.

Dan never talked about that year, he rarely thought about it; full-time teaching had absorbed all of his energy and capacity for memory and reflection. He had absorbed nothing of that year; like a black hole, he had only radiated resentment.

And I will show you something different from either
Your shadow at morning striding behind you
Or your shadow at evening rising to meet you;
I will show you fear in a handful of dust.

The day he had gotten into a Harvard PhD program was the best day of his life, surpassing his undergraduate acceptance to Brown. It wasn't until he finished his first book (*Easy Money: American Modernism and the Critique of Capitalism*) that he felt a similar sense of accomplishment.

Publication of a single book, however, didn't quench his desire to become a public intellectual: someone whose interviews and letters would one day be collected in a book of their own, someone whose every word would be hung upon. His hunger, on the contrary, grew and grew and grew.

The city lights bled over the river.

He was tired. He knew how ridiculous he was being; this wasn't who he was: it was a destruction of who he was.

There was little doubt that he was still grieving for his mother.

Dan would never forget the way she laughed, the way she would throw her head back suddenly, at inappropriate times, before covering her mouth, as if trying to keep the laugh in (the laugh of a crazy person); he would never forgive his father for pretending like nothing was wrong, for insisting that his wife was, for all practical purposes, "normal."

His father did well in those years, the late nineties; the doctor sold his stocks, miraculously, right before the tech-bubble crashed; the family well-to-do-ness increased even as it declined for other families. They expanded the house, added a pool, jacuzzi, got a house on Lake Michigan where Dan spent his summers in high school. Dan's tuition at Brown was paid for by his father's investments (even though Dan had written extensively about the college loan crisis, he'd never actually taken out a loan himself, didn't even know how one went about it—did you just walk into a bank and ask to speak to the person who controlled the money?).

Dan didn't want to be in the *Uber*, which was moving down First Avenue now, nearing Veselka, anymore.

Dan thought about his father's beard: it was always exactly the same length, had the same smell. It still did—even now that his father was elderly. The doctor's beard hadn't changed a centimeter in forty years. The only difference was the color; now it was gray.

He never called his father anymore.

The car, almost miraculously, pulled up in front of Veselka.

Stepping out, he felt incredibly old and tired. The energy just wasn't there. He wasn't sure if he should get out, but he did.

He got out, thanking the driver, smoothing his sweater, checking to see if his belt was buckled, his shoes tied.

Had he even brushed his teeth? He couldn't remember; maybe he would just order mint tea to make sure that his breath was alright (mint had antiseptic qualities).

There were only a few people in the restaurant and Eliza wasn't one of them.

i'm here . . .

Dan sat down at the bar counter. He couldn't believe that he had gotten there first. Was she ghosting him?

This was so stupid.

two minutes . . .

"Are you still serving borscht?"

"Yes, until five."

"Great, I'll have a borscht and an espresso please."

"No problem."

The bartender was a sallow man, close to fifty years old: short, thick around the waist, with calloused, thickened hands. He was exactly as Dan imagined Veselka's night staff.

He had one minute left to collect himself.

He'd been toying with the idea of an affair now for a while. *Tinder*, a brief temptation, had been downloaded to his phone earlier in the summer and seriously pursued for about a day.

He'd used pictures of himself from graduate school, before he had a paunch—which meant that he couldn't really show up for any dates, because the fraud he'd perpetrated would be too obvious. He didn't want to meet anyone; he just wanted to be someone else for a few minutes a day. He wanted a taste.

What he was doing now, however, was more than a taste. Trying to act confident, he sat up straight, and tracked Eliza as she walked in, smiling, awkwardly half-waving from the entryway.

At first glance, she was a little chubbier than he remembered, which was fine. College girls drank a lot. Ate Ramen. Gained weight. Then started a juice-cleanse. Then started over with drinking too much and eating like shit.

Her weight gain made him feel more at ease and his confidence rose.

She seemed to clock his reaction to her body.

"Hi . . ." he said, hugging her as she approached.

She sat down. "Nice to see you again."

"Yeah."

"Can I call you professor? Professor—"

"*Fuck no,*" he interrupted, laughing. "Fucccccck no."

"Okay fine!"

The waiter brought over his bowl of borscht and a small white cup containing espresso. He was afraid it would give him gas.

"It's great, go wild," she said flirtatiously, before turning to the waiter and ordering a glass of Merlot.

Was she really twenty-one? Yeah.

The professor counted to five, six, seven, eight, nine in his head, trying to calm himself down.

Title IX.

Goddammit.

"Okay: talk?" She demanded, smiling.

"About what . . . ?"

"Aw, you're so nervous."

"You've noticed." Dan took a sip of espresso.

"You don't have to be nervous," Eliza said.

"Have you ever done this before?"

"Met one of my professors in the middle of the night?"

"Uh—"

"First time. Does that make you happy?"

"I'm not sure what it makes me."

She was wearing a long black coat, a checkered skirt, knee socks, a blousey-thing, lipstick. He felt himself getting slightly hard again.

"Well, it's just . . ."

"Just what."

"Yeah. Like I dunno. I dunno what I'm doing here."

"Do you have a girlfriend?"

"I'm genuinely worried that you're a little nuts—"

"Hey, fuck you," she said, taking his comment lightly, her eyes still laughing. "I'm confident. That's different from being crazy, I hope—"

He glanced at her breasts. "Fair. Yeah. It is."

"I didn't think you'd be so moralistic."

"What'dya mean moralistic?"

"Like: I can tell you're judging yourself for being in this situation. And me, obviously. For putting you in it."

"Yeah, okay I'll admit it. It's hard to escape those kinds of judgements."

"Why is it hard?"

"Um," Dan chuckled from nervous excitement, "because because because—that's the box I live in."

She was in control of the situation. "I thought smart literary people want to deconstruct those moral boxes."

Her glass of wine appeared as if by magic.

"I mean . . ." Dan continued. "I don't think you have a clear idea of academic life, academics."

"I'm sure I don't."

"So then . . .?"

"But I like romance."

The sound of her voice excited him. She kept smiling, almost as if she had practiced a certain mode of appearance, down the smallest details: eyelashes, forehead, dimples, lips—all the muscles of her face worked in concert.

"I gave you an A minus," Dan said softly, now that he had recalled that particular detail.

"Oh, I remember," she said immediately.

"Oh, you do?"

"Of course. It's uh, haunted me."

"Haunted you—"

"It didn't feel fair, because I remember what you said in office hours when I asked you about it, you said the minus was for unreached potential even though I probably had earned an A. Which means you graded me on a personal curve and not . . . you know it affects future placement, it's not like—"

"Woah. I'm not an easy grader."

"Maybe you should be. I want to go to law school."

He didn't know how to respond to this. There was too much reverberation; he couldn't pick up on her tone.

"What would be the point of that?"

"College is about pieces of paper with shiny A plus's attached."

"Not in my class it isn't."

"Do you grade other students relative to their intellectual talent?"

"Yeah."

"That's bullshit. Just give the A and give out spiritual lessons on the side. If you want students to be interested instead of worrying about grades."

"Are you sure my class is or was . . . interesting?"

"You're interesting; your class, not so much. Or maybe it's the other way around."

"I don't think I'm interesting, frankly."

"You're hot."

Dan laughed at this, embarrassed.

"Your face is kinda angular, like pieces of broken glass . . .. it's thoughtful . . . it *seems* thoughtful."

"It *was* thoughtful."

"And what is it now?"

"What's the opposite of thoughtful?"

"Thoughtless." She didn't miss a beat.

"Well, there ya go."

Dan jabbed a spoon into his borscht, and then dragged the spoon in three consecutive circles around the small white bowl, before drawing the warm, but not particularly hot soup towards his mouth. The borscht was a momentary stay against confusion and fatigue. He swallowed without really tasting. He didn't feel thoughtful: he was telling the truth. He felt inert; his brain received impressions, but didn't record or analyze them.

He was gradually using up his store of thoughtfulness; there were a few years left before he was found out—before he became one of those forgettable campus figures everybody regrets having around, one of those people who endlessly refer back to their first book.

And was his first book, in the end, really that good? No: because it had no meaningful impact. No one read it.

His articles circulated and were read, but that wasn't *an impact*, not in the sense of being registered by the central nervous system of American cultural life. Hundreds of opinion pieces were generated by major publications daily. Maybe more. And whatever the number was it could only rise. And that was a scary thought—that the amount of meaningful information never shrank, that it could only grow. The world was being consumed by the information it produced about itself.

"How's the borscht?"

"Wanna try some?"

"I've never actually—"

"You've never tried borscht?! You're crazy—here."

He pushed the bowl over and handed her the spoon. "I think it tastes good paired with red wine."

She pushed the bowl back. "You don't want anymore?"

"No, I'm full."

It occurred to Dan that she was concerned about her weight.

"Do you have an Instagram?" Dan found himself asking.

"Yeah. Why?" The why was sharp, concerned.

"I'm just feeling my age at the moment," Dan responded.

"You're out of date."

"Like a piece of hardware."

"Basically."

"That's an interesting idea . . . I mean . . . I probably am. I'm probably living in a totally different era . . . in my head . . . which means I'm living a fantasy . . . but then again—who isn't?" he asked rhetorically.

"It's just a question of which fantasy you're living right?" she said, smiling. "Tell me about your fantasies."

"That would be too on-the-nose, don't ya think?"

"Yeah, maybe, but . . ." Eliza trailed over, even while her eyes continued to speak.

Veselka was amazingly quiet. He felt like someone was listening, but who? No one. No one cared.

He watched Eliza shift in her seat. He wondered if, or rather sensed, that she was aroused, or getting there. Maybe she was performing arousal, but there was something striking, distinctive, in her sitting posture; it was like she was extra-sensitive, extraordinarily physically alive—which was arousing to him.

The professor swallowed another spoon of now lukewarm borscht. His attention shifted back to Eliza. He wondered if they were going to fuck; the anticipation was really fucking exciting.

He didn't want to go home empty-handed. He started to think of possible reasons that it wouldn't go down. Roommates were one. She could be on her period. Obviously, she might just not be *that* into him. He could say the wrong thing; he could acknowledge Mariko's existence. There were so many ways to fuck this up.

Maybe not since he was with Amanda, his college girlfriend, had he felt the absolute thrill of not knowing what was going to happen next— but that was because Amanda was fucking crazy. His relationship with Mariko, on the other hand, even from their first meeting, was defined by this very strong sense of certainty, predictability. It was that sense of certainty that he was now attempting to destroy, whether he knew it or not.

"But what?"

"I still want to know."

"My fantasy . . . or fantasies?"

"Yeah, sure, why not?" She was being coy.

"I'm not good at talking about that kinda stuff."

"You're out of practice, that's all." Her confidence seemed a little rehearsed.

"Do you like hearing men talk about what gets them off?"

"I think I like seeing men a little humiliated to be honest," she said casually.

"Um . . ."

"It's hard to explain."

"Try," he commanded, feeling nervous.

"Okay, well like . . . I mean I love tapping into a lover's shame . . . it's like something that can be exchanged or transferred . . . like I can access my own shame . . . like there's this mirroring kind of like thing that happens . . ."

"I'm not sure I get it."

"I'm not sure either."

"Are you talking about like domming men or what?"

"No, not really. Just like making them beg and stuff. Like . . ."

"It's fairly problematic," he continued, hearing the academic tone in his own voice and wincing.

"It's a preference," she said casually again.

"Yeah, but like . . . preferences can be problematic."

"But I don't think it is. It's about power, sure . . . but like. It doesn't necessarily hurt anyone. Some people enjoy groveling."

"I don't. Is that okay with you?"

"Sure. It's perfectly fine."

Uncomfortable.

"Okay . . ."

"Dan: it's okay."

"Okay!" He muttered, still shocked to hear her talk to him in such a familiar way. This was all happening so fast. She was in complete control. He shouldn't have taken the Cialis.

She brushed his leg with her foot. "Relax, bud."

"I'm relaxed."

This made her laugh again. "You're definitely not relaxed."

"I shouldn't have had an espresso. I'm trying to stay awake."

"Aw, is this too late for you? Need to go to sleep? Poor boy."

He took a sip of her wine, feeling a little crazy, over-caffeinated. "I'll be ok, thanks."

"What are you thinking about?"

"Haven't we already established that I'm a thoughtless, outdated almost-forty-something? Whenever I open my mouth, I just prove your hypothesis." Her skin was amazingly smooth and creamy. "But I guess I should just embrace who I am, right?"

"It's hilarious that you think you're old."

"I'm not young."

"True, true."

"Where are you from again?" he asked, already knowing the answer because *Facebook* had confirmed it for him.

"Jersey. But Princeton. So nice. You?"

"Suburban Ohio. Cincinnati."

"Really?"

"Yeah, what's so unbelievable about that?"

"I dunno, I guess —"

"You thought I'd be from a place like Princeton—"

"Yes! Exactly!"

"Snob!"

He wanted to touch her knee, her thighs; he was obsessed by her skin. He was loving making her laugh; he loved laughing with her. What was happening? He hadn't done this in years. He hadn't been on a date in years.

He traced the top of her kneecap with his right hand; he couldn't help it. With her left hand, she gripped his palm. The little subcurrents of potential energy circulating back and forth between them felt amazing.

"Hi," she whispered, as if introducing herself for the first time.

"Hi," he said, relaxing.

"Did you mean to do that?"

"Did you?"

"Yes."

"Then I did too."

She withdrew her hand, took a sip of her wine, and looked out the window.

"I'm really sad. Just FYI. I hope you're okay with me being really sad at random moments."

"What are you sad about? What's making you . . . ?"

"Like, where do I begin?"

"The beginning."

"There is no beginning."

"You don't seem sad . . ."

"*Obviously not.* That's the point. I work very hard to appear this way."

Her hand returned to his like a bird alighting. He had been anxious that she would not touch him again, or let him touch her. It felt disturbingly good.

Young people were extremely good at molding themselves to archetypes, stereotypes. That was what the internet did to people: it destroyed their indigenous interiority, left them vulnerable to external representations of the self. Eliza had no idea who she was, he thought; no idea that this was even a problem. It was just too easy to say exactly what she thought he wanted to hear, too easy to create a pseudo-self as needed with swiping fingers and thumbs.

But maybe she felt that way about him: that he was too easy to manipulate.

Maybe she had messaged him while taking a shit on a whim.

Maybe she'd been drinking.

Maybe she'd gotten really high.

Maybe it was a dare among drunk, high friends.

He was used to being able to anticipate exactly how Mariko's behaviors and moods would manifest themselves. Eliza brought with her an entirely different, or at least, evolved, transformed, set of behaviors, language signifiers—that were essentially meaningless to him, that he couldn't possibly learn fast enough to feel in control of. He was frozen inside his old life like a paleolithic creature with DNA adapted to another climate.

He released his hand from her knee (where it had really hovered close to her groin). He unconsciously bit his lip, sighed, rubbed the side of his neck, looked away.

"So tense." She was teasing him again.

The Cialis.

"I'm not sure I get you, Eliza."

"You don't have to get me, you just have to put up with me."

"'Put up with . . .'" he echoed softly. "Hmmm."

"I'm a *lot*."

"You keep hinting at—"

"Yeah, because I am."

"Gimme an example." Dan turned on his stool and surveyed the crowd: a few old men, a few expensively dressed couples recuperating from a night of partying, a young man in the corner reading a book, a few working-class guys, already up for work.

It was mostly empty seats at this hour. He loved it. It was entirely what he wanted from New York City.

"You don't want to know."

He squinted at her; he almost didn't believe her. He suspected that she wanted to appear more tortured than she really was, if she was tortured at all. But she just didn't have that vibe, that tortured vibe. She struck him as well-adjusted and normal and self-aware. Manipulative maybe, but not a brooding, romantic figure. She was clearly showing him what she thought he wanted to see—but how could he get her to admit this?

"I'm curious though. Like. Is it family stuff or?"

"It's always family stuff."

"Not necessarily. I think the family is kind of an overrated configuration."

"You're talking out of your ass."

"Yeah," he had to admit, "you're right."

"It must be nice to be a white man with institutional power."

"It's okay."

"Really though."

"Let's change the subject." He spooned borscht with exaggerated nervousness, which made her laugh.

"You're funny."

"Well, I *was in* a sketch comedy group in college."

"Oh, that's cool."

"It was like twenty years ago."

"Were you good?"

"No, we were terrible. I was personally extremely terrible," he laughed. "I mean some things were good. But like two percent. The rest was fucking trash."

He heard an artificial note in his own voice; he didn't really talk like this. He was mimicking her diction.

"I'm on Vyvanse right now," she said, changing the subject. "Do you know what that is?"

"It's like ADD medicine, right?"

"Yeah, but it's really strong and I don't have ADD."

"ADD isn't a real condition."

"Yeah, I know."

"What does Vyvanse do?"

"It wakes you up, obviously, makes you hyper-focused and alert. It's like Adderall, but like, probably stronger. Or at least, it has more of an effect on me."

"So you dabble with chemicals."

"Yeah, I like chemicals. They're chill."

"Is Vyvanse and stuff common?"

"Yeah. It is."

Dan watched her swivel back and forth on her bar stool, ever so slightly. He was aware of how much she was in an altered state now. He looked at her almost as if she were already his lover, with a strange tenderness. Though he had just attacked Mariko for depending on him emotionally, he now badly wanted Eliza to depend on him.

"Why are you here again, Eliza?" He felt like was talking to her during office hours about a paper.

"Because I've been curious about you for a long time."

"I'm still trying to figure out why . . ."

"You don't have as much confidence as you pretend to have, bud."

"'Pretend . . .'"

"Like, you strut when you lecture. Do you fuck all your students?"

"All my students? Are you kidding?"

"No."

"Who do you think I am?"

"I think you're you."

"That's true. I am," he said, mechanically. "What do you think you are?"

"I'm smart."

"I know you are."

"How do you know?"

"Because you're paying attention. You notice things."

"Thanks," she said, too easily flattered for his taste.

Now he was saying things that she wanted to hear. Was this what dating was? He'd forgotten.

It *was* true though. He hadn't *really* exaggerated. She was observant, she was sharp; her mind was moving faster than his.

Was it just the Vyvanse though?

He looked at his phone. Still nothing from Mariko. Silence made him feel closer to peril. In a way, he hoped Mariko would text him and tell him to come home.

This was so stressful.

"What do you think about the election?" he asked sullenly.

"I mean, like, it's obvious."

"Yeah. But in-depth—"

"In depth I think Hillary will be good and Trump will be bad."

"That's not in-depth."

"I'm being sarcastic."

"Sure ya are," Dan muttered.

"I don't think you respect my opinion, so why should I give it?"

She had a good point. Dan took another mouthful of borscht. "Who said I don't respect your . . ."

"You never said you did."

"When did I have a chance to say . . ."

"I mean, I was your student . . ."

"But you barely made an effort," Dan demurred. "I'll have a glass of wine," he said to the bartender who was wiping down another section of the bar.

The bartender nodded.

"I'll have another glass too," Eliza said.

There was an awkward pause: the wine couldn't come fast enough.

"Maybe I didn't make an effort because the class wasn't interesting enough to warrant it."

"Sounds like a cheap excuse."

"Probably is, but."

"But . . ." he wanted an answer.

"It's not that the class was boring; it's just that I . . . I've lost the habit of caring about school in general. About things in general. It was interesting, but not interesting enough."

"What could I have done better?"

"Been more dynamic."

"Which means . . ."

"There was a lot of interesting discussion, but I never got the sense that you let things get away from your comfort zone as a teacher."

"Fair."

She smiled triumphantly.

"Tell me what you think about the election. I know you're dying to lecture me."

Dan stared at the skin on her wrist: fat, creamy. He wanted to kiss the inside of her wrist, lick up, along the elbow, kiss her shoulders, her neck.

"I think . . ." Dan trailed off self-consciously. "I've come to realize that Trump is the president that everyone wants: he is perfectly fitted to our era. Jumpy, distractible, constantly bored."

"I'm sick of him."

"He isn't going away until November 8th."

"You think he's gonna lose?"

Dan shook his head back and forth, like a child. "He has to lose. There's no other option."

"He's so fucking stupid," Eliza parroted.

Privately, Dan wasn't sure if he would even vote.

"Hillary's gonna be awesome," Eliza added, as if she knew what he was thinking.

"She's okay," Dan said glumly.

It was strange to think of himself as something other than a young person; he'd only stopped being a young person a few years ago.

Eliza's skin was glowing; the skin on her face, her neck, her legs, what he could see of her shoulders: in a few years the collagen would begin to recede and imperceptibly, even if she remained otherwise the same, that glow would dry up.

It was happening to Mariko even though she took good care of herself. The dewiness was gone.

He felt guilty comparing them.

He signaled to the bartender that he wanted another glass of wine, twirling his finger, attempting to look deft.

He hoped the wine wouldn't fuck with the Cialis.

"I have to go the bathroom, I'll be right back," Dan said, not giving Eliza a chance to respond. Would she still be there when he got back? He wasn't sure. He didn't turn around.

He lifted the lid with his foot and urinated swiftly, flushing with his foot again. He didn't wash his hands. He checked his phone for a second: nothing from Mariko. He also had the urge to check his email—absurdly. Nothing new there either, just spam.

He was exhausted; he just wanted to go home.

He took the second pill.

"Have fun in the bathroom?" she asked wryly when he returned to the bar.

"Oh yeah, tons."

He yawned.

"You gave me an A minus."

"Are you seriously still thinking about that?"

"I could be. Or I could not care at all. I could be fucking with you. You're worried that I'm just here to complain about my grade or something, aren't you—"

"I mean—"

"I'm not though."

"I really have no idea who you are. Like, spiritually."

"So get to know me. Ask me questions."

"What do you want to do after graduation?"

"Publishing?"

"You want to work in publishing?"

"I like books."

"Yeah, but . . . *publishing.*"

"What's wrong with publishing?"

Dan shrugged. "It's pretty pretentious."

"You're one to talk."

"Takes one to know one."

"I like pretentious men. I think it's hot."

Dan chuckled.

"I'm serious," she insisted.

"What are we doing here Eliza?"

"You tell me."

"What do you want from me?"

"I'm still trying to get over my ex. Full disclosure."

"What's his name?"

"Doesn't matter."

"Okay . . ."

"Seriously though, totally does not in any way matter."

"Matters enough that you brought it up."

"Okay, but his identity doesn't matter. What matters are my hurt feelings and my vulnerability." Eliza laughed at herself, which made Dan laugh.

"What do *you* want?"

"I want . . ." Dan had no idea what he was going to say. "Honestly, I'd like to kiss you when we leave."

"*Just* kiss me? And why not kiss me right now?"

"We're in a public . . ."

"So what? There's practically no one here."

"Fine."

He leaned over. Her lips were fat and sweet; he bit them, traced his tongue over them, pulled away.

"That was nice," she said.

"Yeah," he murmured. "Really nice."

"You should finish your borscht."

He pushed the bowl away. "Let's get the check."

Eliza laughed mockingly: "Slow down, champ."

"Okay . . ."

He pulled the borscht-bowl back, shoveled a few spoonfuls into his mouth defiantly. She was toying with him; she knew exactly what she was doing and he didn't. And she was enjoying herself. She was here to enjoy herself, and he enjoyed that.

"I'm gonna pay now, but we can stay as long as we like."

She gave him a serious look. "Do you think we're going to sleep together?"

"Do you?" he asked, terrified that he was being toyed with.

"I'm thinking about it."

"How long did you think about contacting me before you did it?"

"Since last year. Every once in a while. It occurred to me. You intrigued me, like I said."

"I don't remember you saying that."

"Implied."

She leaned over and kissed him on the neck, then the lips; the kiss was slow, and a little sloppy.

"I like how you taste."

He didn't know why she said this. He assumed he tasted like borscht. His image of himself and the claims she made about him kept diverging. Again: he had the feeling of being an imposter. He still felt like he was being trolled.

"Eliza: who the hell are you? Seriously."

"A person. Who are you?"

"I'm a person too."

"The question you want to ask, Dan, is what *kind* of person am I?"

"Exactly. Yes. That's what I want to know."

"I'm, honestly, a deeply caring person. And I want to be cared for by someone who understands me. That's not asking too much, is it?"

"Depends."

"On what?"

"Caring takes the capacity to care and I'm not sure most people, most men, have that. Do you?"

"I don't know anymore. Honestly."

"Why do you say that?"

Her soft little body craned towards the wineglass, as if she were fall-ing over.

"I say it because I know that I've lost parts of myself that I valued. That I ripped out parts of my . . . you know, like . . . I mean . . . my heart. Along the way. So that I could continue along the way. But I'm not sure why I did, or what the point was."

"I think I understand."

"But you're really too young to have started that process yet—"

"Of ripping my heart out piece by piece?"

"Yep."

"I'm definitely not too young for that," she asserted.

"Yeah, but you're too young to understand the consequences."

"And what are the consequences?" she asked, hurt.

"This." Dan pointed to his chest.

"I can't see inside your skeleton, bud."

"Yeah well, it's not pretty. You wouldn't want to."

"I bet it's interesting."

"It'd be a bad bet."

He was feeling antsy. Something had to happen. He wanted her to propose going to her place. The Cialis gave him the feeling of being a sexual athlete; he wanted to show off. He wanted to fuck her really hard, make her forget about the immature boys she'd known before him. He wanted her to call him the best she'd ever had.

"Do you have roommates?" he asked.

"No."

He sat up a little on his stool, cracked his back.

"Why don't you have any roommates?"

"Because, why would I want roommates?"

"Good question. Because money."

"My parents make good money."

"Of course." He wasn't any different. He didn't have any student debt thanks to his dad.

"I still can't make up my mind about you." She was keeping him on edge.

"Then let's keep talking until you do." He realized as he was saying this that he was signaling weakness. She had the upper-hand.

"I'm starting to feel weird."

"Don't!" Dan said reactively.

He took a quick look at his paunch. He needed to start going to the gym if he was going to start dating again. Was that really what he was preparing to do?

"I'm sorry," he said.

"For what?"

"I'm not sure, but I'm sorry."

"That's a weird thing to say."

"Sorry!"

She laughed at this. "It's ok."

"I'm really trying too hard right now aren't I?"

"Yeah man, relax."

"You're just really beautiful, Eliza," he sputtered.

"Didn't you just say that you were trying too hard?"

"Yeah, but I couldn't help myself."

"I guess that's kinda sweet."

"Well, I'm kinda sweet."

Dan *was* an affectionate person, but it had been a long time since he had been able to freely demonstrate it. Plus, the desire to impress someone felt good, and the reversal of power felt even better. He was not really a naturally authoritative person, that was put on in the classroom; it felt natural that Eliza had taken charge of the interaction.

"I feel like a flower in a sexual costume," she said abruptly.

"Interesting image."

"I just feel very pure on some level, almost like I'm having an out of body experience."

"You mean being here right now?"

"No, just in general, like, my life. So much of the time I just wanna be alone in my room and read and water my plants and feel sad and happy and not be bothered."

"What do you need me for then?" Dan asked, genuinely having lost the thread.

"I think I have this idea that there's someone out there who can kind of um—share that isolation with me and make it not isolation—"

"Very romantic," Dan commented blandly.

"That's me."

"Have you been in love?"

"Oh definitely—"

"With the ex you mentioned or—?"

"I fall in love a lot honestly."

"Should I find that encouraging or demoralizing?"

"Both. Do you want me to fall in love with you, Dan?"

"I'm still processing everything that's happening. TBD."

"I'm very fun to have an affair with."

"Is that what you tell every guy? Is that your sales pitch?"

"Oh, for sure."

Dan desperately wanted to leave Veselka's and go to her place, but he didn't want to put her off. Doing, anyway, had nothing on waiting. Waiting was sublime compared to doing.

"I think I'm slightly drunk," he announced.

"Same."

For a moment, they both fidgeted on their barstools. Eliza smiled, her cheeks dimpling slightly. He wanted to kiss her again, but it was more interesting to maintain the silence and distance. He wanted her to think about what he was thinking about (when all he was thinking about was what she was thinking about).

"I'm exhausted, but like, so happy," he drawled.

"I'm happy that I make you happy," she responded gnomically.

"Are you happy that you're here with me—like happy just because?"

"I think so . . ."

He took her hand, stroking the veins, massaging the knuckles. "I know what you mean about loneliness, by the way—"

"Did I use the word loneliness?"

"Or what you implied—said—"

"Yeah . . ."

"I feel that too—all the time—"

"Interesting . . ."

"Is it interesting?" Dan asked, a little anxious.

"I feel like an autobiography of no one."

"Shit, Eliza—"

"Yeah." Deadpan.

"I like your soul," Dan said, trying to rise to the occasion. "It's pretty fucking fascinating slash amazing."

"Wow the amount of smoke up my ass—"

"Insert dirty joke here."

"Slow down, old man."

"So now I'm old—"

"You're getting older by the minute, bub."

"True."

"But the older the better in my opinion," she winked at him.

"I love this time of night in the city, when almost everyone is asleep. I missed this. These kinds of things. Not like—meeting someone necessarily. I used to just come to places like this to write or read. There was a place around the corner called Yaffa's that closed pretty recently. It was 24/7 and was in a basement and was full of kitsch and served shitty coffee and had a backyard; it was awesome. I loved being by myself, in the corner with a book. I guess this was when I first got hired—before I even had tenure or anything like that—a few years ago—like 2011."

"Sounds like you need to spend more time by yourself."

"Well, yeah. Now that I think about it . . ."

"You have pictures with you and a woman on *Facebook*."

Dan hadn't even considered this. "Secret's out then, I guess."

"The non-secret secret. I don't mind being a homewrecker, don't worry."

"I could only assume."

"Do I seem out of control?" she asked somewhat coyly.

"No, you seem pretty calculated actually."

Eliza smiled, raised her eyebrows, and didn't answer. Dan's mind quickly moved from branch to branch of his basic anxiety: she was going to leave; she was just toying with him.

"I think as I get older . . . I uh—I dunno—"

"What don't you know?" she asked coyly.

"I just don't know what I'm supposed to be doing, beyond my existing obligations. I don't know how to be present . . . spontaneous—"

"Seems like you're doing a pretty good job."

"I guess tonight is an exception."

"Do you live with your girlfriend?"

"I don't wanna talk about it, Eliza."

"Okay . . ."

He didn't want to collude or inform against himself; he assumed that the question was rhetorical, that she already knew, somehow, and so all he could do was maintain strategic ambiguity.

"I don't wanna think about it."

"Okay, Danny boy."

There was, he considered, a kind of sweetness, anyway, in the way that she was trying to get him to compromise himself; it was Eliza's way of making him *hers*. He knew that, and he enjoyed that.

"I'm just enjoying this crazy thing we're doing."

"So am I."

"Are you?"

"Immensely."

"That's good."

"I could tell you needed reassurance."

"You could?" He asked, sincerely.

"I can read you like a book."

Dan liked her vigor, her boldness, the directness with which she made him her co-conspirator. Eliza was making having an affair easy for him; and so he felt grateful, almost in awe.

"Oh absolutely. Do you wanna go for a walk?"

"Uh sure."

He stood up, taking her right hand in his, guiding her off the stool. When they were outside, he kissed her again, and they started walking south in silence. He was afraid to ask where she lived.

"Beautiful night . . ." he intoned.

"Yeah." She seemed a little despondent.

"Eliza, what's wrong?"

"I'm just getting tired."

"You're lying."

"Yeah. I'm lying. So what?"

They walked down past Third, Second, towards Houston. He rubbed the palm of her hand with his thumb.

"Tell me about your childhood."

"My childhood?" She wasn't prepared for the question. "It was weird."

"How so?"

"My family is pretty fucked up," Eliza said, looking at the pavement.

"Sounds familiar."

"Yours too?"

"Yup. What's up with yours?"

"My mom has emotional problems, mainly."

"Mine too—or had—like what?"

"Your mom is dead?"

"Yeah—um—but to my question—"

"Uh—well—she wouldn't talk to me for weeks on end, over the littlest things; she's a completely different person around people who aren't her family. Very charming."

"What does she do?" Dan asked, pretending that he didn't know the answer already.

"She's an economics professor."

"Where?"

"Princeton."

"Right. What kind of economics?"

"She's pretty free-market," Eliza said. "Like she went to UChicago when that was like the thing."

"Too bad."

Dan looked down at the sidewalk. He didn't want her to look at him. It was a matter of protecting himself from her inquiring green eyes. He wasn't used to being looked at this way. He had grown so deft at hiding his emotions from Mariko.

The tidal exhalation of feeling from Dan was so great that Eliza stopped abruptly and kissed him. Then they continued to walk east along Houston.

It was a stroke of luck that she lived alone; he'd been imagining embarrassing encounters with roommates. No one wanted to be the forty-year-old among twenty-somethings; twenty-somethings didn't want some guy lurking around their apartment.

"Tell me something you're afraid of," he commanded softly.

"Spiders."

"Emotional things, I mean."

"Oh shit. Do you really want to go there?"

"My mom had issues too."

Was he that eager to talk about himself?

"Like what?"

"Like wanting to kill herself so badly, so consistently, that one day she did it."

"Jesus, I'm sorry." Eliza seemed genuinely sorry.

"Why are you sorry? It's just information I'm sharing; you don't have to comment."

"Were you close?"

He could tell that she was pleased to be let in on something personal; it put her at ease. She wanted him to unburden his heart, and he wanted that too. He wanted her to feel how soulful he was.

"We were close in a way, but she was a hard person to get close to."

"So is my mom."

"Explain."

"My mom? Like I said, she's two different people; she's smart, obviously, and manipulative."

"What's your dad like?"

"He's so in love with her still; he doesn't stand up to her."

"And do you stand up to her?"

"I rebel in my own way."

"What does your Dad do?" Dan was still trying to figure out how she afforded her apartment; a professor's salary didn't seem like enough.

"He's a corporate lawyer. He works in the city."

"Cool, cool."

"Dude, I know you think they're terrible people."

"Why, because—?"

"Yeah, because I took your class—you're a Marxist."

This made him anxious. "True. Let's not talk about politics. Do you live around here?"

"Yeah."

She was guiding him to her place without admitting to him that she was going to ask him to come up; that was part of her game.

Dan studied her face: she wasn't looking at him; she was looking ahead, at the slow trickle of traffic passing them, heading west, or just at nothing: into space.

Dan squeezed Eliza's hand; she looked at him warmly and squeezed back. He was scared shitless.

"Eliza . . ."

"Yes?"

"Nothing."

He felt like a teenager.

They looped back west; he was following her.

He'd stopped thinking about his phone. He'd stopped thinking about teaching tomorrow. He'd stopped thinking about his fight with Mariko.

"I feel like I'm sleepwalking."

"My apartment is the next block."

Ludlow.

"Interesting."

"So. Do you want to come up?"

"Do you really live alone?"

"You're so nervous."

"Of course I'm nervous, Eliza."

"It's fun."

"I feel like an imposter."

"So what? Being an imposter is the fun part."

She was so blithe.

"I'm not sure you really mean that."

"I'm turned on."

"Don't tell me that."

"Why not?"

"You don't have to try that hard," he said coldly.

"It's the truth."

Why did she want him to come up? He wasn't the kind of guy whose presence made women feel spontaneous arousal.

He just couldn't trust that she was attracted to him. No amount of evidence to the contrary could change that basic underlying belief.

"Why are you being rude?"

"Because I'm on edge."

"Why are you on edge? Because you're about to cheat on someone."

"I wouldn't phrase it like that?"

"Why not?" Eliza asked provocatively.

"Because cheating implies that you're playing a game."

Eliza entered the code to the front door of what looked to be a walk-up on a particularly commercial strip of Ludlow two blocks south of Houston.

"This is a funny place to live," Dan said.

"Why is it funny?"

"Because who lives in this part of town anymore?"

"Fintech bros. And rich girls."

"Yep," Dan said.

"You're judging me."

"I'm just thinking."

"About what?"

It was interesting to hear her fluctuate between bravado and fear.

"This."

They were halfway up the first flight of stairs.

"What floor do you live on?"

"Third."

He felt like he was gonna pass out; he was so tired.

"Are you gonna make it?" she asked mockingly.

"Yeah yeah," he responded, trying to catch his breath.

They were there; she was opening the door; he could feel himself getting hard, crazy hard . . . could hear the sound of her breathing, the scraping of the key.

"Goddamn door," Eliza said under her breath.

He just wanted to kiss her, undress her, fall asleep with her. He wasn't even interested in sex anymore, all of sudden, just the warm pressure of another body.

"Hey . . ." she said, standing in the hallway.

He bent down to unlace his shoes. He was not even thinking at this point; he just wanted to get his shoes off.

She took off her sweater; he looked at her breasts.

"Stand up."

He stood up, kissed her; she embraced him. Her body was so much smaller than it had seemed. It was incredibly strange to embrace a body other than the body he was used to.

He felt like someone else.

His hands traveled under her skirt, then moved up along her thighs awkwardly.

"Hey, slow down," she said, pulling his hand away.

"No problem."

She pulled him down on the couch, straddling his waist. They continued to make out. She pushed her tongue into his, pushed her hands under his shirt, then down his pants.

"Do you find me attractive?"

"Yes, Eliza."

"Am I too fat for you?"

This was too much. He didn't want to hear about her insecurities.

"No, Eliza . . ."

"Just say it."

He sat up a little. "Are you crazy?"

"No. Are you?"

He guided her head towards his mouth. They kissed for a few more seconds.

"Stop," she said, sitting back up.

She disentangled herself from him.

He sat up.

"What's up?"

"I'm scared."

"Of what?" He asked, feeling absolutely nothing.

"Having feelings for you."

Dan watched her for a moment, trying to make sense of her statement. He didn't like the suggestion that there could be emotional consequences for this, whatever it was. This was not what they had negotiated, or not what he thought they'd negotiated. Their encounter was supposed to be marked by suavity, lightness . . . not fear, not repulsion or distance.

"I don't think you will Eliza."

"Have feelings for you?"

"No."

"Why wouldn't or shouldn't I?"

"Because I'm just a guy."

"No, but I think you're brilliant."

Dan kissed her shoulder, then her neck. "Just a guy."

Eliza's apartment was filled with flowers; he could see by the streetlight which illuminated the small, but curtainless windows. Everything was arranged with a clean, formal precision. It was so unlike what he imagined: so much more adult, mature. He assumed she'd be a messy teen.

He knew so few people who lived alone. Even at forty, no one could really afford it, and then people who could were largely too successful to be interesting.

He imagined waking up here and drinking tea with her and watching her water her flowers and get ready for class.

"Do you have a condom?"

Her question caught him off-guard.

"No. Do you?"

"No . . ."

"Oh fuck."

"It's okay Dan . . . we can just sit here . . ."

He looked at her, somewhat embarrassed, mind racing, consumed by a thwarted sense of touch. She was warm and small in the lamplight, and she was the last chance he'd ever really have to reach out and touch real beauty: he was sure about that. He did not want to just "sit there." He'd been so unhappy as a teenager, completely unfucked and uncool and alone, and there was something about the possibility that Eliza would reject him sexually that triggered memories of shame and self-loathing. On the afternoon of his mother's funeral, he'd re-read his old journals from high school, and wept until his father came in to tell him it was time. He cried the whole funeral, and afterwards just shut himself in his room. He had told Mariko to stay in New York, which at the time, and still now, seemed like a strange choice, but he was just so ashamed of his family, and everything that surrounded his upbringing.

"Should I run down to a bodega and buy some?"

"No, that's ok. I think I just want to cuddle."

"Goddammit."

"Oh my god, don't get angry with me . . ."

"I'm not angry, sorry."

"Okay . . . I really hope not . . ."

"I'm just so into you; I'm sorry; trying to calm down."

Eliza seemed to have turned off completely; he hadn't even really noticed the shift. They were still on his couch, holding hands, but no longer with the same sense of shared energy and intimacy.

"Are you gonna lose interest in me if I don't want to fuck right away?"

Dan had to hide his frustration. "Not at all."

"I feel like you are though."

"Not at all. I'm very interested regardless."

"I'm a person, not just an object . . ."

"Of course!" Dan exclaimed, undaunted.

"Are you sure you know that?"

"I hope so!" he exclaimed again, caressing her shoulders.

"I told you I get sad easily . . ."

"Is that what's happening now?"

Eliza nodded silently.

Dan was hard, but there was nothing he could do about it. It was depressing. He felt depressed. He wanted to fall asleep.

"I gotta go," he said, sitting up and sliding his feet to the floor.

"You're not gonna stay?"

"No, I can't."

"Okay," she said mournfully. "Are you sure?"

He absentmindedly stroked her thighs. "Yes, I'm sure."

"Come back soon," she said, with an unhappy smile.

"I will, I will," he said, unsure if he was telling the truth.

He had to find his jacket and shoes. He wanted to get the fuck out.

"You're in such a hurry."

"It's really late Eliza."

"I hate when guys do this."

"Leave?"

"Yes. It makes me feel like a whore."

"That's life," he said, without thinking.

Why did he say that?

"It sure is."

She was hurt.

"Okay," he said, kissing her on the mouth, then the forehead. "See ya."

"Just because I don't want to fuck you tonight doesn't mean I don't want to fuck."

"I get it. Sorry about things being awkward."

"It's fine. I'm just feeling sad like I said."

In the hallway, he checked his phone: still no messages. Mariko hadn't woken up. An *Uber* was six minutes away. The brief life cycle of the adventure was almost complete.

Fuck.

What was he gonna do? Did he have his keys? No. They'd fallen out of his pants pocket.

He turned back towards Eliza's door.

Fuck.

No. He was wrong. They were there, he was just panicking, just imagining things.

This was such a terrible idea.

Five minutes. He just wanted to go home.

He trotted down the stairs.

Back there: split open, this young woman's body.

Her heavy breath on his neck.

Almost.

A series of chemical transformations—then the clarity of wanting nothing else.

Four minutes.

Eyes. Dark. Like the windows of a church. Shutting magnetically when he plucked at her body.

He was still mostly erect. His heart was racing.

He felt strangely used.

He hadn't gotten off.

He opened his eyes.

There it was: the pink-orange sun flowering over the river.

How many people had passed away during the night in New York City?

How many people had gone to bed and never woke up?

Blackish, fading night, no stars anywhere. Indian summer air. A sinking feeling.

The city was so quiet in the rabbit-light, just before the sun.

He had to start preparing lies: lies for Mariko, lies for Eliza, lies for himself. There was nothing else to think of.

One minute.

He was anxious to get in the car. He had a text from Eliza. He deleted it without reading it along with their whole thread. He would have to delete the *Facebook* thread too, just in case. He would talk to her later. He needed time to process.

The car was there.

He got in and immediately closed his eyes.

Dan told the driver to take the Brooklyn Bridge. Fuck it. That's what he wanted to take. It was more poetic. The most poetic structure in New

York City, in the whole world. It didn't matter if it took longer to get home.

His eyes were open—but it was like his brain was asleep behind them. Almost nothing was registering.

Black, red, yellow, green.

The *Uber* inched onto the rippling span of the bridge.

Night, death, sea, stars.

Dan closed his eyes.

He saw her again: his mother.

He had been the one to find her: she looked like she was sleeping.

It was all too much to think about.

He felt like a ghost, drifting back into a body. He was a dead woman's child, separated from what he loved by a fissure in time.

The city was a debris field; people were the debris: strange, lost, broken, wandering *things*.

Mother.

He felt tears in the inner-corners of his eyes.

He summoned another image to replace that of his mother.

Eliza.

No.

Mariko.

The Brooklyn waterfront was changing so much, especially in Greenpoint; developers were building an entirely new city in the post-industrial areas.

He was two minutes away. The time couldn't pass fast enough. He was strangely afraid of falling asleep, as if the driver wouldn't wake him up, and he would just continue north, upstate, into a sea of trees.

He felt a stirring in his bowels. He had to shit again. He was so tired that he wondered if it could wait until he woke up.

The *Uber* pulled up in front of his apartment on India St.

He was afraid to get out. What if she was waiting for him?

He didn't want to be seen or seen-through.

"Thanks," he mumbled to the driver.

It took twice as long as usual to ascend the stairs, open the door.

There was nobody waiting. The bedroom door was closed. Without turning on the lights, he took off his pants and sweater in the kitchen, folded them, stowed them under the sink so that it would not appear that he had changed, went to the bathroom, flushed without sitting down, ran the water without washing his hands. The urge to shit had gone away, thank God.

A few seconds later, he was asleep on the couch, away from Mariko, for the first time since she had moved in.

4

Dan watched meditatively as three unwhisked eggs curled and popped in a slick of olive oil.

The windows to the apartment were open, Mariko was smoking on the fire-escape; they had Fats Domino on in the background; the morning was perfect, equilibrium had been somewhat restored, or so he hoped.

And there was the September sunlight—impossible to be indifferent to the miracle of its appearance.

He hadn't had time to shower, his skin had that vague odor of sweat that hopefully masked the scent of sex on his skin.

He wondered if he had been trying to get caught, if he still was.

He didn't want to live in this place anymore; he had a latent urge to leave, to go to a coffee shop with his laptop and research movers and apartments and disappear before the sun set, leaving a note on the fridge.

It wasn't impossible. People did drastic things like that all the time.

He just wished he were a more passionate person, the kind of person who could start all over at the drop of a hat.

The eggs were burning. He could smell the charred fat that was blackening along the circumference of the pan. Dan turned off the burner and moved the pan to another burner.

Soon, they would have breakfast together and would proceed as if nothing had happened, as if they had not fought, as if he had not left the house, as if Akari wasn't coming over to judge them.

He was going to get less and less sleep as long as things remained like this. He could imagine a day when there was no sleep at all, only anxiety. That was his dystopian fantasy: life without sleep.

He hadn't really felt free since his postdoc in Berlin, when he'd really experimented and let go in all sorts of ways.

He could feel himself casting about for a mental belay-point—but there was nothing.

Dan realized his prick was semi-hard, as memories of the night before transitioned from semi to full consciousness. It was just unbelievable that he had touched her voluptuous body.

Eliza had reminded him of his college girlfriend, Amanda, who had had a very similar body type (now that he thought about it); the professor's psyche had conflated the two women: a kinetic store of energy had been released when he kissed Eliza at Veselka's. Dan hadn't even *liked* Amanda, but she had not only taken his virginity but established the foundation of whatever sexual confidence he had. Amanda had wanted to fuck *all the time*. She was everywhere. She activated his sensual body—brought his sensuality into existence like a second mother. And ironically, he didn't even like her; she wasn't even his type. He didn't enjoy talking to her or just hanging out with her. She annoyed him. The fact is, she was incredibly banal, had nothing interesting to say, didn't read, watched TV all the time, was completely *off* when she wasn't *on*.

It was unclear if he was thinking about Amanda or Eliza—distant past or near past. It was unclear if he was layering images from actual porn he'd watched or even just regular movies or magazines. The fantasy was iterative: it could generate endless incarnations of itself; it was self-perpetuating.

In many ways, he still embodied the mentality of an awkward teenage boy. He had never quite caught up to the fact that he was a grown-up. The image he had of himself—the very deep, private image—was not kind: ginger hair, pasty skin, thin build. He had rejected himself around the age of thirteen and had never really reevaluated his opinion. He even knew that he was not objectively *un*attractive now: he had a good jawline, nice eyes—but he had never really given himself permission to be sexually confident or virile . . . sexy.

It wasn't an exaggeration to say that everything he did was a means of compensating for this very foundational insecurity. He sought power and prestige in his professional life, sought it endlessly, and had a bottomless hunger for it simply because he didn't have natural charisma to rely on.

Ultimately, he didn't feel that he deserved love. But did he deserve sex? He had never considered the question so explicitly until now.

Dan took two plates down from the cabinets above the stove and two forks from the adjacent drawers. He placed the forks and plates on the small, circular table in their proportionally small kitchen. Using a spatula, he spliced the mass of eggs in half and slid each half-mass onto each of the plates. Then, sitting down and taking up a fork, the professor called out, "Breakfast's ready!" and began to eat.

He heard Mariko slide in from the fire-escape.

She smiled and he smiled back instinctually.

"Smells good," she said brightly.

"Tastes good too."

Mariko took her seat, brushing his foot with hers.

Did she really have no idea that he'd left—had she really just passed out? Maybe she'd just assumed he'd gone out for a walk . . . that was more plausible than what had actually happened.

He felt agonizingly, volcanically, *insanely* guilty . . . but it was such a beautiful morning . . . what was the point? The apartment felt so peaceful, like it had a life of its own, totally independent of the life they lived within it. The whole city was indifferent to the particulars of the human life it contained.

Mariko gave him a kiss on the forehead before sitting down. She pursed her lips. His guilt spiked. He blinked at her. He felt like he'd traveled a million miles in a few hours to get to that kiss.

He watched Mariko, bathed in sunlight, as she ate. They had done this so many times, sat down to breakfast. Why had he not paid more attention to this ritual? He was so incredibly lucky: the luckiest man on Earth. He was having breakfast with the woman he loved—right?

Should they get married and have kids?

He would love to make oatmeal or eggs for a little boy getting ready for soccer practice in the park; he would love to quiet a little baby girl, screaming while he tried to put her in her carriage.

Their best years were ahead: the years that bore wisdom. He couldn't just throw those years away—could he?

He should have proposed years ago when there was still real trust, when there was a deep physical and mental bond. If he'd asked her to marry him then, she would have said yes, unquestionably; she used to hint at it all the time.

This was it: This was his life, and he was blowing it, letting it slip away. He could just brush Mariko's foot back, reach out, stroke the top of her hand with his fingers, lean across the table, kiss her . . . stroke the hair away from her face, so that it caught the sunlight and framed her eyes.

This was it: this was the moment to heal everything, to make good on the longstanding promise of their relationship.

"You're thinking about something." Her voice was very pillowy and soft.

"I'm always thinking about something."

"Did you get Xavier's email?" Mariko asked.

"I haven't looked," Dan said, raising his thick eyebrows unconsciously, slightly.

"He's got cancer."

Dan put down his fork. "Really? Wow."

Don't care.

"It's aggressive."

"Jesus."

Mariko sat down and began to eat her eggs as if nothing was the matter. Dan reached into his right pocket for this phone and opened his email, pinching the skin between the corner of his eye and the top of his forehead with his left hand.

His girlfriend attacked her eggs with an exaggerated degree of focus.

"I'm really sorry," Dan said, shaking his head sadly.

Mariko put down her fork and looked over Dan's left shoulder, towards the window. Her hair was tucked behind her ears and the muscles of her neck stood out slightly, as if she were quietly straining. She was still so lovely. Even though he could reach out and stroke her hair, her cheek, her neck, if he wanted to, he felt impossibly far away from her.

"I ran into him at Whole Foods a few weeks ago," Mariko said. "He looked fine. I think I'm in shock. Or something. Something like shock. Dunno what to call it."

"You should go and see him today."

"You don't want to go with me?"

Dan continued to pinch the skin between his eyebrow and forehead.

"No. I don't think I can handle it, to be honest."

"Really?"

"He's your friend."

"He's your friend too."

"I'm a friend by extension . . . at best."

"He's dying."

"Which is why you should go see him. Without me."

"I want you to go with me."

Mariko watched as Dan's fingers slid from his forehead down across his eyes, as if he didn't want to look at her anymore.

"I can't handle it. I just can't. My brain feels foggy today and I just . . . I just want to not do anything. Honestly. Not talk to anyone."

"Well, my sister's on her way."

"She doesn't count."

"She doesn't?"

"No. Because she knows how to leave me alone when I want to be left alone."

Mariko got up and carried her plate to the sink.

Once the water was running hot, she began to wash the plate with a sponge taken from a small saucer next to the faucet handle.

"Give me your plate," Mariko commanded Dan, who dutifully passed his plate and fork to her.

"This isn't very fun."

"What isn't?" She asked sharply. "Doing the dishes?"

"*This*." Dan gestured to her, then back to himself.

"What's *this*?"

"Being together."

Mariko laughed, bitterly. She could feel her face getting red. "Do you want to fuck someone else? Is that what this is about?"

"No."

"I don't believe you."

"You don't have to believe me."

"Sometimes I wonder what's wrong with you, Dan—"

"Oh you do?"

Mariko finished with Dan's plate and placed it carefully on the drying rack. She turned and leaned against the sink, bracing herself with her hands.

"I don't know. I'm sorry. I don't think of myself as a spiteful person, but it became obvious to me that so much of the way that I talk to people is on some level, really a way to try to hurt them—talk to you I mean—"

"Well. Ok. Where did you get that thing about my wanting to fuck—"

Mariko just laughed. "No idea. We just don't fuck so I imagine you'd wanna fuck *somebody*."

"Do you?"

"Don't worry. I would never cheat."

"But do you?"

"Figuring that part out."

"Okay."

"My sister's coming over soon. Can you let her in if I'm not here?"

"Sure, no problem." Dan realized he wasn't making any eye contact at all.

"You know how much I care about you right?" The tone was suddenly forgiving.

"Um. I guess?"

"Because I do." She said this with such convincing tenderness that he could only assume she was acting.

"I care about you too."

"It was weird not to have you sleeping next to me."

Dan thought about it: "That's the first time either one of us has ever slept on the couch."

"We had a good run."

"We did . . ." Dan said this with a greater sense of nostalgic finality than he had intended.

"The couch is still so much better than somewhere else . . ."

"True!" He smiled nervously.

Dan realized that Mariko would be absolutely crushed to find out about Eliza; she was so close to figuring it out, sensually or intuitively, but rejected it empirically. She couldn't know or prove it unless she broke into his phone, or had followed him out of the house, and she hadn't done either of those things.

Sex outside of the relationship was a line that had never been crossed: to walk across that boundary was to trigger a set of reactions that could only lead to the collapse of those boundaries, and thus, the whole structure of being-together.

She doesn't want to know, he thought with some relief.

"I love you," she said finally, after an extended silence.

"I love you too." He didn't find himself convincing.

There was another long pause. Mariko got up, and, collecting both their mugs, went to the sink. Dan watched her passively, leaning back slightly in his chair.

They spent so much time waiting for the other person to say something; snippets of conversation always gave way to an equal number of silences, as though according to some law of weights and balances.

"I'm not angry with you . . . I'm not angry with either of us," Mariko began, casually, as she scrubbed at the rings of milky coffee inside the mugs. "I'm not . . . I'm not trying to punish you for our failings as a couple . . . which it might seem like I'm doing. I mean, I see you looking at me and I feel how much you care about me . . . how much you love me, I really do . . ." Sunlight ran through the half-parted curtains. "And I um . . . I feel well, obviously people have to attack the structure they've built around themselves, blow up the foundations . . . I'm . . . you know, you know— this is happening more and more often . . . We're having these fights more and more often. We're becoming one of those . . . . We both want to have kids—like maybe we should talk about that more. I don't know—"

"I don't know if I'm ready."

"But are we ever going to feel ready? I feel like we just have to leap."

"Yeah, but not right now," Dan said with infuriating definitiveness.

"Every day I begin again . . ." Mariko said, as if practicing a dramatic monologue, "trying to answer the same questions I began my adulthood with; and sometimes, many times—often—trying to avoid answers to those questions. Answers are frightening. Answers are facts about the world that drive out your fantasies about the world. And I like my fantasies about the world; I don't know how to live without them, Dan. I'm just trying to keep the unreality to a minimum. At best, I think . . . at best—you can prune an illusion like a bush . . . but you can't pull it up by the roots . . ."

"Alright?"

"Never mind."

Dan felt vaguely, increasingly tense, exhausted, and out of it; the initial optimism he felt when Mariko walked in the room was proving untenable.

He went to the coffee machine on the counter and poured himself a fresh cup. He couldn't functionally wake up; his body was facing a complete adrenaline deficit. More perniciously, he discovered keeping a secret demanded energy, like he had to assign a part of himself to guarding the memory of the night before. Everything was the same but different. Everything was different while appearing exactly the same.

"I think it becomes really convenient to blame your partner," Dan theorized, "for your own disappointment—and I think that's pretty obviously what we're doing to each other—"

"Blaming—"

"Sure . . . and like . . . again . . . I think it has a lot to do with not having kids, not getting married . . ."

"Sometimes though . . . like . . . I just feel like . . . the pressure to be a mother is in many ways the pressure to be a completely different person."

"It doesn't have to be—"

"The idea of getting pregnant is almost like the idea of killing myself . . . choosing to do away with a certain version of me that I've gotten tired of."

Dan poured out the last of the coffee from the pot. "Do you really feel like that?"

"I don't know?! Sometimes—yes—"

"Right now?"

"I think two minutes ago I felt differently and in two minutes in the future I'll feel differently again."

"Oh boy . . ."

"Why don't you fuck me right now, Dan? No condom. It's the right time of the month. Like. Let's just—"

"You're keeping track of that?"

"Actually—I do—yeah—just because."

"Interesting."

"Well, do you want to or not?"

Mariko found herself washing another dish. "I'm a little offended."

"What, that I don't want to breed right now?"

"That it doesn't excite you."

"Dude, a second ago you were saying like you found the whole idea abhorrent!"

"I also told you I keep changing my mind!"

"Babies *just* to shake things up is a categorically bad idea," Dan said in a professorial tone.

"Okay, I guess that settles it then."

When she was finished with the pan, she returned to the table, and folded her hands, like she was about to commence a serious business meeting.

"We can always change our minds tomorrow. The window will still be open."

"No, Mariko. Sorry."

"You seem exhausted. You really couldn't sleep last night, could you?"

"Yeah, I was just up working on my book all night, after you fell asleep."

"How's it going?"

"Meh."

"I feel like it's stressing you out."

Dan internalized this. Maybe his whole almost-affair with Eliza *was* in fact rooted in his own creative-intellectual despair, his own fear of failure. He was expected, he had signed a fucking contract, to write this big, synthetic, poppy book of ideas for Verso (for not very much money), and yet he found that while he could write a thesis and academic book, and while he could write blog posts, he couldn't really write a book for a general readership. The short form and the long form didn't blend into the medium form.

"Yeah, it's stressing me out. For sure."

"I just hate feeling like you're not there . . ."

"I feel guilty . . ."

"Just be here. Be with me. Really be with me—again—" Mariko's eyes were shining. "I would really like that . . ."

Dan yawned. "So would I."

After Mariko left, Dan opened his laptop out of the instinctual desire to think about something other than his relationship. As he clicked through a series of think-pieces, Dan rubbed his paunch, nervously, as if to calm himself.

What would he talk about today? How could he illuminate this very American dialectic between political possibility and impossibility?

He wanted to admit that everyone was simply stuck in this structure (capitalism), but that seemed like cowardice, capitulation.

But what else was there to say? People were too comfortable: too comfortable being too comfortable. Organisms tended towards simplicity, not complexity.

Dan started to write a new blog entry.

All levels of matter are connected: gut, cock, limbs, brain; computer, phone; ecology; economy. Swarming. My brain is just the uppermost level of organization: I extend into other systems. I am a system.

Dan found the tone of most internet writing was basically the same: dispassionate, nerdy, self-satisfied. It was a definitively twenty-first century tone. Writers on the left, writers on whatever side, did not write to change the world, topple governments, upend traditional ideas—they wrote to gently inform or passively complain.

If romanticism was a reaction to industrialization, then what do we call the reaction to digitization—the industrialization of the mind? The dark, Satanic mills are inside us. Are us.

When Dan had done shrooms as a teenager for the first time, he had realized that the mushroom was nature's way of communicating with humans; the human and the mushroom were in a symbiotic relationship. The mushroom made the human more sensitive, and in return, the human cultivated the mushroom. Smartphones did the same thing, except in a perverse way. They increased the power of human perception—through an exponential increase in available information—and the human, in turn, cultivated the phone.

Strange thought.

Dan felt himself almost trembling, perhaps just from the coffee. He wasn't sure if he wanted more coffee or if he should stop. He was aware that he was part of the consuming frenzy, responding to the nearness of easy pleasure and biochemical enhancement. More coffee to read more articles, write more emails, look at more advertising.

He opened *Twitter*.

Twitter made his brain go haywire. It felt amazing.

He felt the urge to shit.

Slipping off the chair, Dan took three steps towards the bathroom that was adjacent to the door, which opened to the kitchenette from the outside. He flipped the seat up with his bare toes, hiked his jeans down with his thumb, and sat down.

The shit slid out instantly because of the coffee. One, two, three, then four long loose stools.

The professor hung on the edge of the plastic bowl, wiping himself.

Scrubbed his hands for seven or eight seconds.

Returned to the kitchenette.

The laptop was still open.

He was aware that Akari was going to arrive soon and that he would be expected to entertain her for a few hours.

He was attracted to Akari. Pixie cut, tight little ass.

He'd become more disposed to those kinds of thoughts lately. He was on the market again, shopping for sensual entertainment.

There was grief in this reversion to nameless hunger, revulsion at the erotic conditions of his life. It made him angry. He wasn't sure whether at Mariko or himself. He simply didn't know what was true and false anymore.

Dan sighed to himself. He'd spent his entire academic career working to deconstruct and deflate *truth* to the point where the word, the concept, only made him feel dead and empty whenever it was invoked. *Truth* conjured up a world of unthought, unanalyzed values—adolescence, childhood, whatever his parents told him, or his teachers taught him.

But now he needed *truth:* needed it in order to feel *okay* about the choices he had made and was continuing to make.

Dan sat down and continued to scroll, as if by scrolling he could unravel his own thought-pattern.

He opened up Spotify on his laptop. Clicked on "Chill" playlist. "Silver Soul" by Beach House came on.

He really liked this song.

Dan rubbed his face and laughed and arched his neck back, in disbelief at his own predictability.

His brain felt fuzzy. He shouldn't have gone online. He stood up and stretched. Where was Akari? She was supposed to have arrived—but she was totally AWOL.

I'd like to spend a whole day watching the sun move across the sky, he reflected.

It occurred to him that he could masturbate. The now closed laptop suddenly beckoned: he could just watch a little porn.

Dan rubbed his face again and turned away from the kitchen table and paced in a circle, his hands traveling over his forehead, through his thinning hair.

He felt ashamed, and horny.

He thought of Mariko and how this was one of the reasons they'd been sleeping together less—porn.

These were the things he never talked to his own students about: his fear that he was just like them, subject to the same forces and pressures and . . . just . . . just *nothing*. A nothing. An annihilated being.

When he was younger, Dan had felt alive in the kinds of ways he encouraged his students to feel alive: intellectually, emotionally, with revolutionary fervor. He'd believed that things could change and sought that change, in himself, and in the world. He started a passionate and popular blog, participated in a strike for higher adjunct wages, read Shakespeare with inmates, gone vegan (before sliding gently in vegetarianism then pescetarianism), stopped using plastics, stopped eating sugar (though he'd given up on that too).

He unbuttoned his jeans, pushed a hand through.

Pathetic.

The paunch, the thinning hair, the estranged girlfriend. There was nothing radical in this. It was so predictable, so obviously what a young person tells themselves *not* to become—so obviously what he had told himself not to become.

In graduate school, he planned to write a history of the loss of faith in progress, in the idea of progress. Now he'd lost faith that he would ever write that book, only notes, sayings, remarks, witticisms.

Tweets.

He sighed again. Paused. Entered a website. Watched images emerge.

"What a fucking asshole," Dan said aloud.

He shut the laptop and zipped up his pants over his half-hard penis.

His body was still buzzing, like Pavlov's dog. There was no meal, just the gentle tinkling of the meal bell.

The objects in the room were prison guards; they had him under surveillance. He felt judged, attacked, discarded.

Guilty.

If this was a crisis, a midlife crisis or whatever, it was sure taking its sweet time. It was strategic, patient, willing to be tedious. It would eat up the rest of his thirties and perhaps his forties. He would become one of those men who started having affairs with other men in his fifties, just to shake things up.

He looked at his phone. Nothing from Eliza.

Maybe he should have wacked off: it would have been more relaxing than reading about politics.

He was anxious. He wanted to masturbate so badly. His cock started to swell again, he unzipped his pants, flipped open the laptop, typed, clicked, clicked.

He closed the laptop again, panicked.

Politics and porn. That was the content of his thought. That stuff of his soul. Power and pleasuring twining together.

He was about to look at trans porn. That was what he always looked at. He could scarcely admit it to himself. Recently, that's what he'd been into. And where had that desire come from? Had it come from porn itself? Or from some latent desire within?

Shit.

Was he gay?

It was just a fear. Maybe even more than that, a little desire . . . an inkling of something—but not an identity. An identity . . . an identity was more than that; it was a deeper, more complex pattern—not an erratic impulse or a squiggle of desire.

He was just curious—just letting off some erotic steam. That was what he told himself.

He wondered how many of his colleagues looked at porn; probably all of them, male or female. The hardcore feminists, the queer theorists, the old white dudes: all of them were probably hooked up to the juice, wanking away.

It wasn't safe to talk about desire in the university; it never was, but now the tools for catching and punishing desire were more effective. To talk about getting off would have meant violating the expectation that education, that intellectualism, be de-eroticized. The result was the warehousing of sexuality: people in boxes watching other people in boxes.

He added another aphorism to his blog entry:

Internet porn means producing data so that the internet can sell you more porn. Watching internet porn is more useful for the markets than having sex in the privacy of your bedroom is because it can be quantified. Porn has nothing to do with bodies. That's what makes it so great.

He was hungry again; he wanted a second breakfast. He'd already had eggs, so it'd have to be something else. What did they have? Cereal?

Dan looked through the cupboards. Kashi Cereal. Okay. But there was no more almond milk; he'd have to go out if he wanted to eat.

He texted Akari to tell her that he was leaving the spare key under the door.

Whatever.

He put on his shoes, the same brand of canvas sneakers he had worn for twenty years. They represented a kinetic link to his youth: as if wearing the same shoes meant treading the same ground, sowing the same earth, freezing time.

The desire to keep things the same was the only reason, too, that he even kept cereal in the cupboard; he didn't even really eat cereal anymore, but the sight was comforting; the cereal in the cupboard was like a pin holding the fabric of daily life together. It was there because it had to be there.

Except that it didn't. It was arbitrary, something that came from the outside; it was implanted, imposed.

There was little difference between hunger and anxiety: the body registered both with a pang, a tightness, in his stomach. The anxiety was so deep, in fact, so ever-present, that it confused his sense-memory, displacing the instincts that told him it was time to eat or drink or fuck or sleep. The only orientation was disorientation; each morning began with the queasy certainty of uncertainty.

There was no self, only this confusion of forces. He, *this*, was just this signal interference in the cortex, this jumble of electrical impulses crying out for coherence. Even his own name: Dan. A short, jabbing sound. A burst of neurological static. Was this the basis for the belief in the soul? Is this what literature and philosophy and politics depend on, this crazy notion that internal noise could be bound together with a name, and thereby become coherent? Whole?

On the other hand, what did it matter what you labeled your internal experience as? Soul or self or brain or Dan or nothing? The name could alter the experience, but couldn't alter *you*, unless you let it.

He was practically running down the stairs from their third-floor walk-up. The marble floors made the enclosed stairway much cooler than the apartment or the day outside. It felt good: it was a relief.

He caught his breath at the bottom of the stairs. For a moment he was tempted to run right back up, just because he could! Because he was alive! Incredibly, unfathomably alive!

He took one step back onto the stairs, as if ready to run.

No: he was being ridiculous. He turned, pushing open the front door, practically tumbling onto the street—

This was real, wasn't it? The light tumble of dry leaves, taxis and cyclists and pedestrians, runners, parents pushing strollers. They were all real and firm in their belief that they were real, those people—weren't they?

Or were they like him? Was it possible that everyone was like him? Anxious, skittering, unsure of what was happening or why. Breathing, shitting, talking, moving about.

Anxiety was the homeland of the digitized twenty-first century in the same way language was the homeland of the chaotic and displaced twentieth century, the century of vast diasporas.

Where to get coffee? He was walking now: south towards Williamsburg. More strollers, runners, teenagers texting . . . bums with cardboard signs and tragic eyes.

This wasn't how things were supposed to be.

There needed to be living feeling, living community, an awareness of others, and the environment, the interconnectedness of everything. There had to be some way to fight back against this structural alienation.

The professor had no meaningful connection to anyone in this city of eight million—not Mariko, not his students, not his friends; if he disappeared, they'd hardly notice. He just took up space, resources, contributed nothing to society except words, made nothing of value. He lived in the fallen world of money.

He tried to remember what he had gone out for. Coffee, he decided.

He had so much on his mind. He felt a little manic. Like the world was ending. But the world wasn't ending, the world was very good at going on, continuing the way it always had, at self-maintenance. It was only that his private world was ending.

Soon he would have to teach.

Soon he would have to get on the L train and go into a room and teach undergraduates about language and ideas. He would have to perform mastery, which was disgusting.

He would just leave a key for Akari, who was always late.

He went into a coffee shop, not even looking at the name, and sat down. All the familiar accouterments of the Brooklyn coffee shop—the optics of white space—helped him calm down.

Where was Eliza? He couldn't stop thinking about her. He had this weird idea that she was nearby. He couldn't text her just yet though, it was too early.

At the counter he ordered a double espresso; he paid with a credit card that gave him one percent back on all purchases.

What was he going to teach?

It was what—the sixth or seventh class meeting? What had they read last week? Hegel and Marx. What were they reading this week? A literary text. Whitman. *Song of Myself,* 1855 edition. All that made sense, right? The democratic, utopian vision; the visions of brotherhood; the sense of something very deep pressing the current of history forward. The spiritual materialism.

His method of teaching was improvisatory: He didn't take extensive notes; he made a syllabus, had students buy all the books upfront, then he let things sit and stew. That was how the really brilliant professors taught. Theory, philosophy, economics, poetry, fiction—it was all represented in his courses. He liked being surprised, he liked seeing new patterns.

He also liked being in control, too, however; the discourse was his—students could provoke new ideas, but he was ultimately the one to give them shape. He was the one who had to give them shape. He was the only one in his classrooms who had done the work: that was why he was the instructor.

Dan sat by the window with his double espresso, stirring the brown liquid with a plastic spoon. In the back of his mind, he wondered if the plastic could melt and release toxic chemicals into his coffee.

It was noon now.

This is what always happened. Akari would arrive and for a weekend everything would revolve around anticipating her bullshit.

She used their apartment like it was a chill Airbnb; seeing Mariko was just a pretense to fuck around New York. Mariko was such a pushover too. She never really directly called Akari out; at most she would nag and mope.

Greenpoint was heating up; there weren't enough trees in his section of the neighborhood along Manhattan Avenue.

He hated these dead periods of the day: the long stretches of doing absolutely nothing, the periods where doing something was only a latent possibility. His life was composed of discontinuous chains of nothing waiting for some catalyzing agent—for a moment of bonding in which the whole chain could light up (otherwise known as happiness).

Whatever the differences between Tolstoy or Dostoevsky, Dan reasoned, their characters had in common the search for, the willingness to search for, God. Great writing was never really nihilistic. Even Thomas Hardy had believed in Fate. And even for a postmodern writer like Pynchon there was the mysticism of The System.

The long phase known as Romanticism always left room for belief or at least ecstasy. But now, Dan reasoned, the Romantic subject was passing away, and something new was evolving.

The professor drank half the double in one sip, having let it cool considerably. He paused then, because he would feel guilty about taking up a seat in the coffee shop without a drink in front of him. He should have just ordered a large coffee just so that he could sit and stare out the window longer.

He got a sudden craving for a cigarette—but he wouldn't give in; it had been too long. . . .

He started to think about the department meeting he had at the end of the week: he was already dreading it. Somehow, people still thought that academic life was glamorous, but what it really was, was total bullshit: full of busy work. At least fifty percent of what he did, as a tenure track professor, was bureaucratic detritus.

How many people were just sitting in offices on *Facebook Messenger*, complaining about their office or reading something stupid? Why was the obsession with employment so great that people were paid to pretend to do something rather to be allowed to do something creative and life-giving?

American capitalism was such that either you were unsuccessful and poor, doing mean, ugly labor—or successful and trapped in easy, but meaningless, soul-destroying labor.

So what was he going to say to his students? For the ninety minutes in which he would do the job that he was meant to do? How could he ascend out of passive meaninglessness and create a deep exchange of sympathies?

"Maybe I should pace more," he thought to himself. "Maybe I should dress up a little more. Dress down a little more. Shave before class. Clean up. Should we keep sitting in a circle? Should we all go out to a bar?"

That's what his coolest professors did—ask the class to meet in a bar, talk about ideas over beer.

Two guys at the table next to him were talking about a pitch they were going to make to Netflix. They were talking about an algorithm that could write TV scripts based on being fed thousands of old TV scripts.

One of the two pitchmen had a villain-mustache, with waxed, curled ends; they were talking about some real bullshit.

Dan kept tuning in and out.

The espresso was gone, he had given in and taken a second big sip. He immediately started to feel restless, like he should keep moving. He had left the apartment because he was anxious, but now he was anxious in the coffee shop. He would inevitably be anxious on the subway ride to Manhattan and would be just as anxious in the classroom too. At every point in the day, he was ready to move on to the next point; he never really felt at rest.

It was possible that he hadn't really rested since he was eighteen, since the summer after high school, which was the last time he truly experienced carefreeness. Since then, he had been sliding, sliding, sliding, unable to grasp on and hold on to an experience, a phenomenological stillpoint. He read and read and wrote and wrote and ate and drank and made and gained practical and theoretical experience and social and professional prestige and still . . .

Dan stood up. The TV guys were still going; he was only half-paying attention to what they were saying. They were talking about someone named Jerry and what he was going to think. Jerry was apparently very important; they had to do everything in service of Jerry's wishes. He couldn't listen to them anymore.

How many times had he wanted to butt into a conversation just to tell someone how stupid they were and never done it? Thousands maybe. It happened every day; it was part of the granular level of city experience.

Assholes, dipshits, motormouths.

"You guys suck," Dan whispered, under his breath as he passed through the coffee shop door, but only once he was sure that they wouldn't hear him.

5

After they paid their bill, Eliza and her friends walked back towards McCarren Park.

"Let's put our shit over there," Parker said buoyantly, the form of her yoga-body clearly outlined underneath her white dress.

"Where?" asked Nina, looking.

"There," Parker said, annoyed, pointing thirty yards ahead, "That sunny spot."

They arrived at the sunny spot. "Here?" Eliza asked.

"Yeah." Parker flopped down. "So are you gonna tell us about last night or what?"

"No. Uh. Nah."

"No, but like you started to tell us in there, so like, finish the story please thank you."

"I'm self-conscious."

"No, but it was so juicy," Nina groaned.

"Too juicy."

"I can't believe . . ." Parker said.

"Are you judging me?" The words flew like sharp spikes out of her mouth.

"Hell no. I think it's hot."

"Like."

"No judgment, I promise."

Eliza looked over at Nina, whose expression was closer to diffident. "You're judging though."

"No. It's a fun story." Nina pursed her lips. "Maybe too fun." Her mouth was small, oval-shaped; her face a little fat, with acne on her forehead.

Ugly girls, Eliza thought, tended to judge sex more than pretty girls. It's not that Nina is ugly actually, just not as pretty as Parker.

Eliza didn't want to think about Dan: that was just a game; it was over. It had been an impulse, a kind of role-play, something she'd done because depression had lowered her inhibitions. She'd felt so lonely and so she reached out to someone who she knew, or assumed, sensed, was as lonely as she was—and she'd been right about that.

It had been unpleasant in the end, even though it turned her on to realize that she had that power over men; she'd only really just begun to understand how to enjoy her body without shame, or without the shame that she'd built up, like credit card debt, as a teenager.

She didn't want to have to admit to her friends that her adventure wasn't as glamorous as she'd hinted that it was (or hoped it'd be). Eliza could see, however, that Parker understood all this and that Nina just wanted to stop talking about it—so she knew that she could escape without being called on her bullshit.

Nina laid out the blanket she had brought, then laid down on her back, took a selfie and started to edit the filter right away. She seemed absorbed in the work of removing blemishes, finding the right angle, the right tag. How many other people in the park were doing the same thing right now? Perhaps a dozen or more? And in the course of the next hour: hundreds would tag themselves here.

Data was rising into the air like smoke from a battlefield.

What was Dan doing right now? He hadn't texted her. Eliza didn't mind not hearing from him, but it wasn't good for her confidence: the whole point was to have him wrapped around her finger, even if she never saw him again. She had planned to lead him on for a few more weeks, because why not? She enjoyed the attention and would maybe give him another chance to fuck her; he would probably get better once his nervousness passed.

It was amazing how quickly one's feeling shifted from one extreme to another. It was like there was a system of weights, checks and balances, in the brain. No feeling became too dominant; there was constant transformation.

Nina posted the picture; Eliza watched from over her shoulder; it was clear just from body language alone that Nina was immediately concerned with the response the picture was going to get. Warm weather would be gone soon enough, and the bright, sensual optics of summer would soon disappear. There was nothing like the glow of sunburnt flesh.

Eliza received a text from her Mom: *hi honey just wondering how the new school year is going . . .*

She didn't feel like answering.

"What's that guy doing?" Parker asked nobody in particular.

"He's riding a unicycle," Nina explained, deadpan.

"Dudes are so weird."

"Yeah they are," Parker agreed.

"I'm sweating balls out here." Nina was so self-conscious.

Eliza glanced at her phone, which she pulled from the pocket of her high-waisted jean pants: no message from Dan.

It dawned on Eliza: Dan's girlfriend, whoever she was, was a real person, out there . . . someone whose relationship she'd invisibly altered . . . someone who had no recourse, no means of changing the situation (if this person was even aware of it). Had she been unconsciously competing with this woman? Had she unconsciously wanted to cause someone pain (just to demonstrate that she had the power to do so)? Eliza hoped not.

Was Eliza's behavior influenced by her mother, who had cheated on her father, several times in fact, knowing that her father would not be strong enough to confront her? She asked herself this too. Was she, in fact, not turning out to be exactly like her mother? Was she not actively, almost in a muscular fashion, refashioning herself in her mother's image?

Her parents hadn't spoken directly to each other in three years, even though they were still married, lived in the same house. There was something so ruthless and determined about her mother, a rashness. She splashed the people around her with napalm. Her mother didn't play games with power: either you had it or you didn't and she had it. It was that simple.

Eliza was worried she had a hickey (even though she'd checked several times in the morning). She wanted to erase all signs, visible and invisible, of the affair.

A frisbee sailed a few feet over their heads; a barefooted, bare-chested man with a beard dashed by to catch it.

Parker looked the sweaty frisbee bro over. "I'd do it."

Nina looked away, embarrassed. "I wouldn't."

Parker took out a beer from her purse and a keychain with a bottle opener and a Sierra Nevada (she had good taste in deli beers).

Nina took another selfie. There was something off-putting about the way people constantly examined their appearance in the camera of their phones: they could not grasp how ugly it was, and how ugly the irony was too. Still, Eliza wanted to like Nina, who was intelligent and thoughtful one on one, or even in the media theory class they currently shared. Nina had potential; she just needed confidence.

"I'm gonna go get a beer," Eliza said, "I'll be right back."

Now she was on her feet, walking west, towards the water, tilted slightly towards Greenpoint, where generic bodegas were strung like pearls along the street.

It occurred to her that she could just walk away and not come back.

Friendships in New York City among people her age were often a matter of triangulating who knew who and how that might matter in the bigger scheme of winning money and influence. Parker was rich; Nina knew cool bands in Bushwick, and so on. Was that why she hung out with them?

"Can I have a pack of cigarettes?" Eliza asked the bodega man. "And this." She took a little vial of ginseng extract on display next to the register. It seemed like a good idea. Healthy.

The bodega guy nodded, and she handed him her credit card. Cigarettes were so fucking expensive.

She was terrified of post-graduate life, of the real world. What a strange concept. Who came up with these things? Who decided that life had to be this way?

The cigarette tasted good. American spirits.

She crossed the street back towards the park.

Were they even still there? On one level, she was sure they were (she'd only been gone for a few minutes); on another level, she worried, was even convinced, irrationally, that they had left. People just hurt you for the sport of it; she'd been hurt so much, especially by other girls growing up. You were formed as a person by these little cuts, these little social rebukes; even elementary school social groups could make permanent changes in your character, molding you and forming you into a personality with a place in a hierarchy. Childhood was a giant sorting process where you figured out if you were passive or dominant or somewhere in the middle, a solid beta.

Parker and Nina were both on their phones when Eliza returned.

She felt relieved. More than anything, she just wanted to have a lovely afternoon, and to really connect. She wanted to open up to her friends, and to have them open up to her.

"You can get a fine for smoking in the park," Nina said anxiously, as Eliza flicked her lighter.

"Fuck if I care."

Cigarette smoke wafted over the picnic blanket, mixing with the smell of lukewarm beer, grass, and mud.

"I wanna get drunk tonight," Eliza heard herself saying.

"Get drunk right now."

"I didn't get enough beer."

"You're thinking about that T.A. you fucked," Parker said mockingly.

"He's not a T.A.; he's a real professor."

"T.A.'s are real professors."

"No they're not."

"Whatever."

"The point is—he's not a T.A."

"I still can't believe you *did* that," Nina said.

"Yeah because it's not something you would do."

"No, it's not."

"Judgmental voice."

"A little. I guess you can tell."

"I can definitely tell," Eliza said sharply.

"Well, it's kinda inappropriate."

The fact is that Nina was the kind of person who didn't want to deal with her drives. So what she did was demand other people shut down theirs. She didn't want to see it. She wanted you to pretend to be a rational agent. It was suffocating to be around her.

"Define inappropriate." Eliza asked defensively.

"How is it not?"

"I mean, we didn't even fuck."

"That's not the point . . ."

"It's interesting that you're being moralistic about this—"

"I don't mean inappropriate on your part—just his."

"Takes two to tango."

"He should have known better though . . ."

"Why? I'm hot and we had fun."

Nina raised her eyebrows in Parker's direction. Parker shrugged, as if to say, "this isn't my business."

"Everybody needs to—" Parker took a swig of beer, "—chill."

"I'm fucking exhausted." Eliza lay back in the grass, blowing smoke into the air.

"From fucking the T.A." Parker laughed.

"Oh my god shut up."

"It's funny."

Eliza thought about the outfit she had worn to Veselka's; it really was like playing dress up, like playing a role she'd created. At the time, it had really just been about having fun, and about exploring a fantasy. And she'd done that: she'd explored the fantasy all the way up the point at which it had become too real, the point at which Dan went from someone who she looked up to, to just another sad, old man who might get way too attached way too fast.

"Yo, look at this dude who's been trying to slide into my DMs all day," Parker said, pleased with herself.

"Who?" Eliza asked robotically.

"This rapper."

"What?" Nina giggled.

"This shitty white rapper that my sister knows."

Parker's sister was an editor at *The Fader*.

"Did you respond?" Nina asked, concerned.

"Uhhh."

"Oh my God, you did," Nina said, giggling again, this time more nervously.

Nina loved this shit.

"This person is singularly hilarious," Parker said, returning her focus to the screen. "I can't believe he exists."

"Yeah, he's unreal," Eliza said.

"Yeah, but still."

"Should I hang out with him?" Parker asked.

Was she serious?

"Go for it," Eliza said without enthusiasm. "Why not?"

"I can think of reasons why not!" Nina responded, almost programmatically.

A subtle zone of tension was created by their willingness to see the worst in each other and sustained by their politeness: their unwillingness to say the worst.

Parker folded her long, tanned legs together, tucking her right white Ked neatly inside the instep of her left. "Can I have a cigarette?"

"Yeah, sure." Eliza extended her pack and her lighter.

Parker lit a quick, bright flame, then inhaled with pleasure, and released the smoke in a thin stream. "We should go to yoga tonight."

"I can't drink and do yoga," Nina said, shifting on the blanket, looking annoyed that there were now two smokers in her group.

There could be more than this (friendship) Eliza thought, but it always seemed to evade them, or evade her, personally. She worried that she was incapable of bypassing the small differences of habit and temperament that mediated her experience of others, especially women her own age, and that, consequently, she would never have that warm, comforting feeling of being surrounded with care. It was painful to think about.

"I'm getting fat," Eliza announced.

"No, you're not," Nina interjected, concerned.

"My legs are fat."

"Come on . . ."

In Nina's mind, Eliza had nothing to complain about, because she was naturally beautiful, or at least, very attractive. In Eliza's mind, she was wasting her genetic potential. She used to be hot, like Parker, but she had let herself go in college.

Eliza noticed that Parker didn't second Nina's remark; clearly, Parker thought she was getting fat too—which was not surprising (Parker used to have an eating disorder). Parker never said anything about it, but Eliza had heard through friends that she'd gone to rehab in high school—had to leave Exeter for a semester.

UPPERMIDDLECLASS.

Eliza used the term as a fortress against the possibility that she had too much privilege.

Eliza watched her friends, as if they were animals in a zoo or tribespeople in an ethnological study.

Nina looked across the park, at nothing in particular. She seemed acutely unhappy, and Eliza wondered what she was thinking. Eliza couldn't help but think she had said the wrong thing, or framed the Dan experience the wrong way. Maybe Nina was jealous, or maybe she was disgusted, or both. Nina never really talked about her personal life beyond ideating about boys; it was possible she was a virgin; Nina seemed positively frightened of the psychosexual drama of human socialization.

Parker and Nina, Eliza was beginning to understand, represented the two symbolic poles of her own moral development. Parker was outgoing, buoyant, sarcastic, cutting; Nina was demure, judgmental, insecure; Eliza, herself, was all of those things, and shifted back and forth between modes more readily than her friends, who seemed to have a clearer, more fixed idea of what their personas should be, which Eliza was almost jealous of.

Yet, it was possible, as well, that they felt the same way about her.

She slipped off her shoes, wiggled her toes in the sun, and then put her shoes back on.

"La la la," Parker sang.

"Are you guys going out tonight?" Nina asked.

"No idea," Parker answered.

Eliza shifted the position of her ass, which was half on the blanket, half in the grass. She realized that she had to shit: the feeling was unmistakable.

"I have to go find a bathroom," Eliza said.

"You should have gone when you went for cigarettes," Parker said.

"I didn't know I had to shit ten minutes ago."

"Uhuh. Bye."

Eliza headed back west where there was a row of bars lining the street across from the park.

Eliza hated going in public; she couldn't use a public bathroom until living in New York made it a necessity.

A random association: her dad always had literature in the bathroom: used to read history books on the toilet.

She was worried about her dad. She wished her parents would reconcile and put an end to sleeping in separate rooms (with Dad in the basement like a college student).

Eliza put in her earbuds, opened Spotify, opened the "Chill" playlist. She was trying to assuage the anxiety that had settled in that morning when she woke up after three hours of sleep, feeling like her space had been violated.

"Fuck me!" Eliza thought.

The whole thing was so stupid.

God damn.

His cock was on the big side, and it had momentarily excited her when she'd felt it pressing against her when they kissed on the street, but something about the rest of him had turned her off. He was clumsy; his hands slid all over her body without any real direction; he used too much tongue. And worse, he seemed to lose control. She was certain he would have cum right away if they had fucked, which was one of the reasons she had called it off. She had wanted a more sensual connection, a slowness, an intellectual bond, that never formed. The longer the night had gone on, the more she had had to lead, which was fucking boring: the total opposite of what she'd wanted.

Eliza hit next on her Spotify playlist. It was something ambient. The music made her feel like she was floating in a soap-bubble.

Eliza went right into a bar-restaurant that was packed for lunch; she didn't notice the name, it didn't matter; it was cavernous, the patrons all seemed to be enjoying themselves.

There was a short line for one of the four private bathrooms that were available to her. She was relieved to discover that she wouldn't have to poop in a stall next to some other flatulent bitch.

Eliza tapped her phone impatiently. She hadn't had her regular coffee shit this morning. She had been so discombobulated, so out of body.

The woman ahead of her was scrolling through her phone, looking at Instagram.

Everybody everywhere was on fucking *Instagram*.

Waiting to shit my brains out. #fiber #vegan #sewage

God, she was in a bad mood.

She received a text from Dan, which immediately produced a complicated sensation. Her pride required that he follow up and prove that he was obsessed with her, couldn't stop thinking about her.

Hey!

hey Dan . . .

Using his first name was patronizing, turning him into an old, highly unerotic friend. It was hard to say why, but it did.

I'm on my way to class. I just wanted to touch base.

He was writing in complete sentences now, which was a change from the night before. It was like he had decided to act like a proper adult.

Saving face.

It was probably killing him that she hadn't texted him. He probably imagined that she would be his sex-buddy, a permanent fantasy: a dream that he could make manifest whenever he wanted.

But there was a deeper problem too, a deeper discomfort, only she couldn't name it; it was a subconscious irritation: there was something *about* him that made her panic and not want to be in a room with him again. She just couldn't define it.

She had been so manic the night before, so certain of herself. There was no foundation for her decisions.

What's up?

just chillinnnnn

Yeah?

with my friends we're in the park

Washington Square

This was a lie because she knew he lived relatively close to McCarren.

Cool. Getting coofee, you?

coofee lol. made plans with my friends for breakfast . . .

Oh so you barely slept . . .

yep . . .

That's interesting.

it sux

Yeah?

yeah

She'd pursued him. She'd gotten him out of bed, or whatever, out of his apartment, in the middle of the night. She was responsible. She'd wanted it. She'd gotten off on it. Now she was stuck with him without having even gotten off. It was unsettling.

Next in line.

She really had to go.

Women take forever just to pee.

So annoying.

There should be a law against taking five minutes to take a piss.

The door opened.

She took out her earbuds, closed the door behind her. The relief was immediate.

She started to think about all the other shits she'd taken in public bathrooms in New York. The Strand was probably the public bathroom she'd used the most (unless you counted different Starbucks as one Starbucks, because then it was Starbucks by far).

She flushed, and went to wash her hands, a process which took at least forty-five seconds.

Maybe that's why women took so long, in addition to the obvious reasons: they spent more time washing their hands than men did.

Eliza put her earbuds in as she opened the bathroom door; she just wanted to get the fuck out of there.

Why couldn't she stand up for herself, or make up her mind? Why was she even responding? It would have been a moral victory if and only if she'd used Dan and then discarded him. Drama was no good. She didn't have any time for it; and besides, there was Nate, her ex, who she was very much not over.

Her thoughts were racing. The fresh air felt good.

i'm not sure im in the mood to chat . . .

why . . . what's going on?

nothing
i want to know . . .
no Dan.

She walked faster, brushing her hair away from her forehead with her hands, which was a response to stress.

The obsession with Nate probably had a lot to do with the fact that there wasn't much to him: she could fill up the image she had of him with whatever she wanted.

Nate got off-campus early; he'd always acted older, hung out with older people; he was going to make a lot of money in real estate; he had already developed the right connections and was already prone to spending a lot of money on coke.

Dudes were so awful.

Eliza took the long way back to the park, looping south. She thought about calling her dad but didn't.

She watched a pudgy Latino guy make an incredible catch on the run, arms outstretched, in the outfield. His teammates cheered wildly; the other team scowled while the hitter stood on first base in disbelief.

The pudgy Latino guy got up, his belly spilling over his belt, smiling; he couldn't have been happier: it didn't seem possible for a human being to be happier than this guy.

What the fuck. Was that all it took?

Eliza noticed she had a notification on Bumble.

Not right now.

tell me . . .

Dan wasn't going to leave her alone.

She kept walking faster; she almost felt like running (maybe she was). She was beginning to panic.

Fuck fuck fuck.

stop.

ok . . . then a second text: *have I offended you?*
just respect my boundaries

i'm still learning what they are . . .

clearly

hey . . . be nice

sorry man

oof . . .

yea

Parker and Nina were both on their phones when Eliza got back; they only half-acknowledged her when she sat down.

"Fall in?" Parker asked.

"Yeah, head first," Eliza said dryly.

The sun passed briefly behind the clouds, casting shadows over the grass.

"What'd I miss?"

"This guy started talking to us."

"Who?"

"He's over there—"

Parker waved at a good-looking guy who must have been in his mid-twenties.

"Blake."

"Blake . . ."

"Yeah, Blake," Nina said dismissively.

"He's pretty cute."

"He asked if we wanted to go hang out at his place with his friends; I guess they live in one of those condos around here. Do you wanna go?"

"I'm going home," Nina asserted.

"I'll go," Eliza said, realizing that she was more interested now that Nina wasn't going. Nina seemed to notice this. "When?"

"They said like in an hour."

Parker was pleased with herself. She liked attention.

Eliza took out another cigarette from her purse. The weather was so nice. September was one of the best months. She was just one body out of a thousand or two, lounging in the sunshine.

Her phone buzzed again. She ignored it; she'd look at it later; she needed a break. Nina was packing her stuff up; the girl was in such a sour mood.

Eliza looked at her phone again.

It was just her mom.

6

Mariko had gone on a few dates with Xavier when she was twenty-two and he was fifty-two; they met at Spoonbill and Co. in Williamsburg, browsing in the Drama section. The director was of medium height, thin, his eyes were blue, and he was someone who never seemed to blink, so intense was the quality of his eye-contact. Like a dancer, he seemed to live on cigarettes and coffee: yellow teeth, steel-wire hair, wrinkled skin, boyish features. She'd found this very attractive.

She had just graduated from Tisch, and he was well-known, and known to her, as a director at the time, and she considered the affair that began with him that day the final and better part of her aesthetic education. He was courteous, tender, and as she was to learn—distant, bordering on indifferent or aloof.

"I like living alone," he told her. "I've always been this way. I just think it's better to be clear and honest with people from the beginning; that way there's no confusion. That's the only basis for a genuinely sophisticated connection."

What "sophisticated" entailed, for Xavier, was Film Forum dates, walks along the river, expensive bottles of wine, slow-burning sex, long emails. The relationship was evolved along clear, aestheticized lines; there were rules of engagement. She could tell him about other men she was seeing; he could give her advice on her career; she would always be a guest in his world, his apartment.

And maybe, because he was so scrupulous in shaping expectations, she never expected anything else.

He was an eager, skilled lover; he worked hard to please her; and her beauty—the natural, careless beauty which she had then taken for granted—was always at the center of the experience. Xavier indexed and desired every part of her—but his desire was middle-aged and tempered. He made love in a focused, practical way, teasing out all the points of connection between her mind and her body, pushing on her will, her strength, her means of expression until she was in a state of soft seizure.

After a few months of this—after months of French wine, Russian movies, slow, gentle sex—he suggested they be friends, that they consider the relationship, like a technical problem, resolved.

"I'm too old for you, Mari—it's for the best."

And she'd agreed, because it seemed sensible, at least at that point in time, and because she was getting a little bored by his seduction script, and because she wanted to work with him—something he said was impossible while they were sleeping together.

And, for a little while, they became collaborators. Xavier, who had inherited a fortune from his mother, largely funded his own work, which he staged in a converted warehouse in Gowanus. His company, "Passing Strange," was going through a period of turnover at the time as older actors left, or retired, and Mariko inherited the ingénue roles: Masha in *The Three Sisters*; Hedda Gabbler; Isabella in *Measure for Measure*.

Xavier's shows only paid the Equity minimum, but she never resented having to supplement her income with restaurant shifts, which seemed like part of the magic of being a young stage actor in New York City. She felt that she was paying her dues, that her work was growing, that, even if bigger things were in store, she was happy to do the granular, exacting kind of work that Xavier demanded.

But after a few years, she met Dan, who was, if not jealous of Xavier, judgmental ("Does he fuck all his actresses?"). Xavier, for his part, just like he had let her go as a lover, intuited that it was time to let her go as a collaborator; no grief was given; he stopped offering roles, and she stopped asking for them simultaneously.

While they remained friendly and would occasionally meet for coffee or a drink to catch up, they were both aware that they had stopped working together strictly because of politics—or at least the threat of politics. Their friendship, which was the third and final phase of their relationship, was cool, therefore, though cordial.

Mariko, however, from a distance, continued to admire Xavier: his intelligence, his temperament, his generosity, his art (she continued to attend the shows—always catching opening night).

Over the years, he never expressed any resentment, never chastised her for breaking off their collaboration, never said a negative word about Dan (who would dutifully attend the productions—maybe just to share his criticisms after).

And for *that*, for Xavier's forbearance, Mariko was grateful.

In the days following his diagnosis, fucking was all he could think about: thousands of fucks between the ages of sixteen and fifty-seven split between hundreds of lovers (ninety percent of which were women)—futureless, mindless, animal rutting. There were other things, too, that he cared about—friendships, family, his many projects—but his anxiety, his grief, concerned the imminence of the loss of touch, the death of the sensual subject. The libido died last: the evolutionary logic was obvious. He couldn't really comprehend that this decades long phenomenological thread—him, his decades of touching, breathing, desiring—this refined, self-organizing aesthetic sensibility, this catalogue of existence, would be *destroyed*.

He had emailed or texted or called other exes, but in so many cases, they were as old as he was; they had kids in college; there was a sweetness and wistfulness and nostalgia in saying goodbye, but nothing else. It was like taking a last look at a painting before leaving a museum before it closed.

Mariko, who was younger than the rest, still, was a different story; and while, a decade before, he'd felt no regret—and, rather, relief—in letting her go, now, with the prospect of months of chemotherapy ahead, all he could do is think about, and replay, in his mind, their two dozen or so nights together, their conversations, their natural congeniality. He was even beginning to feel that his instinct to seduce her that day in the bookstore, to ask her what she was reading, to ask her to coffee, was an early premonition of death, an uncanny function of the death drive; he needed her then because he would need her in the future—*which was now.*

He didn't, consciously, expect or plan to sleep with her again, but when she responded so promptly to his email, when she essentially demanded to see him, he'd gotten excited, and allowed himself to feel, at least, that he would find comfort in her presence, her closeness: the afterimage of ten years prior. And while his own bodily decay was at hand, it had only been a few days since he had been to the gym; he still looked young for his age; his symptoms were not yet advanced; there was still a physical basis for denial and repression. For a day or two longer, or at least for one more afternoon, he could feel, if not young, normal.

The director lived in a loft near Nitehawk Cinema; he'd bought the space before the Williamsburg boom and the entire floor was his. The decoration was minimalist, almost like a white-box theater. The only exception were the vases of cut (the florist had come by that morning) and potted flowers which were found in every room, on every surface.

Unable to sit still, or focus, he laid on the carpet, his arms and legs splayed out, and meditated, focusing on deep breaths into his belly, and consciously feeling sensation in every limb and digit.

Finally, there came a buzz at the door, and he rose slowly to answer it.

"Xavier . . ." she said in a hushed voice when he opened the door.

"Please!" Xavier said, embracing her, getting a sense of her body (she'd filled out a little, which pleased him). "No pity!"

"I'm overwhelmed."

"How do you think I feel!"

Mariko looked away. "Sorry, yeah. I can't imagine."

"Sure you can—"

He gave an odd laugh, guiding Mariko to the living room and the couch. On the adjacent coffee table were two porcelain cups and an ornate, decorative teapot, as well as a dog-eared Folger edition of *Cymbeline*, and his phone.

Before sitting down himself, Xavier, who had been listening to music all afternoon, went to flip the record that had been playing softly in the background: Glenn Gould's *Goldberg Variations*, the 1955 edition. There was an unparalleled purity and precision in 1955 recording, like light through ice.

Not incidentally, he associated Bach with Shakespeare: both were metaphysically charged strings of language: changeable, fluid, mercurial; strict, pure, and formal. He needed them both now more than ever.

"Coffee—would you like some?"

"Sure."

Xavier leaned forward and poured two cups.

It was simply incomprehensible that he was *here*, at home, drinking coffee with a beautiful woman.

"I start radiation tomorrow, so this is my last day with a functioning body, and, solemnly, with hair. So I plan to enjoy it."

"I don't know what to say."

"You don't have to say anything, Mariko."

"Okay, maybe I won't."

"Starting now."

"Starting now."

Mariko slipped her hand into Xavier's; he immediately wanted to kiss her. He almost felt, irrationally, that he loved her—but he reminded himself, had to remind himself, that she felt bad for him: that's why she was here. He was a paternal figure, a mentor, her director—not a lover anymore.

It was all so absurd. In a few weeks, he would really start to deteriorate. Then, the deterioration would deteriorate into the endstage; slowly, his body would start shutting off, like an office building at the end of the day. He wasn't prepared for that, not if he was being honest with himself. The only useful consolation was Mariko's hand—her warmth.

"Can I say something, actually?" Mariko asked, her voice soft.

"Go for it."

"It really shook me up to hear . . ."

"That's gratifying to hear—"

"You mean something to me, Xavier . . . I could have taken you for granted. . ."

"Taken my continuing to exist for granted . . ."

Mariko winced. "Yes."

Xavier laughed, though forcing it a bit. "So did I."

"The way you committed your whole life to crafting something that could change peoples' lives . . . the like almost spiritual aspect of the way you ran rehearsals, like—"

"I didn't change many lives. Let's not pretend. Pretentious theater for fifty people at a time—it's not um—"

"Well, you changed mine."

"That's very generous."

"No, you did."

"I'll take you at your word."

"Does it help at all?"

"Does what?"

"Like—all the work you've done—like *Antigone, Hamlet*—like . . ."

"Does it help me die?"

Mariko winced again. "Yes."

Xavier shook his head: the question was naive. Mariko wanted to idealize him, to see him as a figure of deep, living wisdom, but he wasn't sure he hadn't any; to the contrary, he felt exposed by cancer. Three decades of directing tragedies had not equipped him for seemingly terminal illness. Tragedy was an onstage, not offstage, event, something that happened to somebody else; and death itself, its actual meaning—was always offstage, was always somewhere else.

He'd been to maybe fifty funerals in his life, including those of his grandparents and parents—friends, teachers, students, colleagues, lovers— and he'd never really thought, never really let himself think, about what it must have been like for them, *the dead*. He remembered watching his father die—even that had seemed abstract, and almost genial or benign. He remembered spouting cliches about how nice it was that his father had died in his sleep, but now that *he* was the dying one, he understood how mind-numbingly cruel those end-of-life cliches were.

Xavier leaned back into the sofa cushion, sighing and closing his eyes. "Did I mention that I plan on just enjoying today—for its own sake?"

"You did, yes; I'm sorry."

"No, it's fine Mariko—I just—I struggle . . . I'm struggling with this too . . . how little it's all meant . . . *Antigone* and *Hamlet* and *Hedda* and the whole crew of tragic heroes whose wisdom cannot help me in this moment, who can't redeem me from the darkness."

"What can redeem you?"

"Why—nothing at all . . . in the long run . . ."

"But in the short run?"

"You're sitting here next to me."

"That's sweet."

"I mean it." And he did.

"What are you thinking about right now?" she asked, squeezing his hand, and he couldn't answer honestly: touching her, undressing her, kissing her neck, her breast, her stomach.

"Nothing." His eyes were still closed. This was his life. This was the last day of his life before he started dying. How did he get here?

He started to rapidly flash. Fragments from every phase of his life. Childhood, youth, early adulthood, middle-age, the beginnings of old age which he was just beginning to enjoy . . . All of the injury, embarrassment, disappointment, smallness, frustration, disappointment, exhaustion, longing, ecstasy, terror, joy.

"I feel like the answer isn't actually nothing."

"No it's not, but let's pretend."

To animals, Xavier thought, death just happened; there could be physical suffering, but no anguish. Animals were biological. The mystery of death was rooted in the way human beings represented it to themselves; the mystery came in thinking about the mystery.

"Maybe today wasn't the best day," Mariko offered.

"Today is the perfect day." Xavier smiled slightly, the corners of his thin lips pulled upwards as if by wires descending from the ceiling. "It's good to see you, Mariko . . . really, really good."

The actress felt strange, almost like she was playing a role she didn't have the script for—like he was directing her. "It's good to see you too . . ."

"Don't be morbid," he insisted, "that defeats the point of seeing each other."

"Is it selfish of me to be sad?" she asked, without fully knowing if what she felt was sadness, or closer to pity.

"Extremely selfish."

"Well, then I guess that's just what I am . . . *selfish*."

"I didn't mean to upset you, Mariko."

"The truth is . . ." Mariko said, hiding her trembling voice in the music, "I might not have made time to see you otherwise . . . if you hadn't."

"And I might not have provided time to meet, either. So in a way, I'm lucky . . . I'm grateful you're here."

"Are you?" she sounded like a little girl to him.

"Immensely."

"I feel like I am a disappointment to you."

"Not at all."

"Because I'm not really onstage anymore."

"That could change."

"I'm not really trying."

"That could also change."

"I'm battling so much inertia."

"There's light in you, Mariko; I have always felt it very intensely."

"Corny."

"Merely accurate."

"I don't feel much light inside at the moment."

Xavier smiled, warmly—blinking, breathing slowly, as if he were trying to influence her own respiration, her own heart rate. "I'm at a better vantage point to see it than you are."

"I'll have to take your word for it."

"Please do."

"How can you be so calm? So self-possessed?" Mariko asked. "I mean, I'm sorry if that's a rude question, but—"

Xavier's brow crinkled like tinfoil; the skin around his ears was pulled towards the cap of his skull; the whole musculature of his face seemed to work in concert to convey a very deep kind of ambivalence. "Oh, don't worry; I'm not calm; I'm losing my mind—but it's all internal . . . so very, very internal."

"Ah."

"That's the reality."

"It's really upsetting." Her voice was still trembling.

"You're telling me, kid."

Mariko took his hand, innocently. "What are you going to . . . do?"

"As much as I can while I can."

"Are you going to keep working?"

"They'll have to carry me off."

"I don't want to be there when they do," Mariko answered honestly.

"Time disappears in direct proportion to the amount of energy we spend trying to hold onto it, I think. So when you stop wasting energy clinging—it's sorta liberating—I feel sort of liberated—in a way—"

"What are the odds you can beat this?"

"Oh well, sure; there are different timelines, but . . . my hatred of doctors sort of caught up to me . . ." Xavier coughed again, half-laughing at the timing of the cough.

"How long did you ignore how bad you were feeling?"

"At least a year," Xavier said with a little smile.

"It's almost like you wanted it . . ." she whispered.

"No," Xavier corrected her, shaking his head. "I didn't want it—I really just don't like being medicalized, don't like the idea of it. I'm a purist in some ways."

"What purity is there in cancer?"

"Well," he said, adopting a patient tone, "it's *mine*—it's my body's cancer—"

"What play do you want to do?"

"I'm not sure yet. That's another answer I'm waiting for from the cosmos."

"I can't wait for whatever you choose."

"You'll be in it."

"Will I?"

"Yes. Of course."

Mariko noticed, as she raised her coffee cup to her mouth again, that her hands were trembling. Xavier noticed too.

"Are you sure about that? Like, I'm rusty—there are better actors."

"Nonsense."

"You're just saying that because . . ."

"Because I still wanna fuck you?" he said, breaking the tension.

"You do?"

"Mariko."

"You're one of the few people I look up to."

"Is that a warning?"

Mariko edged away on the couch. "It's just a statement of fact."

"I see."

"I asked my boyfriend to come with me, but he refused."

Xavier looked towards the window, avoiding eye-contact. "What's his name again?"

"Dan."

"How are things going?"

"All over the place; I don't know."

"Code for bad."

"Not necessarily bad . . . just . . ." Mariko searched for the right formulation. "Something's off."

"I never found him particularly compelling."

"How many times have you met him, like twice?"

"Yes, I've run into you with him a few times."

"I don't like feeling judged."

"That's sort of my nature . . . not much I can do about it . . . especially at this point . . ." Xavier ironized. "Anyway. Forget I said anything. About anything."

"I don't think I like this," Mariko admitted, picking at her cuticles.

"What is 'this'?"

"I think there's a reason I stopped working with you . . ."

"What's that, Mariko?" Xavier said, feeling nothing, wanting nothing, barely evening listening.

"The way you break people down . . ."

"Did I break you down?"

"Many times."

"That's my job."

"We're not in a rehearsal right now."

"All I said was that I didn't find him particularly compelling . . ."

"*That's all you had to say.*"

"I'm not going to lie to you."

"Sure, but you simply don't know the man well enough to make those kinds of judgments."

"I see people in a flash, you know that."

"You also said you wanted to fuck me."

"I'm experiencing things very intensely right now; I'm sorry; I wish I could help it. But I also have so little reason to . . . care about politeness . . . you know?"

"A part of me knew this would happen," she admitted.

"I know."

"So I felt guilty in rushing over here . . . because it excited it me . . . there's something romantic about it . . . which is insane but . . ." she trailed off.

Xavier stroked Mariko's neck, gently, with his knuckles. Then, without looking at her, he took her left hand, the hand nearest to him, and kissed her neck.

She leaned away. "Stop."

The director turned towards the window and squeezed her hand.

"Sorry if that was unwanted."

"It's not unwanted . . . it's just . . . I don't know. I don't know. It's a lot."

"I know . . ."

Through the window, Mariko could see two children stepping out of a car. They wore red and blue fall jackets. They looked like brothers, each with a head of curly blond hair. The trees, which lined the street, were beginning to bloom, white and pink.

Mariko took Xavier's hand, which still held her own, and kissed it. First softly, then harder, pressing her lips to it. She held still.

His hand ran down along the hem of her sundress.

"Don't."

"Why not?"

"It's not very flattering to be invited to fuck you just because you're going to become medically impotent soon."

"I never said it was flattering."

"It's actually remarkably crass."

"I understand that," he said calmly.

"I just don't see the point."

Xavier closed his eyes, smiling slightly. "The point is that there isn't a point. You're here and I'm here. That's it."

Xavier kissed Mariko on the neck. "That's not it."

She felt like she was being directed, like she was playing a part.

She felt a hand under her shirt, another on her knee. Her nipples were hard. "Stop . . ."

"Okay . . ." Xavier pulled back immediately and smiled—totally under control.

"But now I'll wish I hadn't asked you to."

"I'm confused, Mariko."

"So am I obviously."

"May I kiss you again?"

She froze, then found herself saying, "Yes. You may."

A charge passed between them. He started to unzip her sundress; she opened her legs slightly; she was breathing heavily.

Then she pushed him away.

She looked at him: he was so old; he carried the stench of death. It would spread to her.

Vampire.

He shifted away from her on the couch, his body twisting like a piece of silver wire. He didn't seem upset or disarmed.

"Mariko . . ."

"What!?"

"You wouldn't have been able to kiss me, kiss me back, like that—if . . ."

"I'm an actor, so I think I could convince you of whatever I wanted to convince you of."

"I'm a director—"

"What's your point?"

"I can tell when someone's faking it. And you're not faking it."

"I'm extremely confused."

"I don't think it's that confusing."

"When I was younger, I could act on my impulses; or even create impulses to act on . . . but now . . . not really."

"From my vantage point, the nagging, pseudo-moral voice in your head that tells you to stick to conventions is not very interesting or smart."

"I'm not seeing things from your vantage point."

"Maybe you should," he said with a shrug.

If it had not been for the fight with Dan the night before, Mariko might have told Xavier to fuck off, but her psyche was already worn down, its defenses considerably reduced.

"Why are all men children?" she asked.

"Ask their mothers," Xavier snapped back.

"Dan's mother died last year. She killed herself."

"How's he doing?"

"He doesn't talk about it. He found her."

"You weren't there?"

"I was in California."

Xavier's thin, birdlike body was tense, as if he was waiting for the subject to change back to something he was interested in.

He stood up and walked to the record player. *Goldberg* had finished. He searched through the scattered record sleeves and picked one out.

Mahler's *2nd Symphony*.

He pivoted in place, so that he could lean against the table while directing his attention at her; she was looking out the window.

Mahler instantly changed the mood of the room.

Mariko was still extremely attractive, maybe more attractive than ever: fuller, more womanly, more self-aware; slower, more sensuous. She carried herself with the grace of disappointment.

"I just don't understand why all of a sudden you're interested in me," she said.

"I've always been interested in you."

"That's not true."

"I think giving you up and losing interest are different things."

"You were hard to get ahold of back in the day, Xavier; you'd see me like once or twice a month. It was never necessary that we see each other."

Xavier shrugged. "I'm not the possessive type."

"You weren't even the caring type."

"I care in my own ways. I hope you can see that. I'm bad at showing it directly . . ."

Mariko bit her cuticles again nervously. "I think Dan might be cheating on me."

"Have you said anything to him?"

"Of course not."

"Why not?"

"I'm not good at confronting people."

"You seem pretty good at it with me."

"I can defend myself when provoked."

"It sounds like he provoked you though—"

"No, he was trying to be sneaky. He was trying to avoid provoking me."

"Interesting."

"He's never done anything like that before. I think that's why I bit my tongue. Because I have no context to situate his behavior in."

"But how can you know without asking him about the whole story."

"I guess I'm afraid to find out."

"Well there ya go."

"Well there ya go. So now what? We have sex and I get my revenge? You think that's how this works?"

"That would be far too simple," he said smiling. "Wouldn't it?"

"I don't know." She threw up her hands. "You're being opportunistic."

"Or maybe you are." Another knowing glance.

He sat back down, this time very close to her, and kissed her again, pushing her back into the couch; she kissed back, relenting, opening her mouth and, a second later, her legs, so that his hand could pass under the lip of her dress.

She emitted a little moan.

Then he stopped, pulled away from her, edging to the other side of the couch.

"Now I'm turned on," she said in a throaty voice, while brushing her dress back down to just above her knees. "That wasn't fair or nice."

"I wasn't trying to be either of those things," he responded dryly.

"*Ugh.*" Her whole body shuddered, as if some particle had been released at the base of her spine and had traveled up through the crown of her skull. "No—don't look at me like that, I know what you're thinking."

"What am I thinking?" he asked dully.

"You have sex with so many people . . ." she said with considerable resignation.

"I used to. I've been out of the game."

"Still."

He kissed her again. This time things moved quickly. He pulled her dress over her head, went down on her, pulling her underwear down with his teeth—a man possessed.

She stood naked in front of him while he fell to his knees, kissing her shins, her kneecaps, her belly.

She stroked the top of his head; he felt like his whole body was suddenly very relaxed.

"Are you on birth control?" he asked.

"Yes," she answered after a pause.

While he fucked her, gently, slowly—reprising his old role as the older sensuality-teacher—Mariko kept her eyes closed, feeling sleepy (like it was late at night, like she'd been drinking, like she'd been waiting tables all night). But she was none of those things. They were making love in the middle of the day; they had been drinking coffee.

She felt like a car that had run out of gas on a desert highway.

"Is this okay?" he said, kissing her neck, biting her shoulders, digging his nails into her back. "Do you mind?"

Though he was still fit, his skin was saggy; he was undeniably old, beyond his prime. His body was soft and slack.

"I don't mind," she said, which was true. She didn't mind because she didn't care. She had given in to a feeling that had been breeding inside of her a long time, many years: indifference.

She was just one of the many big potted plants in his apartment, lazily sucking up the sun.

And, in turn, he was draining that life from her: the ambient, warm life of the light.

He pulled out for a moment (he had a big cock, even semi-hard), and she turned over on her stomach, opening her eyes. She didn't want to look at him. She couldn't.

"Does that feel good?"

"Yes."

"Good."

Rhythmically, steadily, he fucked her, at first doggy, then he collapsed onto her back, breathing heavily; she could feel his sweat on hers. She could feel him sobbing, slightly, too, so that the tears slipped down the channels of her back.

An hour later, Mariko was in the shower and Xavier at the sink, brushing his teeth. He put the brush back in its holder and ducked his head under the faucet, as he had done since childhood, in order to rinse.

He looked at himself in the mirror, smiled, examining his gums, which were bleeding slightly. Unconsciously, he laughed at himself, and shook his head slightly, running a hand through his thick, steely hair. Soon it would be gone. First his hair, then his fat, his muscle, collagen, teeth—then everything: skin, blood, brains.

If he were directing an actor to play him, he wouldn't give himself any hope. *Be brutal,* he'd tell the actor. *This person is being brutalized.* But he'd also say: *a character can't be noble if they don't have hope . . .*

Xavier began to hyperventilate slightly.

Holy fuck.

He placed a hand on each of his temples, creating temporary blinders. He felt like he was going to pass out.

"Hey, is everything alright?" Mariko called from the shower.

"Yeah yeah yeah."

Mariko stepped out of the shower. Xavier handed her a towel from the far side of the white-tiled bathroom.

Her body was pear-shaped; full and slim at the same time—perfect, to the director.

Now, wrapped in towels, they passed into the short hallway and into the bedroom, where their clothes were scattered across the bed and floor.

Quickly, Mariko covered herself, pulling up her black thong (had she worn it intentionally?), her sundress. Her body rippled with a new and subtle confidence.

"You're staring at me,"

"Yes, why wouldn't I?"

"I don't know, it makes me uncomfortable."

Xavier shrugged, as he often did. "Do you feel guilty?"

"Of course I do."

"You shouldn't."

"Don't be callow," Mariko responded brusquely.

"You have to realize I don't care at all about your bourgeois relationship—"

Mariko sat down on the edge of the bed, deflated, suddenly as timid as she'd been earlier in the day.

"I don't know what to do."

"Go home, continue with your life."

"How can you say that?" Mariko asked with more curiosity than hostility.

"Because you still have a life to live, and I don't."

"Oh."

"It really is that simple, Mariko."

Xavier sat down next to Mariko, took her hands in his, kissed her neck gently.

"You should go."

"I know," she said, "I really should. But."

He pushed his hand into her hair, gripping a handful by the roots; he pulled her head back, kissed her, then shoved her onto the bed. He remained standing, watching her. She lay back and closed her eyes; she felt so empty—and she knew that he felt that way too.

She started to cry, while the director remained above her, impassive.

There was a certain point between people when you knew communication was not only impossible, but inappropriate. You just had to be present. Aware.

He stroked her head, looking out the loft windows. The sun was strong—a midday sun. Warm and aggressive. Clear. Clarifying.

Dying was so absurd, Xavier thought, as absurd as life. It was incomprehensible that, after death, he would lose contact with this warm, reassuring light.

"Mariko . . ."

7

Eliza hovered near the edge of the balcony, avoiding any attempts at small talk or, God forbid, real conversation. She didn't understand why she'd said yes to this gathering (maybe it was just the novelty of someone going out of their way to invite them). They were all victims of the attention they enjoyed.

Their collective decision to attend this party was an extension of *Instagram*-thinking: it was (and this was truly bizarre) like they were being "liked" in real life. They were more receptive to the physical contact because they'd grown so accustomed to digital contact. The internet softened them up to being hit on.

Another song came on. Not Kanye. Something else she didn't recognize. It was shitty.

Eliza just wanted to go home and take a nap.

Blake approached her, leaning against the railing next to her. "Hey hey."

"I think I'm gonna go," she said to him, as if they were old friends; she could have just left; he didn't matter at all.

"You just got here." His voice was low, forcibly manly.

"I have to get up early tomorrow."

Blake burst out laughing. "It's four in the afternoon."

"Do you even know my name?"

"No, honestly."

"Eliza."

She looked over the railing towards the lush green that ringed the park. She scratched her neck unconsciously and then cracked her fingers.

"Why are you talking to me?" She had decided to use a different, "cut the crap" tone.

"You seem interesting."

"That's a generic answer."

"I guess I'm a generic guy then."

"Hell yeah you are."

He looked a little hurt. He wasn't used to being talked to this way. She touched him lightly on the arm. "I'm just playing with you."

"Okay."

He was doing the whole stoic thing. The whole manly thing. And it was working a little bit, she had to admit. He knew how to leave room for her imagination to work. He could be whoever she wanted him to be: a cipher, just like Nate. It occurred to her that he *reminded her of Nate*.

"I'd like to think that you're more interesting than you appear."

He raised his eyebrows. "Like, how so?"

"Just like, you have this generic guy face and this generic guy name."

"Thanks."

"It's not your fault. It's your parents' fault."

"Fuck you," he said, laughing a little.

"I'm sure they're nice people from Connecticut."

"Virginia."

"Close enough."

"You don't know me," he said bravely.

"I don't need to."

"How do you know?"

"Because why would I?"

He laughed at this, then laughed again—which made her feel like he was being condescending or wasn't taking her seriously. She was making him insecure, so he was answering in kind.

She did a half-spin, looking for an opening in the crowd. "I gotta get out of here."

"Right."

He was like 6'3" and probably had a big dick.

"Do you want another drink?" he asked.

"Yeah," she said, despite her own best intentions, "I do."

"Come with me."

She followed him back into the apartment through the small crowd into the kitchen. He poured whiskey into a glass, bypassing the red solo cups that everyone else was drinking from.

They clinked glasses; she noticed no one else was in the kitchen.

"Cheers."

He kissed her.

"Dude!" She choked up a little whiskey, half-laughing.

"What's wrong?"

"Just *no*. Not so fast."

He stepped back, leaning against the counter, looking around, clearly a little embarrassed, but also, clearly, enjoying the challenge.

"Whiskey isn't, like, the key to my underpants."

"I get that."

"You're a man of few words, aren't you?"

"I guess. Yeah."

"Seriously though. Like, holy shit, *talk*."

"You'll just make fun of me."

"True. Guess the plan is just: awkwardly drink in silence."

"Guess so."

Eliza took two more big sips and put her drink on the counter heavily. "Okay now."

He leaned down and kissed her, grabbing her hair and giving it a light, but firm, pull.

He was a good kisser—but she pushed him away, exaggeratedly catching her breath. She picked up her whiskey glass and took another sip.

"Are you happy?" she asked under her breath.

"Are you?"

He wanted affection so badly: she could tell.

"I'm chill. That was chill." She didn't like the sound of her own voice. Why the vocal fry?

Parker floated into the kitchen to pour herself another drink. Eliza couldn't tell whether she was relieved or disappointed. Probably relieved. This guy was moving way too fast. Eliza felt like such a slut.

"Hey."

"Hey . . ." Parker said, making a rapid survey of the room with her eyes. "What's going on?"

"Just havin' a little chat," Eliza said.

"Oh yeah?" Parker raised an inquiring eye at Blake.

"Yeah."

"I'm gonna go back in," Blake said, responding to Parker's subverbal suggestion that he leave. "Cya," he said to Eliza.

"Ciao."

"He's pretty attractive," Parker commented.

"No doubt. Also, Nina left."

"Did she?"

"Yeah, she said the party sucked. But I think she was upset that no one was talking to her."

"She didn't say bye."

"She's been in a mood all day."

"I think my escapade offended her; like it has anything to do with her; like?"

"Yeah . . . I'm not sure I get it either . . ."

Eliza furrowed her eyebrows without responding. The whole triangular friendship was bound up in this weird uncertainty.

"I think on some level Nina is just like . . . you're making her think about certain things that like she would wanna have the courage or the balls or whatever to try."

"I wonder why we all just can't be different and into different things without having to like align values."

"Impossible."

"It's frankly disappointing and weird."

"Just talk to her about it."

"Well, she left."

"I mean later."

"I don't see the point."

"Yeah that's your prerogative too," Parker acknowledged. "Are you into that guy or? Like should I make myself scarce?"

"I'm honestly not sure."

"I haven't had sex in two weeks; I wanna jump someone."

"I'm pretty sure you can have your pick."

"Lots of horny bros, it's true."

She thought about the kiss from Blake: it had been a good kiss—an unusually good kiss. She was kinda pissed at Parker for scaring him off. She needed an erotic palate cleanser after Dan, who she couldn't, in the end, even bring herself to fuck.

"Go make it happen."

Eliza glanced at her phone. Another message from Dan. *thinking about you . . .*

"Do you think you're gonna stay?"

"Yeah, I'm thinking I'll make some moves as well."

"Nice, well, let's go back in.

Parker led Eliza back into the living room by the hand, passing through a crowd of faceless bros.

can we talk?

in person? she wrote back, unlocking her fingers from Parker's.

yes . . .

when?

maybe tonight.

I'm not sure that's what I want.

what do you want?

I'm not sure.

The whole exchange took maybe a minute. In that time she hoped Blake would approach her, but he was nowhere to be found. Parker had melted away too.

She should leave. This was ridiculous. Her head hurt a little bit. She felt very, very numb . . . and useless and vaguely depraved.

She turned towards the door and at that moment saw Blake come downstairs from the second level of the condo. Was he with a girl? No: that would be crazy: she had only been away for a few minutes.

Blake raised his chin at her in a vague gesture of acknowledgement.

"Hey!" Eliza asked bouncily, "where'd ya go?"

"I was just in my room for a second."

"Doing what?"

"I changed my shirt. I was sweaty."

"It's so fucking hot today."

"Yeah it's hot as balls."

"Do you want to show me your room?" Eliza gave him a little ironic smile.

"Later."

What the fuck.

"How much later?" Eliza asked, her voice turning slightly shrill.

"Depends."

"On what?"

"When everyone goes home."

"Who cares about other people?"

"It's my party."

"No one cares if you disappear for an hour."

Eliza constantly underestimated her own insecurity. She was more grateful for the attention than anything else; she liked that this tall, muscular guy found her attractive; she had concealed from herself how much she wanted him to want her. Desire in the body and desire in the mind were completely different things.

"I care."

Eliza laughed bitterly. "You have a funny code of ethics."

"You can stay after," Blake said dutifully.

"I can't stay after."

"Why not?"

"I have class in the morning."

She noticed how fit he was: his muscles were clearly outlined under his blue shirt. His physique, however, seemed to immobilize him as if the cost of such raw strength was not only a loss of flexibility, but a loss of expressivity.

"I'm really confused," he mumbled.

"About what exactly?"

"You."

"Oh god. What's confusing?"

"Pretty much everything." He said everything so matter of factly.

"Like what?"

"It doesn't matter." He had already shut down.

Men all wanted the same thing: they wanted to be adored and cared for. They wanted their cheeks stroked; they wanted you to coo in their ear. They wanted a sexualized mother.

"I think we're making this too complicated. Just tell me what you want?"

"You should stay."

"And what do you expect to happen if I stay?"

"It depends —"

"On what?"

"On what you want."

"Okay. What I think I want is to leave." As Eliza said this, she realized how true it was. She could have easily talked to one of his friends and gotten essentially the same result.

Her thoughts were all over the place. She kissed him on the lips. "I'm gonna go. It was nice meeting you."

"Do you wanna exchange numbers?"

"Find me on *Instagram*," Eliza offered. She showed him her handle, holding her phone up to his eyes. "DM me."

Before he could answer, she was gone.

The elevator pinged open, and she stepped in.

Don't know how people live in these fucking condos.

As if on cue, a text arrived from Dan: *so . . .*

so nothing, she typed.

I feel like we left a lot of things unsaid.

like what?

like feeling-things.

no Dan we didn't

Are you sure about that?

No but let's pretend I am. Yes. Yes I'm sure.

I sound crazy.

wtf . . . where are you right now?

i'm on my way home . . ..

can I come over?

no

why not?

why not? because I said so.

I'm really anxious about last night. Want to talk.

cool but not right now.

cool . . ..

what are you anxious about?

just the fact that it happened?

do you regret crossing a line with a student?

probably but also no because it's you . . .

ok . . .

She could imagine him receiving her message and freaking out at its inscrutable tone.

you're afraid that i'm gonna tell someone

Yes, he wrote, before adding, *I am.*
ok. cool. i'm not going to. so chill
ookokok let's meet up!!
we can but not right now
What are you doing?
walking to the L
I'm in Manhattan can I meet you?
Eliza sighed. He was so persistent. *fine*

She was walking south along the eastern edge of the park, passing by the softball fields, tennis courts. On the far side of the street people streamed in and out of the trendy bars which lined the street. She felt flush with whiskey now. Her life had been like this since high school: drink, hang out, fuck around. New York only sped up the rate at which her centrifuge spun; the city was a sadness generator.

Why had she agreed to coffee? It was the last thing she wanted.

She was tempted to stop at one the bars along Bedford Avenue, which she now angled onto, before heading back into the city. There was plenty more that could be added to her bloodstream. Her thoughts were still painfully clear: she was still too aware of herself. She felt like both rider and horse: her legs carried her forward, while her brain resisted, or tried to resist, where her legs were taking her.

Blake was already a memory, a bad joke.

The trees were so dry. A cool wind rolled down the avenue, alluding to the autumn to come. Cool nights, warm days.

She associated autumn with going back to school: field hockey practice, parties in empty houses; a significant part of her psyche was still fixated on high school and childhood—reenacting their drama on the stage of city life. Even the condo gathering she'd just left was really her subconscious attempt to recreate the joy of mingling, drinking, and flirting for the first time—of getting cornered by, or cornering, a guy in the kitchen, just to see what happens.

And now she was going to see a former teacher.

She hadn't properly integrated her adult self with her adolescent self. Everything was happening *to her* and she didn't really know why—outwardly, she was smart and put together. "Chaotic neutral," as her *Tinder* profile said.

Even now, she found herself walking towards the Bedford L with only a dim sense of why she had just agreed to meet a man who made her uncomfortable—a man whose intentions and apparent goodwill she distrusted. On a deeper level, she had even begun to panic. Dan didn't have charisma, or charm: he had *power.*

The only question was—what kind of power and why?

She didn't know why she messaged him, met up with him, almost fucked him, lost interest in him altogether; why she went to school in the city and not a small liberal arts college like she'd originally planned; why she drank so much, smoked so much, watched so much Netflix.

She really didn't do anything that she believed in, anything that she respected. The less she respected something, the more she was attracted to it. Her own very poor self-image was constantly searching for correspondence, likeness, in the world. If she didn't hate herself, she was trying her best to become the kind of person who did.

It was better to give up hope, to renounce everything extraordinary about oneself, than it was to be stranded inside the deceptive paradigm of self-actualization—of a growing, overflowing, inner-life. The young woman didn't know anyone who was *that*, who had *that*, who was ever going to be *that.*

She jogged down the stairs at the entrance to the Bedford L at the corner of Bedford and North 7th, deftly taking her Metrocard from her purse and swiping through the gate almost without pausing or even slowing her pace.

A train was coming. Compared to the other lines, the L was almost reliable.

She took a seat in the far right corner of the car that could only seat two people. She opened her phone.

Where do you wanna meet?

there's a Think Coffee on 6th ave

I'll meet you there

k

The subway car passed under the East River. She always wondered if it was possible, like realistically possible, for the tunnel to collapse. It was so strange that no one questioned the constancy of these marvelous engineering feats. She felt the same way when she got on a plane. She couldn't grasp why every plane didn't at some point drop out of the sky.

First Avenue.

I'll be there super soon. wbu?

I'm nearby. It's close to school.

Third Avenue.

She closed her eyes and took a deep breath, as far down into her belly as she possibly could. She hurt a little bit from drinking on an empty stomach. She wondered what her breath smelled like.

It didn't matter.

Union Square.

She kept her eyes closed. One more stop. She was starting to really feel anxious about this meeting.

The more she thought about him, the more he disgusted her. She was not the same person she had been the night before; she had totally disassociated from that version of herself.

Sixth Avenue.

She hoisted herself up, feeling the train break hard, feeling as though the subway car were gagging, trying to vomit her up onto the platform. She passed into the busy, claustrophobic crowd stepping off, and onto, the L train all at once.

She wanted to go home and nap, but there was something tempting in the idea of not stopping, drinking more coffee, flirting more, playing another game: that was her idea of city life—that was what adults did.

She was tempted to text her old professor and call it off, but something held her back; she sensed that if she didn't meet him now, that she would have to meet him again, that there was a debt to pay for being so uninhibited the night before. She also considered whether, in fact, she wanted to have sex with him. The encounter at the party had left her a little horny, but there wasn't anyone else at the moment (although it wouldn't be hard to find someone if need be).

She was on the street now, walking towards the coffee shop. He wasn't there, but there were plenty of tables; she ordered an espresso and sat down and took a book from out of her purse. Nietzsche's *Genealogy of Morals* (for her Ethics seminar). The class was supposed to read it for the following week.

We are unknown to ourselves, we knowers: and with good reason. We have never looked for ourselves, —so how are we ever supposed to find ourselves? How right is the saying: 'Where your treasure is, there will your heart be also'; our treasure is where the hives of our knowledge are. As born winged-insects and intellectual honey-gatherers we are constantly making for them, concerned at heart with only one thing – to 'bring something home'. As far as the rest of life is concerned, the so-called 'experiences',—who of us ever has enough seriousness for them? or enough time? I fear we have never really been 'with it' in such matters: our heart is simply not in it—and not even our ear! On the contrary, like somebody divinely absent-minded and sunk in his own thoughts who, the twelve strokes of midday having just boomed into his ears, wakes with a start and wonders 'What hour struck?', sometimes we, too, afterwards rub our ears and ask, astonished, taken aback, 'What did we actually experience then?' or even, 'Who are we, in fact?' and afterwards, as I said, we count

all twelve reverberating strokes of our experience, of our life, of our
being—oh! and lose count . . .

Eliza put the book down, spine up, on the table, because her espresso had been deposited on the counter; she stood up, took the coffee with a quick "thanks" directed towards the barista, and sat back down.

The book had a blue cover with orange lettering—ugly, but endearingly academic and plain.

It was not unimaginable that she could follow her mother into academic life; she had always been good at school; she could have even gone to Princeton if she'd wanted to—but she'd decided against staying at home (and honestly didn't give a fuck about the Ivy League, unlike so many friends from high school). Part of her semi-attraction to Dan was the possibility of learning from him, networking with him, becoming him.

Kids who grew up in Princeton were generally super successful: returning home, especially around Thanksgiving and Christmas, was a frustrating and unpleasant experience for this reason (being vaguely into critical theory at The New School was not on par with what her friends were doing at Harvard, Yale, Williams, and Amherst, among other places). A few years of college had already transformed them: they had internships, mentors, serious plans for the post-graduation years.

She had nothing: an internship with a publishing house from the summer. Babysitting jobs. Nothing that added up to anything. Her declared majors? Literary studies and philosophy—neither of which were particularly practical. Her mom might push her to go to graduate school, but Eliza doubted that she could successfully be pushed. She was too comfortable, and she knew it. She knew that there was no real threat of her parents cutting her off, of having to give up her apartment. Her Dad made a lot of money working at Chase, her mother did well as a tenured professor; a job wasn't about financial security, but dignity and independence.

She was destined to fall into the massive pool of young people who were artistic, but not really artists—intellectual, but not really intellectuals.

That was scary. Was it even avoidable? It seemed culturally determined, structurally determined. She could ask Dan what he thought.

It seemed fairly easy to go on like this until she was twenty-five or twenty-six; God knows—maybe thirty. There was no practical crisis, and any deeper, existential crisis could be deferred by staying busy and having fun. That was obvious enough.

She had gone prematurely dark: a shuttered power plant.

Dan came through the door, looking exhausted and anxious. He sat down across from her (she was sitting with her back against the window) without ordering anything.

"Hey . . ." he said, looking at the table or at his feet.

"Yo."

"Thank you for meeting me."

"No problem."

"I wanted to talk . . ."

"That's assumed."

"Yeah. I just. I dunno. Last night was weird and unexpected . . . and—"

"I want to know what your motivations were like . . ." Eliza interrupted, "what it was like for you I guess . . . I still . . . it's still fairly mysterious to me . . . It was so spontaneous . . . "

"Yeah . . ."

"But nothing is spontaneous, you know?" She countered, feeling tense. "Everything has its roots . . ."

"Okay?"

"Like, I'm trying to say that nothing just happens magically, for no reason—that there are reasons that we found ourselves . . ."

"Sure there are. What's your point, Eliza?"

"My point is just that I'm thinking about it . . . thinking about like what was going on in both of our heads."

"Is that why you agreed to meet? To try to figure that out." Dan tore little scraps of napkin into pieces, rearranging the pieces on the tabletop.

Eliza could tell that Dan seemed startled by how rational and forth-right she was being, like he couldn't track the transformations between the person she was the night before and the person she was now. He hadn't read her very closely, and, as a result, his picture of her was static, rather than dynamic. Or maybe it was the other way around: he didn't read her very well because he'd insisted on a static picture of who she was.

"That doesn't feel good . . . or right . . . or something like that," Dan said, dejected.

"Yeah. Probably"

"I feel kind of, um, like, if not set up for failure, misled."

"You're being such a baby," Eliza rejoined coldly.

"It's not like I'm not a vulnerable person—just because I'm older or have status or whatever—it's not like—"

"I get it: you bleed, blah blah blah. You cry, you have manly emotions. Boo hoo."

"I want to know why you enjoy seeing me on the defensive—"

"I don't enjoy it *at all*. I'm not trying to hurt you. I was fascinated by you . . . in a way I remain fascinated by you . . . but I'm not sure what to tell you . . . like, I'm here . . . that should be enough to show you that I'm trying to like . . . be a decent person about this . . ."

"I think I have feelings for you." He wasn't making any eye contact.

"That's silly," she said, feeling deeply uncomfortable. The possibil-ity that he had emotionally bonded to her in some way frightened her. She didn't want to be *saddled* with him; she didn't want his problems, his needs, his insecurities, his fantasies. She didn't need anything, in fact. What she *had* wanted, she had already gotten; everything past that point was too much.

"Is it?"

"Absolutely. Extremely silly."

"Maybe—but it's also true Eliza," he said pedantically. "*Real.*"

They could go back and forth all evening, she realized, which was probably what he wanted. For her part, Eliza had no idea what she wanted, other than to establish a link between the precocious and seductive person she had revealed to him last night, and the decisively normal, *normie*, college student her friends and family knew. If this link could not be established, then she would be in trouble (but what kind of trouble, she could not say).

"Maybe it's true—maybe your 'feelings' are real—but it's also irrelevant to me."

"Fuck. Ouch."

"What? do you want to be my boyfriend?"

"I'd take plain old lover."

It was ridiculous the way he said the word "lover."

"It's possible I'll eventually fuck you, but don't count on it."

"I'm not—"

"I feel like that's the sole reason you wanted to meet up."

"You're being so accusatory."

"How so?"

"I dunno. I'm just exhausted. I need to go home."

"Yes, you do. Get some sleep."

"I'm gonna get a coffee."

She didn't say anything, just rolled her eyes. He got up and went to the counter. She watched him with considerable consternation.

He came back with a large drip coffee.

"Hey . . ." he said, sipping the lukewarm and not particularly good coffee.

"What?"

"I don't want you to feel pressured."

"Then stop."

"I feel like I fell off a cliff and am still falling."

"I take it you haven't been with a lot of people recently. Or something like that. Like, you've just been with your girlfriend."

It was the first admission by either party that he was *with* someone else.

"That's accurate."

"I get that it's a lot to process . . ."

"It is . . ."

"But regardless: stop pressuring me."

"Okay, okay."

"You don't think you're pressuring me, but you are, so stop."

He was clearly taken aback by her tone. "What exactly," he asked in a dry, academic way, attempting to conceal his anxiety, "changed between last night and today?"

"Perspective."

"As in . . ."

"I had an experience that changed my expectations."

"Okay so . . ."

"So I thought this would be more exciting than it is."

"An inappropriate sexual relationship—"

"Correct."

They were both defensive.

"Was excitement the point?" He asked unconvincingly. "That's so suburban and depressing . . ."

"Come on—"

"Yes so I get that it was a factor, but was it the only factor?"

"Are you gonna tell me that you have feelings for me again?" she asked, rolling her eyes.

"*Yes. I am.*"

"Oh God, Dan."

"I mean I think I do."

"How romantic."

"You love this . . ." he sounded angry. "You love that you have me at your mercy."

"Absolutely," she agreed.

"That's kinda fucked up."

"Fucked up? I mean dude . . . like . . ."

"What?"

"You lusted after your own student . . ."

"You initiated it!"

"But still, you *lusted*."

Dan sat back, breathing in through his nostrils into his belly, as if trying to center himself, prepare himself. "But what's wrong with lust?"

"It's more the student part."

"Okay, sure; well . . ."

Eliza examined her professor across the table. If she was being honest, and she wanted to be honest in this moment, there wasn't anything, in her opinion, objectively, or universally, wrong, with a teacher and student hooking up, past a certain age, but there was still, simply the matter of poor taste. Dan had acted in poor taste; she had rejected him, in the final calculus, not because he had broken some social taboo, but because he had been clumsy and graceless.

She reached across the table to steal his bits of napkin, arranging them in her own style.

"I think uh . . ." she whispered. "What's wrong with it is that you didn't know what to do with me. I wanted to be *handled*, Dan—and uh—you didn't know how to handle me."

"Has anyone? Has uh—anyone ever properly handled you before?"

"No dummy—that's why I called you in. Or that's why I thought I did."

"Well, sorry to disappoint."

"I'm sorry too. Man—I feel kinda bad for you . . ." She said, staring at him, like he was a specimen behind a veil of glass.

"Why's that?"

"Because you really thought you *could*."

"I think I still can . . ." Dan suggested with pathetic earnestness.

"No—" she stuttered. "I think uh . . . I was hoping for something that didn't require work or . . . uh . . . coaxing . . . or even much explanation. I wanted to be understood—*apprehended*—by someone."

"I did 'apprehend' you—I mean you're so beautiful, Eliza—"

"I'm just a lil fetish object . . ."

"Isn't that what you wanted to be—" he fumbled.

"Are you kidding?" she said, her voice pitched higher, sensing his own barely latent hostility rising.

"Like, didn't you want to play that role?"

For the first time, she began to really feel what her nerve-receptors had been telling her: that someone was stroking the top of her hand. She felt a little chill run up her spine. She turned away from the window and faced him. "No . . . like that's the opposite . . ."

"Okay okay okay—sorry—misstep—"

"Yeah. Very telling."

Dan gathered back the bits of napkin from her side of the table and started to recreate his original patterns.

"I just want to know what to do about this incredible loneliness . . . you know? I'm sorry if I'm saying all the wrong things . . ."

"I'm sorry too, Dan."

"I'm realizing that there are a lot of things about myself that I have to work on . . . like . . . uh . . . probably should go back to therapy, yada yada . . ."

"Everybody could use therapy," Eliza echoed without any real idea whether she believed it. "I mean, I should go back . . . I haven't since high school."

"What happened in high school again? Did you tell me?"

"Eating disorder, obvi."

"Ah."

"Too real?"

"Not at all."

Eliza blew the scraps of napkin off the table. "You want to be an authority on everything associated with the good, so it kills you to realize that you might be a shitty person—"

"You think I'm a shitty person?"

"No, I think you think you *might* be."

"Oh."

"It's not unreasonable to think that if you play with the feelings of a twenty-one-year-old that they're gonna get confused."

"True. I admit that. But I think it's also fair to say that you're playing with my feelings too."

"We're an emotional Escher drawing I guess."

"Cute."

"Confusing."

"That too." Dan scratched the bridge of his nose. "I'm certainly confused."

Eliza almost wished she'd invited Parker to sit at the table next to them and take notes on the conversation; she craved a witness; she craved a record. The thought occurred to her: was this whole episode with Dan just an attempt to give her life substance, to create a situation worth dramatizing later . . . to create a self through creating an antagonist out of her old professor? Did she owe him an apology? Did she owe herself an apology?

"I'm um . . ."

"What Eliza?"

"I'm so fucking tired, to be honest."

"Yeah, I didn't get any sleep. I'm running on less than empty."

"I feel like I wanna catch a train back to my parents' place tonight."

"Yeah, it's good to get out."

"I love just the feeling of being on a train at night with no one on it. I love the last train out of New York."

"It's pretty convenient to be from Princeton," Dan said, missing the point.

"Yeah."

"I never go home," Dan continued. "It depresses me."

"Why's that?"

"It's just a very dull place. Suburban Ohio."

"America in general is a dull place—"

"Hallowed out wasteland, yeah," Dan declaimed.

"Or just a boring non-wasteland."

There was something about the way he was looking at her that made her uncomfortable. She realized that lust hadn't left his eyes for a single second of the conversation. "Maybe both. I need to pee," Eliza said, standing up abruptly. "I'll be right back."

Dan, for his part, was beginning to realize that there wasn't a path forward with Eliza; seduction would not be as easy as it was the night before—but was that what he even wanted?

No.

"Did I offend you in some way?" he asked when she returned.

"No," she said curtly.

"Because you're acting like I have."

"I'm just tired."

"Just tired—"

"I'm going through some stuff?"

Dan perked up. "Like what?"

"Stuff."

"I'd like to know."

"I don't give a shit what you want, honestly."

He laughed anxiously. He didn't know if she was kidding. There was something so cruel in her voice at certain moments, he'd noticed; it seemed like a learned behavior—something she'd picked up from her parents: say whatever will hurt the most.

"You think I'm joking—"

"No no, I believe you." He could feel himself shutting down, closing off. "You shouldn't have sat down and started attacking me," he said, "I don't respond well to that."

"I'm not attacking you, why do you keep saying that?"

"Because you are."

"I still think you're cute, dummy . . ."

Dan didn't believe this at all. There was something a little creepy in her reflexive flirting. It was like she couldn't stand to be disliked even if she didn't really like him. She wouldn't push him so far away that he couldn't give her attention, that he couldn't need her and lust after her. He understood this implicitly. He felt like he was being presented with a contract.

Dan traced the edge of his coffee-cup with his pointer-finger, staring at the oily surface of the liquid.

"I just think that maybe we shouldn't have rushed into things," Eliza continued.

"Easy to say now."

"Yeah. I know."

"You shouldn't pretend to . . ."

"To what?"

"I dunno, Eliza. Be someone you're not."

"And who's that?"

"A confident person who knows what they want."

Eliza looked away over her shoulder towards the window. "Yeah. I guess I should stop."

"I'm not trying to be . . ."

"It's not hurtful —"

"I'm just hoping that maybe we can communicate . . . share responsibility for what happened last night and . . ."

"You're not gonna fuck me tonight." She ignored the part about responsibility.

"I know that."

"Do you?"

"Based on the hostility levels at this table right now: yeah, I do."

"I'm just really tired of being an object that other people pick up and put down whenever they like."

"I hear you."

"Stop acting all sensitive and mature."

"Oh sure thing," he shot back sarcastically. "I'm so sorry."

"It's manipulative."

"What could I say that you wouldn't automatically register as manipulative?"

"I have no idea," she mumbled.

"So every direction I turn—"

"Yeah—"

"I'm screwed."

"Yeah."

The situation was oppressively ambiguous.

She shifted in her seat, brushed his foot with her foot. "I'm gonna stand down for a second. Give you a second to catch your breath. I'm acting . . . I'm a lot. I'm being a lot. I hear myself being a lot. Kay?"

Quizzically, he squinted at her. "Kay."

"I like sitting with you, I do . . . I liked being in the same room with you in class . . . I liked the feeling of messaging you and meeting up with you on the spur of the moment like that . . . I like seeing your gears whirring . . . and I like how indecisive and cagey and neurotic you are—"

"You think I'm neurotic?"

"Fuck yeah you are."

"If you say so."

"I think you second guess yourself. I think you overthink things."

"The classic attack on thinking."

"Classic?"

"As in it's been going on as long as civilization has existed. The complaint against people who think too much."

"Don't flatter yourself."

"I'll try not to for your sake."

"Thanks."

As a teenager, Dan used to masturbate to girls like this: girls who treated him like this, mocked him, made him feel like a piece of shit; he always went for the pretty girls who were popular, but still good in school. Essentially, Eliza had just tapped into a deep insecurity.

"Are you okay?" Dan looked at her sympathetically.

"Why would you ask that?"

"Because you look upset."

"This coffee is so shitty," she mumbled, ignoring him on purpose.

"I like it," he said, smiling, trying to be charming, sensing, or hoping, that things were turning in his favor.

"I really just don't know how to talk about what I'm feeling," Eliza said tonelessly.

"Who does?"

"It seems like absolutely nobody does. It's wild."

Dan shifted in his seat. "What are you reading?" He flipped the book over on the table. "Nietzsche. How sophisticated. This is probably the best Nietzsche. Is this for a class?"

"Yeah. Ethics. It's an upper level class."

"I wonder if I know the— "

"Dr. I forget his name. He's Italian."

"I think I know who you're talking about. All the philosophy people are European."

"Do you like Nietzsche?"

"I mean—you know, at the end of the day Nietzsche believed . . ." Dan, who didn't know Nietzsche very well, began, "that you could write off most people as 'the herd' and what I believe is that you have to stick up for those people. The herd is just a smear word used by the upper-classes against anyone who demands justice or fairness."

"So Nietzsche's a snobby bitch?"

"He's a lot of things. But yeah. That's one of the things he is. That's a prominent feature of Nietzsche."

They were in his comfort zone now. Finally.

"So who should I read? Ethics wise? Who should instill morals in me?"

"Levinas," he said, trying to name someone who sounded exotic, someone she didn't know.

"How boring. Let's get face to face and stare into each other's souls and feel transformed by it."

Dan tried to hide his disappointment. "Oh, so you've read—"

"Uhuh." She stared at him, as if to make it seem obvious that she'd read Levinas already. The fact was, she'd just read an excerpt of Levinas the week before in class.

"Bravo."

"So give me someone else to read—"

"Ask your professor for a reading list; I mean, he gave you one, right?"

"He's boring."

"No, I know that guy, he's super smart."

"He's lame."

Dan was beginning to notice her body again—just the way she spoke with her hands, bit her lip, smiled, crossed and uncrossed her legs, leaned forward in her chair.

"I'm not sure what counts as ethics. There are different traditions . . . but . . . you could try Spinoza, if you haven't already. Or, if you want to go in a completely different direction, more my direction—read George Eliot. *Mill on the Floss*. Or *Middlemarch*. Or even better, anything by Thomas Hardy."

Eliza looked at her phone: she had an *Instagram* notification.

"What?" Dan asked. "Ex-boyfriend or?"

"Seriously—you expect me to tell you that?"

"Why not?" Dan was really curious. "It's clearly affecting you."

"It's nothing. Some dumbass guy I met earlier today."

"How many people have you slept with since school started?" he asked abruptly.

"Five," she said, when the number was really seven.

"Since late August?"

"Yeah."

He shrugged. "No big deal."

"I don't know if you understand that I wasn't asking for your opinion," she said, withdrawing back into her defensive stance.

"Sorry." He stroked her hand.

The coffee shop was close to campus, but he didn't care; he was increasingly willing to take risks.

"I'm not trying to be an asshole . . ." Eliza explained. "I don't like getting off on being mean or bitchy. I um. Yeah. I want to say so much to you . . . I really do . . . and I like the idea of you helping me and of me helping you too . . . if you're a little bit like me which I think you are but . . ." She half-watched the traffic passing up and down Sixth Avenue. "But . . . small things are vast to me . . . being myself from day to day feels like pretty fucking tragic . . . Like, I have this friend who's a barista at this coffee shop in Bushwick, and the other day I guess this police car smashed through the storefront. It was a cop in training and he sideswiped some-one and then tried to speed away, like he panicked, but he lost control of the vehicle . . . that's why I can't stop looking out the window . . . appar-ently, this woman who was in line for a like, fucking latte, got her leg pinned to the wall and now she might lose it; like things like that happen every day, and you're lucky if you're not one of the people who get fucked up by random acts of fate."

"I guess."

"Don't you feel any anxiety about that?" Eliza asked, still looking out the window. "About the unknown, the out of nowhere, the unpredictable? In some ways, I feel like it's hard for me to take a single step out of bed sometimes because of that . . . because of all the things that could go wrong."

There was an important part of contemporary anguish in her eyes: the heroic absence of any certainty.

"Hmm."

"What?"

"Have you ever had a period in your life when you believed in any kind of higher power?"

"No, not really. Why?"

"Sometimes when I'm feeling like that, I think—gee, it would be nice to believe in God . . . but I just have no capacity for faith whatsoever."

"Were you raised religious at all or? I wasn't—"

"I was raised Episcopalian but that's basically nothing. What about you?"

"I mean, I'm half Jewish, half Catholic, but I never went to synagogue or church or anything; I just got the cultural residue, so."

"If you could press a button that would magically give you faith in something, would you press the button?" Dan asked.

"For sure."

"Why?"

"Because of what you said—it would make things easier."

Dan pinched his chin between his thumb and forefinger. "I guess I would too."

"Isn't radical political commitment supposed to like supplant religion?"

Dan wasn't sure if she was mocking him. "That's what I think I was doing, if I'm being completely honest, during Occupy and such. But—"

"It didn't do the trick—"

"No—nothing's 'done the trick'."

"Sad."

Dan nudged Eliza with his foot under the table. "Hey—"

"Hey . . ."

"You're cute."

"I try," she said listlessly.

"I'm boring you."

"I'm boring myself."

"I have this intense desire to lean across the table," Dan said, muting his own inner-protest, "and kiss you."

"Have at it."

Dan leaned awkwardly, and their lips met briefly. For a split second, he felt her tongue dart into his mouth, before they both sat back.

"Interesting," Dan said.

"Essentially, I want you to see through me and call me a fraud. I want you to analyze all the contradictions in my behavior; I want you to be mean to me, but you don't. You want me too much."

"Well, it's not like . . . I don't see the contradictions—" Dan said, trying to pivot.

"Are you sure about that?"

"They're obvious."

Eliza laughed. "Then what are they, dude?"

Dan took a belly breath and then exhaled. "You want to be dominated, in some way, but on the other hand, you're too anxious for that, so you put up new boundaries and walls even while you're tearing the old ones down."

"Mr. Gorbachev, tear down this pyscho-sexual wall!"

"Pretty much," Dan said, amused.

"You don't think there's anything problematic about you wanting to be the one to do that—even if you're currently not doing a good job of it—?"

"Yeah, it's problematic. Okay? I'm problematic. What do you want me to say? I watch porn and am sad and repressed and depressed and I have socially unacceptable lust for you—"

"Are you sad and repressed and depressed?"

"Clearly!"

"What kind of porn do you watch?"

"Mostly lesbian stuff."

"Pretty typical."

"Sure."

"I like to watch lesbian porn too even though I don't fuck girls; there's something more aesthetic about it. I dunno."

"Modernity is really fucked, isn't it?"

"Oh absolutely."

"What's your favorite memory, Eliza? Like what's something that makes you happy when you think about it?"

Eliza scratched her nose. "The freshness of summer nights in high school–any number of them. Sneaking out and driving around with my friends. Smoking in cemeteries and stuff like that. It wasn't long ago at all, but shit just wasn't that complicated. Going to concerts and stuff. I played in a little pop punk band. I think between fifteen to seventeen was just like prime good stuff."

Dan took another belly breath; she was so young, emotionally—so so young. "And now you're looking for the adult equivalent of that kind of romance."

"Precisely, precisely."

"Makes sense."

"Do you think that's lame or that I'm lame?"

"Not at all," Dan said matter-of-factly.

Even while a part of him wanted to say "yes—it's so lame," he had to admit that he was, and always had been, seeking his own forms of romance, that he had never stopped trying to dress up his own life, make it more heroic or memorable than it really was. He had already admitted as much in talking about his time in Occupy. His whole interaction with Eliza had demonstrated that, as a teacher, he was, in a sense, recreating his own failed romantic projects as if they were still alive; his teaching was a form of self-mythologizing, in which he fused with radical texts and thinkers, in which his pedagogy was falsely linked to his life practices. Eliza, at least temporarily, had actually believed in the mythical person he presented to his students, and to some degree, in his writing. She had hoped that he could help her create her own self-myth.

"I just really want to be vulnerable with someone."

"Same."

"In some ways . . ." Eliza scratched her nose again. "I just feel so fucking isolated. Like it's easy to make friends—but—"

"Do you like your friends at school?"

"They're fine. They're nice. But there's like a missing element of trust. Like when I did a study abroad program in Germany this past summer, I couldn't help but notice how much better Europeans were at friendship. Like there was an aura of trust and intimacy that just doesn't like happen here. There's always a secret chill to people in the city. I dunno. I feel the chill inside me. I've been cold—and I kinda like the power that's come with being cold—the protective armor . . ."

"Yeah, I get that."

"I wanna be emotional. I feel like sobbing right now."

"I'm not gonna stop you."

"Dan, I think in a lot of small ways, you are stopping me. Blocking me."

"From crying? Oh? How so?"

"Because our interactions are conditioned by your fantasy idea of me, not who I really am."

"I'm trying to figure out who you really are."

"So am I."

"Wow . . . uh that's quite the Mobius strip of an explanation . . ."

"I don't understand . . ." Eliza whispered.

"You want me to figure out what you don't know about you so that I can stop seeing you the way you wanted me to see you in the first place."

Eliza smiled a wan smile. "Oh yeah, right. That."

"Pretty bizarre."

"No. Pretty normal. I feel like that's a good description of most human interactions."

Dan thought about this for a moment. Eliza's mind moved as fast as his own did—or faster. He had to admit that a part of him wanted to punish her for being, pedigree and learning-time aside, cleverer than he was; subliminally, his mind rejected the idea that she could easily surpass him if she committed to the same kind of academic track that he had. "I think I'm afraid of you, Eliza," Dan said after a moment. "Like really, really afraid."

"I know you are," she said. "I think that's the point."

8

Akari was on the couch, scrolling *Instagram*.

Her body was small, but she was very toned and lean from yoga and pilates classes, so she appeared longer than she was. And though her eyes were cast down, she was aware that Dan was staring at her, studying her very intently.

"You look like someone, actually, who really needs to talk," she said, without looking up (she was on the couch, he was on the floor).

"Well, sure I do, yeah."

Dan laid down on the rug in the small common area, groaning slightly because his back was stiff; exhausted, he didn't think he could or would get up. He didn't want to move. He smelled a little sour; his pits were damp from the humidity trapped in the apartment—and from the general stress of the day. He needed a shower, but he just wanted to lay there.

Akari cracked her knuckles and took a sip of beer from the can she had on the end table. It was a nice, quiet night in Greenpoint, and she planned to enjoy it; it was clear that her almost-brother-in-law wanted sympathy or conversation, but she wasn't going to offer it merely to appease him or make the moment more comfortable. That wasn't her game. She wasn't going to let his mood affect hers. She had taken a nap after getting back and felt refreshed; she'd even mustered the willpower to turn off her phone.

She felt deliciously disconnected from responsibility.

"What are you thinking about?" he asked.

"Nada."

"Are you still with that—"

"We broke up," Akari interjected curtly.

"Oh that sucks, I'm sorry."

"It's whatever." Akari took another sip of beer and burped. "I mean, it tore me up for a while—um. I'm not someone who really . . . I sort of experience my emotions objectively, like they're someone else's. I know what I'm feeling but I'm able to analyze it and compartmentalize it and get on with my life."

"That seems dangerous."

"How is it dangerous?"

"Because there's no such thing as actual objectivity in regard to . . . to the um, self. I'm kinda realizing that—that's what I realized today. You can't lie to yourself forever. It catches up to you. You think you understand why you're engaging in a certain behavior, but the behavior's tricking you."

"I'm surprised you're not watching the debate tonight," Akari said, ignoring his little rant.

"We don't have a TV."

"But it's not like you couldn't find a way to watch it."

"Sure—but uh—I find it all so fucking depressing; I can't bring myself to care."

"Huh. I thought that was your thing."

"I guess . . ." he mumbled, lamely. "But—not lately. I feel remarkably apathetic."

"Interesting."

"I need to go to bed." Dan stretched out on the floor, yawning.

"Then go to bed."

"I'm physically tired, but my mind is very *not* tired." He sat up as if to prove his point, making uncomfortably direct eye-contact.

"What is going on, my dude?"

He laughed bitterly. "You have no idea."

Akari, for her part, thought that she *did* have an idea. She had snuck around before; she had cheated before; she knew all the symptoms. What happened was that you started to feel bad for yourself for letting things get so complicated and absurd; you started to feel like a victim of your own impulses; you felt kind of divided in two: into the person who did the doing and the person who had to deal with the consequences. Besides, she was pretty sure she could *smell* the sex on Dan; there was a faint, but distinct odor.

"Do you wanna tell me about it?"

"Do I?"

"Are we gonna be all high school about this or can you just spit straight facts?"

"I think it's better that some things are left unsaid."

"You're not leaving anything said though; you're just being a weirdo."

"Akari, I literally cannot tell you what's on my mind—ok? It's just not something . . . like—I mean, you probably can guess. I'm guessing you're guessing—"

"I mean I have an idea based on the way you're acting and looking at me."

"So why not leave it there."

"Because you *want to tell me.*"

"Yeah, I do."

"But you won't. You want to but you can't bring yourself to at the same time."

"Correct."

"Because a part of you doesn't know whether it's a brag or a confession."

"Correct."

"Do you think I'm judging you—that I'll judge you?"

Dan took a moment to think about this before asking, "What do you think of the whole situation?"

"Your relationship? I really don't want to comment."

"I'm just like dying for an objective perspective."

"I'm not objective."

Akari laid back on the couch, sighing, breaking eye contact with him. Sometimes, she was down, or in the mood or whatever, to indulge Dan's little games, but tonight, there was just something depressing about him; he was actively making her depressed. If she kept engaging him, she'd end up just like him: an emotional grifter.

Besides, she had her own issues, to say the least, and getting involved in the politics of Dan and Mariko's relationship was only a distraction. They were fucked up—in increasingly obvious ways—but there was only so much pleasure to be gained from comparing her thing with Suzanne to what Mariko had with Dan; the comparison, in fact, offered diminishing returns: after a while, all she could feel was pity.

"Okay . . ." Dan said after a moment, "I don't even need an objective perspective. Honestly, I'll take *any* perspective."

"My perspective is uh—" Akari, studying Dan's body language, sensed that he was trapped between self-loathing and self-pity; he didn't know which posture to choose, and he didn't really know what was appropriate. He didn't really know who he was or what he was becoming. He had, furthermore, no interest in ever really knowing. Dan wanted to remain suspended between self-knowing and unknowing forever. "My perspective is that you can't ever really resurrect the intensity of the beginning of a relationship, so you sure as hell better have mutual respect and trust . . ."

"Easier said than done."

"Then maybe it should be done."

"Oof."

"I hate to be the bearer of bad news, but . . ."

"I'm not in a great headspace," Dan admitted blandly.

"I can see that."

"I think I'm having a panic attack."

Akari sat up a little, not really interested, but willing to at least feign baseline concern. "Is that so? Are you ok?"

"I don't know. I feel like I'm going to die."

"Take deep breaths into your belly."

"Okay."

"Do you want to talk about it now?"

"Fuck no . . ."

The poor guy was really suffering (for whatever reason).

"Dan . . ."

"I really messed up, I think."

"In what way?"

"Just dumb choices. I've made some really dumb choices."

"It happens man . . ."

Akari studied her almost brother-in-law, whose body language was almost wholly discounted from the things he was saying. He seemed so weak, almost like a little boy. She almost felt like his mother, or more specifically his aunt: a somewhat more distant, but still maternal figure. The cool aunt.

She didn't want to be unkind to Dan, but she struggled to take him seriously; though the possibility existed, as well, that engaging with his feelings, and inner turmoil, would instigate, or spark, her own process of self-evaluation, which was not exactly what she wanted. If she could keep Dan at an emotional and psychological distance with understatement and implied scorn, then she could minimize the expectation that it would be *her turn to share*. She wanted to punish his attempts at vulnerability to demonstrate that vulnerability had no place in the conversation or the room.

"How's your panic attack going?"

"I'm not sure if it's a panic attack; I'm not sure I've ever had one, so I don't know if this is one."

"Is your chest tingling?"

"A little, yeah."

"Are you having trouble breathing?"

"A little, yeah."

"Probably a panic attack, yeah."

"Oh great, great."

"I'll just hang with you 'til you're feeling better."

"A part of me is like, too exhausted to even panic. I barely slept."

"Yeah, I took a little nap when I got in, but otherwise the red eye kinda fucked me up."

"I forget—are you here for a gig or just to visit?"

"I'm shooting a commercial tomorrow not far from here; I should go to sleep soon."

"I thought maybe Mariko called you in for emotional reinforcement."

"I mean that's what she expects of me in exchange for putting me up, but . . ."

"I think you're a calming presence . . . and obviously a part of you relishes the role you play—advisor, referee—whatever—"

"I mean, I'm not going to deny that," Akari responded, "but I think the whole question of roles is pretty complex like . . . I think it's very easy to start enjoying what other people have conditioned you to be or pushed you into like . . . with my sister I've had to do the moral support thing for so long that like . . . obviously my own self-esteem is bound up in it in certain very fundamental ways, like . . ."

"I think like Mariko . . ." Dan started, relishing the opportunity to analyze, and indeed, talk shit, "is charming enough that her default assumption is always that she's going to get her way . . . which is not to say that she's literally manipulative but like that uh—that uh—well I think we're both taken for granted in certain ways."

Akari raised her eyebrows skeptically. "That's a conveniently self-serving interpretation, but also not wrong."

"Did you ever cheat on Suzanne?"

"Suzanne and I were non-monog, so not really, no. I guess I lied in certain circumstances . . . um . . ."

"I had the realization today that I started watching a lot of lesbian porn after I met you and her."

Akari whistled. "Whoo eee. That's uh—that's total TMI."

"Sorry," Dan said like a little boy.

"It's cool; it's dope being a fetish object for my sister's boyfriend."

"We flirt—admit we flirt—"

"In our own strange way, sure."

"Are we flirting right now?"

Akari whistled again. "Well, I understand now that you're trying to."

"I'm self-destructing; I'm not sure if that's the same thing."

"Flirting with the wrong people is definitely a tool of self-destruction."

"Are you a wrong person?"

"Of course, Dan."

"Yeah. I think—honestly—what's happening right now . . . what I'm realizing . . . is that I'm reacting to the possibility that Mariko actually really doesn't love me anymore . . . I'm just flailing . . ."

"I believe that's called a self-fulfilling prophecy."

"I know . . ."

"I masturbated on your couch today," Akari found herself saying.

"Is that supposed to mean or indicate something?"

"I figured I needed to share something embarrassing to bail you out a little bit."

"Is that embarrassing—it's kinda hot?"

"*Daniel*—"

"Sorry . . ."

"I do think it's embarrassing or like in poor taste."

"No one was home or harmed by it—why is it embarrassing?"

"I find uncontrolled desire or lust slightly shameful; doesn't everyone?" Akari asked.

"At the moment, I certainly do."

"What happened tonight, Dan? I'm very curious."

"I absolutely cannot say."

"I won't tell her . . ."

"It's just that I'm not spiritually ready to confess. Somehow not saying it preserves it . . . from I dunno . . . just preserves it . . ."

"I guess I understand that."

Dan stretched out, wiggling his toes, his increasingly expressive face in profile. "I've felt frozen for so long—frozen in so many ways and now I'm worried I thawed out too fast—like frozen salmon or something . . ." Dan started doing crunches on the couch. "I need to get in shape."

"Feeling old?"

"So old."

"Poor Dan."

Dan jumped up from the floor and punched at the air, shadowboxing. "Why wasn't I an artist or revolutionary? I think about that all the time— like, *man*—why did I choose to be me and not someone?"

"Did you choose?"

"I made the choices that led me to being me—the me that I am—"

"Did you?"

"I hope so."

"Choosing is weird." Akari made a funny face. "I'm not sure it's what humans really do."

"No, I'm not sure either," Dan said forlornly. "I'm not sure that that's what I've been doing the last thirty-six hours."

"What would you call it then, if not choosing?"

"Just reacting reacting reacting reacting reacting," Dan chanted, punching the air with each word.

Akari thought of her text exchange with Suzanne from the morning. "I empathize."

"Last night," Dan began, sitting back down on the couch, "I felt like Mari and I were really connecting again . . . really getting somewhere . . . in this conversation we were having . . . and it's like I just pressed explode on all that—"

"Not necessarily . . ."

"You think I can just like—I dunno—?"

"Is total fidelity to truth for its own sake your goal or having a harmonious relationship?"

"The latter."

"Then hope that you got out of your system what you needed to get out—and you can return to your relationship . . . like . . ."

"I'm worried that it's not so simple."

"Well, control what you can control."

"I guess. I'm still anxious."

"Anxiety is human nature, human destiny bro."

"No. I don't think so. Anxiety is mostly a function of a petty bourgeoisie mentality," Dan explained, "which, if I'm being honest with myself, I embody: the obsessive desire to preserve small comforts and routines . . ."

"Um, yeah."

"Sorry."

"Do your thing, Dan. Be you. Talk the way you talk."

"I saw a *Twitter* 'thread' today about how Millennials will be lonely if they give up on childrearing into their forties—and a part of me doesn't disagree. But I can't help but wonder if the reason parenthood is the only way forward is because an urban single's range of experience has become curtailed, predictable, Yuppified, and, um, boring. Like. Maybe the problem with urban Millennials is not that they've, or um, we've, not settled down, but because we've never grown up—"

"Honestly, probably."

About ten minutes later, after they heard the sound of someone rattling keys, Mariko entered, looking haggard and a little nervous. Akari immediately could tell that her sister had spent the evening getting fucked; whether Dan noticed or not, however, was unclear, because he was busy avoiding making eye-contact; his eyes were half-closed on the rug.

"Hey hey," Dan mumbled.

As Mariko walked by Akari on her way to the kitchen area, Akari could have sworn her sister smelled like sex too.

What a shitshow.

"How is everyone?" Mariko asked listlessly.

"Just dandy," Akari said.

"How was your day?" Dan asked from the floor.

"It was fine," Mariko declared with forced casualness. "Nothing special. What about you guys?"

"I'm just chillin—did not sleep enough," Akari stated for the record.

"Just got a beer with a friend," Dan said, as if it were true.

"Nice, nice. Well—Akari—you should get some sleep."

"Ya'll are in the living room, so."

"That's a good point. Sorry. Dan—my love—let's go to bed."

"I think I'm gonna shower first."

"I was gonna shower, but—you can have the first shower—"

"You can go first . . ."

"No you go; it's fine."

"Okay . . ." Dan said, shrugging.

He disappeared into the bedroom to get pajamas and a towel, returned for a moment, then closed the bathroom door behind him. The apartment never felt smaller.

Akari raised her eyebrows knowingly; her sister declined to meet her gaze.

"Let's go out on the fire-escape . . ." Akari whispered.

"Why?"

"Let's just go?"

"What is this?"

"Mariko come on."

"Mariko . . ." Akari whispered harshly, "It's so obvious."

"What's obvious?"

"Let's just go out to the fire-escape," Akari said, this time in a normal voice, as if to lay bare the situation for Dan in the other room.

"I prefer not to," Mariko said.

"Okay . . ."

"Can you not do this to me?" Mariko pleaded, gripping her sister's arm (they were both on the couch now).

"I'm trying to help you."

"No you're not; you're cornering me; I don't like it."

"Cornering you how?"

"Morally."

"Yo, relax relax. Can we just go out and have a cigarette?"

"You're being a weirdo, Akari . . . like, just chill . . ."

"I'm chill."

"You're being strange . . ."

"I'm like, just a little pissed that you wanted me to come out here to hang out, then start an affair . . ."

"What what?"

The shower was loud enough that they could just bump their speaking volume from about 1 to 4. Akari could really smell the sex on her sister; it excited her a little bit—which was disturbing—and she tried to push the sensation out of her mind. Shit was twisted.

"You heard me, Mari . . . Like I'm here because you'd been calling me telling me how lonely and sad you were, so like . . ."

"I mean fair—I just got caught up in something—"

"In what?"

"I was with my mentor who I found out has cancer."

"All day?"

"He's really sick—so—"

"You've been fucking—"

Mariko's eyes flicked towards the bathroom instead of responding.

"You two are crazy."

"What does that mean?"

"You're just wild—wild wild wild. What a shit show."

"Sorry."

"It's fine; it's just like—holy shit."

"Have you talked to Mom and Dad lately?" Mariko asked abruptly.

"Last week."

"You went home?"

"Briefly."

"Why?"

"Why? Because I wanted to."

"Okay."

"Does that bother you?"

"I haven't seen them since Christmas."

"Well then get on a plane."

"I can't afford to."

"Yes you can—"

"No," Mariko said sharply, "I really can't."

"I'll buy you one then."

"Please don't."

"Okay, whatever you want."

"Akari . . ."

"What?"

"I need to tell you something."

"I know you do . . ."

"I um . . ."

Dan appeared from the bathroom in his towel; he looked around, as if in a daze. "What's going on?"

"Just chatting," Mariko said, fully an actress.

After a certain point, living wasn't active, Akari thought, but passive: a habit, like picking your cuticles. The human organism, from the perspective of a truly evolved species, was utterly pathetic, like a mosquito: a buzzing, vampiric nonentity—an evolutionary perversion.

"I see." Dan slipped back into the bedroom, closing the door.

"You two need to talk."

"Fuck no."

Akari had to laugh at this. "Okay . . ."

"Eventually we will."

"'Eventually' is such a cope."

"So let me cope."

"Okay."

Seeing that there were tears in Mariko's eyes, Akari leaned forward and rubbed the tears away with her thumb.

Mariko sat still for her sister, like a child at the doctor's, until her tears were gone.

II

Remember: there are no small parts, only small actors.

—Stanislavski

9

Mariko watched Dan nervously tip cigarette ash onto the sidewalk outside IFC. His hands were shaking, and he looked like someone who had rehearsed the action so much that he had forgotten how to be natural. He looked so much older, in general, and it made her uncomfortable; it was like he'd come back from war.

Starting with a movie had been an odd but good choice; the theater was a transitional space, allowing them to become comfortable with the presence of the other without too much direct confrontation. She didn't even remember whose idea it was; it just sort of happened.

It was a cold night, but the air felt good.

She just kept looking at him and he kept looking at her—quick little glances.

She knew he was taking a lot of Klonopin these days.

Wrested from the context in which he was familiar to her, Mariko was actually able to see Dan now: a palpable mass of biological life, an innocent creature badly in need of emotional security, trying to make sense of his fate. She wanted to stroke his forehead, whisper in his ear; she wanted him to cry in her arms. And this was so strange, because, for more than a year now, she had wanted nothing more than to see him punished.

Her own past behavior was incomprehensible to her, as if she had been following a set of ethical codes written for life on another planet: barren, pitiless, harsh. Now, she was like an astronaut, approaching green earth from space.

It was so fucking emotional being together again (but she couldn't let him see that).

"Where should we walk?" he asked.

He looked anxious.

For whatever reason, after the long phone call with her therapist the day before, and after a lot of journaling, she had just wanted to call him, to do something with him, to hang out, to let him be a normal ex with whom she was on good terms. And, of course, she kept dreaming about him; he appeared to her many nights, as if he were one of the dead.

"Doesn't matter to me."

"We'll just go west."

She knew he didn't like being this close to school, but there wasn't much they could do; it was New York after all.

Imagining what it was like for him made her uncomfortable.

She wanted to keep things at the level of pity, but it was clearly not going to be that simple: there was another inference—buried in the situation itself—that she couldn't quite articulate. It had to do with her own role, what *she* was responsible for: she'd failed to stop him; she'd let him dig his own grave; she'd been indifferent. She felt a little guilty.

"Do you want one?" he asked, offering her a cigarette.

"I don't smoke anymore, not even a little."

"Really?"

"Yeah."

"Okay Mariko."

"Your hands are trembling."

"I'm cold."

"You're not that cold."

"Actually," he drawled, "I am."

It occurred to her that he had lost a lot of weight; he was quite gaunt.

Wildly, she felt the impulse to kiss him—to grind her pelvis against his.

Togetherness 2.0.

Dan took a long drag of his Marlboro and exhaled. "Man, the ending—"

"What, you liked it or didn't like it? I can't tell—"

"Oh no no no. I fucking hated it. Hated it."

"Why?"

"It should have just ended at the karaoke bar."

"I think that would have felt abrupt."

"So what?"

"What's wrong with happy endings?"

"I think that's obvious."

Dan stamped out the cigarette with his boot and reached for her hand, which was gloved, and brushed her fingertips with his own. It had been at least a year since they had physically connected in any way. She felt nothing, but didn't say anything; it couldn't hurt to just be nice to him—not really.

"How would *you* have ended the movie?"

"Like," Dan began as they started walking, "I would have had them run into each other on the street and not say a thing—blow each other off."

"Interesting you say that—"

"Well, we planned to meet tonight, first of all—"

"Anyway—"

"Okay—anyway—I would have had the divorce battle destroy them— like—I would have had the kids get depressed and suicidal. I would have them stop being hot. Otherwise you never forget who the actors are. You never believe that they're a real couple with real problems. They never get scuffed up. It's just Brooklynite fan fiction; it's honestly disgusting."

"Who are we to judge?"

It wasn't *just* that Dan had been fired and humiliated, subject to public scorn, but because both of their lives, according to the values and ideals with which they had commenced adulthood, were *failures*. They were only able to live in New York City, to have a night off to meet, to stroll, any- way, because their parents had both, separately, agreed (out of pity) to help them out financially. They were living their own fictions: independence, dignity, self-sufficiency.

Mariko watched her ex rotate his neck at its base and heard the little crack of air pockets between his vertebrae. They crossed Sixth Avenue. It was all absolutely surreal to her; a part of her just wanted to cry.

"I uh—" Mariko sniffled, fishing for a tissue in her pocket. Her nose always got so runny in cold weather; it undercut the whole dramatic effect she was trying to summon. "So many people just think I should never speak to you again."

"They're probably right."

She stopped cold in the middle of the street. She didn't even know where they were, the streets got so confusing around here and she had taken her contacts out after the movie because they had been hurting.

"Dan, I have no idea what to do—okay? I have no training for this—and I'm someone who likes having training."

"Do you think I'm a predator?"

"I've told you many times—no—not exactly."

"'Not exactly . . .' You've told me you see both sides of the situation—"

"You made a mistake . . ."

"I think people are capable of all kinds of conflicted behavior. So."

"It's possible I'll just keep changing my mind for the rest of my life."

"I don't know if you realize—"

She started up walking again, unconsciously, as if her feet were setting the pace for the whole conversation. "Realize what?"

"How badly I just need someone to tell me I'm still a decent person."

"You're an extremely decent person. You just did something deeply embarrassing."

"According to current mores, I'm a bad person."

"Well, I don't agree."

"Great, thanks."

She didn't continue the conversation for at least two blocks.

"Someone sent me a screenshot of your *Tinder* account," she said, finally.

"Who?"

"Doesn't matter."

They were waiting for the light to change so they could cross the highway and reach the riverpark.

Dan focused on the traffic. "Haven't I been shamed enough?"

"I can't help it if someone sends me a text out of the blue."

"Was it Akari?"

"Uh, yeah. It was."

"Yeah, I saw her on the app; so I could surmise."

"How's that working out for you?"

"*Tinder?* Mariko, I have no idea; I just downloaded it out of curiosity. . . . It seems kind of cruel of you to pry."

"I guess I'm feeling cruel then, yeah."

"You're confusing."

The attempt at closeness was destroying proximity; the absence of separation had revealed an almost infinite distance.

"Can we sit down on a bench?"

"It's too cold to sit," he said, somewhat childishly.

"I need to center myself."

They walked in silence and took a seat on one of the benches that looked out from the concrete thoroughfare that ran along the water.

For several minutes, they were silent while Dan smoked another cigarette and shivered. Mariko was perfectly still (as if she had been directed to be still).

"You know—" He started as the cigarette tapered out.

"Yes?"

"Nothing. Nevermind."

"I'm worried about you."

"Worried how exactly?"

"You know."

"I mean, would you even be upset—?"

"Come on—"

"No really."

"Dan, I'd be upset."

"Okay. What bothers me is that I'm just quite simply too scared not *of* dying, but of *being* dead—like I started to try to imagine nothingness, not existing, not thinking, and my whole body sort of reacts, instinctively— like my brain calls my guts on a direct line, or the other way around. I just can't do it."

"Have you tried?"

"I have some pills but like—"

"Dan—" Mariko cut him off, using a kindergarten-teacher voice; she really couldn't listen to this: it was too much. "Either don't try to manipulate me into levels of sympathy I don't want to give or be completely honest with me. One or the other. You choose. If you need help, if you're a threat to yourself—let me know. Say it. If not. Don't play. Okay?"

"I'm not a threat to myself." His voice was clipped.

Mariko pulled her coat tightly over her chest. She had gained about fifteen pounds since he'd last seen her; she was careful to dress in a way that could mostly conceal it. It wasn't that she minded the weight—she liked her body this way—it was that she didn't want him to think she was letting go, that she was anything less than she was. She wanted him to believe he'd lost the most desirable woman he'd ever have (which must be true!).

"I'm not—" he repeated, unaware that she'd stopped listening.

"Okay."

"You know, the other day, I sent my Mom an email just to see what would happen because it was her birthday. 'Happy birthday, wherever you are.' It actually went through, which was eerie. I guess the account is still active. . . . That really made me feel something . . . I uh—I started to read old emails from her too—the real borderline shit. 'You're a terrible son. You kissed Aunt Rosie but not your own mother at the wedding. You hate me.' So—I definitely understand that there is some shit with me and women. I know there is. But I can't change what's happened . . ."

She turned to face him directly. "Is it weird that I like you better like this?"

"Like what?"

"Deeply chastened."

He covered his face with his hands like he was about to blow out birthday candles and took a deep breath. "No—it's not weird; it's depressing to hear," he said, exhaling audibly. "Makes me wanna off myself."

"Fair."

He rotated his head left to look at her, pursing his lips, running his hands through his hair (the remnants of which he had let grow quite long) and then down along the nape of his neck. "How are there no second chances?"

"There are plenty of second chances. Just not in academia in 2019 for teachers who tried to date their students."

"I've been branded as a creep."

"You weren't branded: you were fired."

"My career was cauterized. I mean, it's all scar tissue. Don't act like there's some amazing menu of alternatives for me."

"Don't act like there's no menu at all."

After she said this, she watched as he considered if this were true; it was a bit like watching a child be told "no." It was like he was trying to find his way around a rhetorical fortification—or under or over it.

"Has it ever occurred to you—" Mariko's voice cracked with sudden anger, "do you ever think about . . . like—the fact that she suffered, that you brought suffering into her life too—"

"I think about it every day."

"Then don't you think that you deserve to be fired?"

"I think I can regret my behavior . . . and also regret my liquidation—"

"You're so self-pitying—"

"Fuck off."

Mariko sat back, surprised at the amount of raw anger in his voice. She waited a moment while he rubbed his gloved palms together.

"Also Mariko—like don't use *her* as a vehicle to express your anger at me, your personal anger—okay? Your sense of betrayal—that's bullshit."

"'Vehicle . . .'" Mariko shook her head in disbelief. "Okay, Dan. I won't. I'll just be angry at you—generally—because of how you treated me."

"Thanks."

"You're welcome," she said, smiling a little, unable to help herself.

For whatever reason, he reached for her hand with his free hand and for whatever reason, she didn't resist (maybe just because it was cold).

They leaned together a little.

"Can I tell you something?" Mariko asked meekly.

"Sure. What?"

"Actually—"

"What?"

"Nevermind."

"Really?

"Yeah."

"Alright," he said, resigned. "Can we keep walking? I'm really shivering my balls off."

"Yeah, we can keep walking."

"Cool."

They started walking north with no apparent aim other than to keep warm and keep talking, hands still intertwined.

"What were you gonna tell me, Mariko?"

"Ah fuck—"

"What?!"

"It's not a pleasant thing. Or, it wouldn't be for you."

"You fucked someone else too."

Mariko didn't answer.

"I remember having suspicions," Dan said in a hushed, meditative tone. "But I had other stuff going on, as you know now."

"Do you want to know who?"

"No. I already know who it was, I think."

"Okay."

"Do you miss him?"

"A lot. Immensely. It's horrible to think that . . . uh he's gone. But . . . it's not what you think. We only slept together once. He was a friend."

"Okay, but was it just . . . ?"

"No. It became several people. You can hate me—"

"No, I can't."

"Are you sure?"

"Positive. I can't hate you any more than you hate me."

"I used to hate you, but I didn't have much basis for it."

"Really sucks that you let me believe that I was the only one doing the betraying. Really sucks that we broke up because of that."

"We broke up because . . . we're not meant to be together."

"Are you sure? Even now—I mean—are you sure?"

She couldn't deny that some kind of bond remained, but it was unclear what kind of bond it was. In a perverse way, Mariko thought, it was like you couldn't really appreciate a person until you could properly peer beneath the ego-layer, and just see them as a raw being, a raw creature.

Across the river, the condos and office towers arrayed along the shore of New Jersey gleamed dully.

"I love you, Mariko," Dan said, his teeth chattering.

"No, you don't."

"In this moment I do. Maybe for the first time ever, I mean those words."

"Why? Why would you say that now?"

"Because I can show you forgiveness now too—"

Mariko felt a sob rise in her throat. "Oh, wow . . ."

"What?"

"I literally believe you."

"Do you?"

She squeezed his gloved hand without looking at him, as if her hands could express what her eyes and mind resisted. "Yes. I can feel it, somehow."

"Okay then . . . what do you feel exactly?"

"Just that we're here—really here—"

"Yeah, I guess we are."

"I remember reading that girl's *Facebook* post about you—and just getting so angry not just at you, but at her, for being so utterly tactless."

"What's really fucked up is that on some level I still have feelings for her—"

"Damn, Dan."

"I know, I know."

"I think that's natural too though, in some way I can't articulate," Mariko said, looking down at the water.

Cyclists and a brave, bundled up runner passed behind them.

Dan drew her to the railing and tried to press her against it. His teeth glinted beneath his drawn-up upper lip. "Can I kiss you, Mari?"

"No . . ."

Anguish. "Why not . . . ?"

"That's not what this is supposed to be."

"I was so excited when you agreed to see the movie with me."

"Just to break the ice, not to get back together."

"Valid."

"We weren't happy together; that's why all these things happened in the first place. All of this just unfolded out of our shared misery, Dan— really we were making each other just so miserable."

"I don't know if misery *is* the right word . . . maybe it is for you? *Was*—"

"In so many ways I believed in us right up until the moment I didn't; it's only in retrospect that I'm able to recognize that I was not a happy or fulfilled person."

"Ah."

"I'm actually booking roles now. I'm dating. I'm not unhappy now."

"You're dating?"

"Only less surprising than the fact that I'm booking. Of course I am though, in all seriousness—aren't you?"

"I mean, I'm going on dates—like—I feel like a criminal. I'm afraid they'll find out."

"You're not a criminal and like regular people in the world do not conform to Title IX okay? You're fine."

"I feel like a pariah."

"Operative word is pariah. It's such low level stuff, it's like—just live your life man."

"Easy for you to say . . . like . . . I'm trying, I guess . . . I feel like we're talking past each other."

"What I'm saying is: repair, retrench, move on, yes. With my support. With my offer of kindness and renewed respect."

"I've had enough HR language . . ."

"That's not HR language, that's just how I talk."

"It sounds very put on."

"I'm being sincere."

Dan leaned against the railing. Another cyclist went by. "There are two types of relationships . . . I think . . . those that leave you with a feeling of regret, and those that leave you with a feeling of gratitude."

"Which one were we? Are we?"

"I can't decide," he said.

"Alright."

"I'm full of pent-up irony. I was going to say frustration—but irony is more accurate."

"Do you plan on being demoralized for the rest of your life?"

"I don't plan on anything."

Mariko took the cigarette from between his lips and took a drag. "There was another part of me that was kind of proud that you could seduce a student—that I was dating someone with that kind of appeal. I admitted that to my therapist recently."

"What'd the therapist say?"

"That I lacked self-esteem. That I gave you permission to transfer your attractions to a much younger women because I felt that only young women were worthy of affection."

"Sounds accurate."

"It is accurate. I have a good therapist. Do you?"

"I've been seeing a Lacanian but it feels like a waste of my father's money."

"Your father's been helping you?"

"For the first time in my life, he sees me as sympathetic and worth helping, weirdly."

"Are you working?"

"I don't wanna talk about it."

"I wish you'd keep writing your blog."

"I don't. It was stupid. I'm stupid. The biggest epiphany of the past year has been what a fucking idiot I am."

"Why did she wait until after she'd graduated to report you?"

"Because cultural conditions changed; I dunno; people are inexplicable."

"I thought maybe you would just get suspended."

"I didn't have tenure. I was DOA."

Mariko tugged him away from the railing, so that they kept walking; she got cold whenever they stopped.

"I think you were always a little jealous of me," Dan said, cutting her off. "I think you resented me for my little place in the world."

"Yes, because that's what I lacked: a place. Sorry."

"But you're doing better now . . ."

"Marginally. A few TV things. An indie feature my sister shot. In the running for this off-Broadway play. I'm not sure if you've followed . . ."

"I don't go to your *Instagram* page, if that's what you're asking."

"I guess that is what I'm asking; not that you have to . . . I just don't want to tell you things you already know, that would be obnoxious."

"Understood."

"Can we sit down somewhere for like a glass of wine; I'm really cold," Mariko said.

"Yeah sure. Let's spend $93 bucks for four drinks in the West Village."

"Okay, we don't have to."

"No, I'm fine with it. Fuck it."

They veered back east, crossing over the highway, both parties having fallen into a protective silence. Mariko trailed alongside Dan, who was walking quickly. She couldn't stop thinking about how thin he looked: like how she imagined characters in Russian literature. He'd become a monk, of sorts, a recluse. He was a completely different person. Was that a good thing?

Once ensconced in a wine bar on 8th avenue, Dan took an extended moment to check his phone. "I've been buying Bitcoin," he explained.

"Really?"

"Yeah. I put whatever savings I had in it, so. Rolling the dice or whatever."

"Unexpected. I think my sister lost money on Bitcoin in 2017 when crypto crashed."

"Rough."

The waiter came over and they both ordered Merlot.

"What have you been reading?" Akari asked.

"Uh just living in nineteenth-century fiction. It's very nice. Right now I'm re-reading *Mansfield Park*. I just walk to Prospect Park and read most afternoons."

"Are you really not working at all?"

"I mean I'm doing some online tutoring and stuff; it pays pretty well; college essay prep, that kinda thing."

"How is it?"

"I mean it's a functional income, but yeah, my Dad's definitely helped me off and on."

"Is that awkward?"

"Yeah, it's pretty awkward. I'm turning forty. Like."

The wine arrived. Mariko felt a strong urge to get drunk. She needed to loosen up. She took two big sips.

"I think we shoulda had a kid," Dan said solemnly. "I think that was what we needed, and we missed the boat."

Mariko traced the top of her wine glass with her forefinger, thinking about Dan's claim. It didn't really strike her as true, just a mixture of nostalgia and insinuation. She sensed that he wanted to blame her for crushing their relationship from within and driving him towards his student (she refused to refer to Eliza by name). Dan wanted to say that an abundance of caution about commitment had led them to where they were now, or led him to the low state he currently occupied, but that struck Mariko as a selfish interpretation on his part, one which completely elided his own hubris. He hadn't needed her at all when he could take her for granted, and when he had career stability. Having kids was something he'd talk about once in a while; it was never something he'd *seriously* pushed for. No. If anything, she'd always felt that he would bring up having kids just to demonstrate that he wasn't against it in case she ever wanted it. He'd been so calculated; he'd never had any real passion for togetherness or family, but could she tell him that now?

"I guess, uh . . ." he said, when he could tell for sure that she wasn't going to say anything, "I guess I'm looking for a narrative that's something other than like . . . we destroyed each other . . . I'm looking for little slivers of . . . undestroyed . . . hope . . ."

"But what's the point of that?"

"I just want to feel like there were other trails in the garden of forking paths that didn't lead us where we are now."

"Sure there were. We didn't take them. But there were."

"Humor me then: what was a best case we missed out on?"

"Uh," Mariko stuttered. The truth was, she had long since stopped imagining alternatives to the way things were or had turned out between them. "Maybe just becoming amicable friends, and dating people who excited us more."

Dan's face dropped. "Ah."

"You might be reading Jane Austen my friend, but I'm not; I can't mentally project that world onto this one. What I see are two lonely, aging Millennials who couldn't figure out how to enjoy the consumption lifestyle together."

"Ah."

"Is that like, too harsh?"

"Well, it sounds like something I would have written if I was still writing. A material critique."

"I do think you influenced me to see things differently; I can tell you that."

"What a relief," he said dryly. "I'm not sure I even could call myself a socialist anymore actually."

"Really?"

"Yeah."

"That's hard to wrap my head around."

"I don't know what I am. Politically homeless."

"Makes sense given what happened."

"It's not because of that."

"I call bullshit."

Dan shrugged and downed his wine (he was drinking even faster than her). "On the road to $94."

"Seems like we could blow through that total at this rate."

"I fucking hate the West Village. Fuck."

"Are you alright, Dan?" she asked, peering across the table.

"Oh, I'm great. Amazing. Fantastic."

"Doesn't seem like it."

"Mariko, I honestly didn't know what loneliness was like until the past year . . . but I've just become insanely lonely. I told you about reading in Prospect Park, well, that's because I'm desperate for someone to ask me what I'm reading, same with coffee shops."

"Does anyone ever ask."

"Extremely rarely, and usually old people who like my taste in books."

"What's wrong with old people?"

"Nothing. But that doesn't solve my loneliness problem."

"I suppose not."

Dan gestured for another round, as Mariko finished her glass. "I don't think I realized how great it was just to have someone."

"I think you're in danger of saying having anything, anyone is better than nothing, which doesn't make me feel like I was valued for being me, more just like for being a warm body. I dunno."

"Can it be both? Could inherent warmth and inherent you-ness both be reasons to miss the past?"

"Uh . . ."

"I guess not."

"I never really felt like we could genuinely *be* married. I was watching the movie tonight, and I was just like: this isn't us. We were several steps away from *that*."

"I mean we were practically common-law married."

"No we weren't."

"I said practically."

"Why didn't you just value me when we were together, Dan?" Mariko said venomously, a little drunk off one glass.

"I didn't know how," he said truthfully.

"It just feels manipulative to sit here, running through all these scenarios in which we could have stayed together, when the reality was, we had lost something essential long before we both started acting up."

"I sorta wish you could get punished by society for having sex with an older man the way I got punished for having sex with a younger women."

"She was your student, Dan . . ."

"He was your director at one point . . ."

"You don't honestly think it was the same thing. I was in my thirties . . . We weren't working anymore."

"Not the first time you dated him . . ."

"Oh my god, really?"

"Why did I get wrecked, when other people got off, get off, literally, scot-free?"

"Dude, I don't make the rules."

"Sure, but you don't also seem to think about the contradictions in them."

"You might have a point there; I never thought about that particular point."

Dan nodded smugly, drinking the second glass of wine which had arrived. "I know you haven't."

"Alright, calm down."

"I'm calm."

"I'm not here to persecute; I've made that extremely clear; so you don't have to persecute me."

"Well, for a long time, I think you very much did join the prosecution."

"I was upset; it's true . . . but like . . ."

"No, you just reacted; you didn't stand up for me at all."

"What power did I even have to quote stand up for you?"

"I dunno. You could have even posted something on social media or something. Or even like, stuck by me in some definitive way."

"Oh wow. All you can really do is think of yourself, huh? And how I can best serve you . . ."

"No, I'm just saying you could have shown some backbone . . ."

"You're getting drunk."

"I'm not drunk; I'm totally lucid about what I'm saying."

Mariko thought they both were getting and sounding a little tipsy, but she was also aware that maybe there was a tiny kernel of truth, even with his flagrant narcissism, in what he was saying: she had immediately jumped ship; she had never considered doing anything else. It was a little ignoble, a little opportunistic, since she hadn't had the courage to end the relationship naturally. "Okay, I hear you."

"Do you?"

"I'm trying, yes."

"Sometimes, in my head, I curse my Mom, like, scream at her . . . I really feel like I regressed after she died. I started to become a teenager again in so many ways. I think I wanted you to be my mom, and I wanted to date teenagers; I wanted a second chance at adolescence, symbolically."

"Uh. Well. Okay. Okay."

"You don't have to respond to that, I know it's a weird thing to say."

"No . . . it's just a lot to untangle . . ."

"Life's hard."

"Yeah it is . . ."

They both drank in silence.

"I'm so sorry . . ." Dan exclaimed, putting his arms over his head, starting to cry. "I'm so so sorry. I'm so ashamed."

"It's okay . . ." Mariko murmured, reaching across the table, while looking around to see if anyone was watching. "It's really okay . . ."

"I'm such a jackass . . . I'm so so sorry. I fucked up something beautiful."

"It's okay . . ." she said, stroking what was left of the hair on his head. "It's okay . . ."

"It's not . . ." he sobbed. "It's so not . . ."

"Dan . . ."

"Adrenaline has been getting me through everything. Nothing is ever easy. Nothing is simple. I was so excited to see you tonight for some reason. Irrationally. Now I'm just crying. Wow."

"Dan, I love you."

"I love you too, Mari."

"But I can't be with you."

"I know. I don't think I can be with you either."

"I know."

10

Maybe it was all in the water, Dan thought, still groggy, turning the bathroom faucet (to drink from): moods, metabolic health, disease. Maybe it was all in his water, his food, in the plastics he used, the air he breathed.

Maybe the creature he was was a product of a century or more of ecological crisis: disorder, toxicity, breakdown.

Maybe he was drinking nothing but pesticide runoff and birth control.

His face was gray. His hair was going gray. He was prematurely aged. His body was the body of a poisoned environment: his testosterone was low; his serotonin was low; he didn't have much muscle. He looked like a prisoner of war.

After he lost his job, after his book contract was canceled, after he spent two months working as an Amazon labor organizer for $13 an hour, after tutoring Russian immigrants in Brighton Beach for $30 an hour, after failing to set high enough prices for the essays he had sold to graduate students (only $200 for fifteen pages?)—he gave in and started taking money from his father.

It would have been possible, perhaps, to have found a new academic job, but that would have meant leaving New York, hoping that the story didn't follow him; Title IX cases were closed, but rumors floated, reputations were vulnerable.

More importantly, it—taking money, not working, and finally allowing himself to tap into his father's latent guilt, into his own family tragedy, into his own social tragedy—felt *fucking good*. It felt good on mornings when he didn't have to prepare lecture notes, or nights when he didn't have to grade papers; it felt good to no longer spend enormous amounts of spiritual capital on the question of career advancement; it felt good to ignore the culture industry and give up his place within it.

Freed from having to earn, at least for the time being, he could be anonymous rather than one of the meritocratic elite.

But the doctor's capital was more than just a lifeline; the money he received from his father felt *productive of itself.* Money spawned money; it was talismanic, magic. Money wanted to be the only value and it spent itself ruthlessly in order to erase the memory and awareness of other kinds of wealth: spiritual, emotional, aesthetic. Money was covert metaphysics—and that was its appeal.

Dan climbed back into bed and spooned the shape that was half in the covers and half out. It barely moved.

"Morning."

Allison, his *Tinder* date from the night before, finally stirred, more than half asleep. Her hair was short and blue, her arms tatted. "What's up?"

"Do you want any breakfast? I'll happily make some"

"Aw. That's sweet, but I'm not really that hungry."

"Cool."

Dan had imagined a cozy breakfast together, potentially in bed, and he was a little disappointed that Allison didn't seem very enthusiastic. He wanted a slow, nostalgia-infused morning, a kind of relationship role-play. It was hard to deprogram the desire.

The night before, at a bar on Nostrand Ave, there had been a lot of talk about exes. Allison had just broken up with someone named Chris who worked as a bartender and she had moved out of the place they shared in Ridgewood. There was just too much about himself that he refused to work on, according to Allison; he wasn't changing or growing and he insisted on playing video games whenever he had free time. She and Chris were still fucking; the sex was still good, but it wasn't worth the moral and emotional costs of entrapment. That was the story at least.

For his part, Dan had devised an elaborate series of small lies that managed to elide the pith and substance of the last ten years of his life. Instead of an adjunct, he was a tutor; instead of a single long-term relationship, he had described a series of intertwining, unfulfilling affairs. And weirdly, he had begun to convince himself, at least over a few drinks, that he *was* the person he described to Allison (a person he wondered if he preferred). He really became Joseph—his middle name—and with considerable relief.

For a moment when she had asked for his IG, he'd panicked, but she bought the excuse that he simply didn't have social media; she just took it for granted that he was a geriatric, jaded hipster who was suspicious of the internet. What he didn't tell her was that he loved, *fucking loved*, the internet (loved the cognitive texture of it, loved the feeling of refreshing his *Twitter* feed)—and that Joseph (the offline guy) was the detritus, the fragment, the figment, of the deplatformed Dan (the ultimate online guy).

He was just worried about being Googled.

"Is there any coffee?"

"Yeah, I have a pot going."

"Rad," Allison said in a flat, affectionless tone, as she swung her whole body out of bed. "I'll def take some."

"How do you like it?" Dan asked as they both made their way into the kitchen, a small, narrow room wedged between his living room and bedroom, which had a tiny, circular table and two stools. There was good light, but not much of a view on the fourth floor.

"Do you have any stevia?"

"Stevia?"

"Yeah."

"No, sorry. I don't."

"Okay. No worries."

Something about Allison's presence made him nervous, even though he was too skin-hungry to disavow it and politely send her home.

The progressive lexicon Allison had used at dinner made him nervous. Each statement seemed to come with an adjacent threat: signal that you strongly agree—*or else*. In order to fuck, he had to pretend he agreed with her—just as he would have, unreflectively, proudly, a few years before. A progressive pariah, he had little choice but to act as if he were still one of the righteous.

In a sense, Dan had become an amphibian: liberal and reactionary— outwardly sympathetic and yet inwardly very, very angry and resentful. In a way, he had gone out with Allison because she resembled the type of woman he had started to hate, or had always hated all along. Joseph could be pleasant, accommodating, funny, even seductive, while Dan smoldered inside.

Dan began tapping his foot on the kitchen tile. "You still want coffee, right? Even without sweetener?"

"Yes please, lovely."

"Here ya go," Dan said with rote hospitality, taking a mug down from the cabinet and pouring out the French press.

"Well, thank you."

"Where do you live again?" Dan asked cooly.

"Crown Heights."

"Nice. Have you lived there for a long time?"

"Uh, like a year. I was in Bushwick before that."

"Bushwick sucks."

"Yeah, I'm over it," she said. "How long have you lived here?"

"About a year."

"Do you like it?"

"Definitely," he said sincerely. "The apartment's pre-war; there are trees outside; super lovely."

"What neighborhood is this again? Kensington?"

"Ditmas."

"Ah. I'm never down here."

"Yeah, I never was until I moved here."

They had nothing to say to each other. Observing her face closely in the morning light, it was clear (he'd had his suspicions) that she'd had at least lip filler and maybe a nose job at some point, which seemed increasingly standard for women in New York. This observation made him miss Mariko, whose beauty had always seemed effortless to him.

"Last night was fun," Dan murmured, brushing her neck with his lips.

"Totally."

"You don't sound enthusiastic."

"No, no—it was nice; I promise."

He wasn't sure whether she was just too groggy to make a quick exit, or whether there was some kind of genuine, repeatable connection. He felt genuinely out of his depth.

He moved his hands up along her arms and shoulders, massaging her briefly before pulling her close and kissing her on the neck and then the mouth. Her tongue slid into his mouth, and her hand reached for his dick. She was actually still into him.

"I have trouble getting hard in the morning unless I've had something to eat," Dan said after a minute of making out, aware that he wasn't responding properly and starting to panic.

"No problem," she said, with complete indifference, as if a second ago she had been anything other than moaning into, and licking, his ear.

"I uh—"

"Uh oh—"

"What?"

"You're gonna give me some sad simp story about your ex—"

"I already told you all about her—"

"Yeah, but it's always the morning after that the guy admits he still really loves her."

"I don't still really love her—that I can promise."

"Then who do you still really love?"

This struck him as an odd question. "No one."

"I don't believe you?"

"Why?"

"Because why else wouldn't you want to fuck me?"

The closeness of her body, even while it didn't turn him on, still kind of excited him in an abstract, almost intellectual way; it was still unbelievable that he could share intimate moments like this, with a total stranger, floating free of the gravity of his own reputation, experience, and social network.

"Coffee's cold," she complained between sips.

"This isn't a coffeeshop . . . sorry . . ."

"No. I just hate cold coffee. Sorry—that sounded bitchy."

"It's cool. No worries."

He listened to the platitudes pop out of his mouth, casually, into existence. Was it this easy? Was this simply how you dealt with people you weren't in any meaningful way tethered to?

"I hope you don't mind . . . that I'm like . . . you know I'm adjusting," she said, pitifully. "Like to this—like *Tinder*—just like you are, I mean."

"I totally get it."

"You're a sweet guy."

"I'm not sure if that's true—but that's kind of you," Dan said, staring at the floor.

The irony of his affair with Eliza, and the subsequent fallout, was that, after the initial despair, the initial sense of total annihilation, of atomization and alienation, he had begun to understand why the affair had happened in the first place; he had begun to understand how he had violated himself, denied himself a chance at real, romantic and erotic actualization and fulfillment, and how Eliza's decision to go public with their interaction was rooted, ultimately, in his own self-repulsion, in a self-hatred and disgust that he had transferred onto her through sex.

"Joseph—"

"What's up?"

"It's absolutely fine if you don't like me that much."

"Whaddya mean?"

"I mean, if you found me wanting physically or something, like—"

"I think you're super sexy."

"Well thanks stranger."

"You're welcome."

Dan kissed her on the nape of her neck. "Does that feel good?

"Yes . . ."

Allison *was* pretty hot (Dan had to admit) and good at fucking. Turning her on her belly and fucking from behind made him feel super good, confident. "I'm so into you."

"I don't really like to pretend." There was something so cold about her voice.

"Pretend what?"

"Well, that this is going to be anything."

"I would be stoked if it did," he said, lying again, but lying in such a way that he forced himself to believe it. "Go somewhere—"

"If I'm being honest . . . it just annoys me when dudes pretend they want like a relationship when they clearly don't—"

Dan bit his bottom lip nervously. "I'm not trying to be manipulative, but I do think a relationship is something I want," Dan reiterated, really beginning to convince himself. "I mean, it's something I've always wanted and I've never really wanted things to end when they do; I think relationships are good for people. I'm old-fashioned, I guess. Or I am now. I've become old fashioned with age."

"To be completely honest, I'm always a little dubious of older dudes who are perpetually single."

She was the erotic merchant; he was the buyer, and they were haggling.

"Why do you keep saying 'dudes'? It's a little alienating."

"Men. Boys. Penis-humans. Whatever you want, *dude*."

"Also, I'm not perpetually single; I'm just single right now."

"Gotcha."

"I'm gonna start cooking breakfast."

"I still want you to fuck me again, just to be clear?"

He got up and opened the fridge. "Do you mind if I make breakfast first?"

"I wouldn't love it," Allison said, taken aback, "but it's your house."

"You wouldn't have eggs right?"

"I've been a strict vegan since I was seventeen, so no thanks."

"Gotcha, gotcha," he mumbled passive-aggressively.

He took the eggs out of the carton, cracked two in a bowl, took a fork out from the drawer, whisked, and put the fork down. Then, taking a knife from the door, he lashed open the packet of cheap bodega bacon and threw it into the pan (which still had the remnants of bacon grease from earlier in the week and which had not been cleaned).

Out of the corner of his eye, he watched Allison and tried to gauge how put off she was. Maybe regular, functional, undamaged men just spent mornings in bed fucking; maybe that's what she was used to. Maybe they had cool record collections and fancy coffee and made funky plant-based scrambles and rode scooters to work and all that shit. Or maybe everyone was fumbling and unsure.

"I'm gonna go chill in the living room," Allison, who had taken out her phone, announced, "while you go cook."

"The smell is intense, sorry . . ."

"Yeah, I'm trippin."

Dan stabbed at the now mostly crispy bacon with a fork, lifting the six or so strands onto a plate, pouring the battered eggs into the now vacant pan. The eggs popped and sizzled in the heavy grease. Bacon grease was the best way to cook eggs. In the intense residual heat, the omelet would be done quickly.

Dan wasn't really sure why Allison was still there, and he wasn't really sure whether he was hoping she'd excuse herself or stay. He felt completely at a loss about what "connecting" with another person really entailed, any-more, and it seemed better if he didn't try at all. They had used each oth-er's bodies—it gave him a thrill to think someone would want to use *his* body—and that was that, that had to be that.

When he was done with the omelet, which he ate rapidly, barely chew-ing, Dan ducked his head into the bathroom, took a swig of Listerine, and returned to the living room, where Allison was patiently waiting, reading the most recent issue of *n+1*, which Dan stubbornly refused to stop subscribing to even though he had long since ceased to read more than the Editor's Note.

"Yo yo."

"Hey caveman."

"You're still here."

"It's not like you heard me leave."

"In my head, you were dying to go."

"No, but I want you to fuck me. Like stick your cock deep in my pussy and fuck the shit out of me. You've got a nice cock, by the way—"

"Really?"

She smiled. "Yes really."

"You're trolling me."

"Wow, low-confidence."

"Guilty."

"Come sit next to me."

"Alright," Dan said, sitting beside her obediently.

She stroked his greasy hair back and kissed him flush on the mouth. He felt his cock stir, to his immense relief, and kissed back, running his hand under the back of her T-shirt (really his T-shirt). Impatiently, she rubbed his cock through his boxers and moaned. He moaned, echoing her and trying to work himself up.

"God I want you," she whispered in his ear.

He was stuck at half-mast. He closed his eyes while she kissed his neck and continued to rub his cock. He tugged her shirt off and kissed her breasts, which lay flat against her chest in a kind of prematurely aged, matronly way. He regretted throwing away all his Cialis, which he had blamed, probably rightly, for his own overt aggressiveness with Eliza.

Eliza.

Her body kept flashing before him like a jump cut.

Eliza.

He hated her so much.

Perversely though, thinking about Eliza with his eyes shut, while Allison touched him all over had the right effect: his cock swelled past the threshold of functionality.

Allison slipped from the couch, pulled off his boxers, and started to blow him. He was completely inert, submissive. The more he tried to move, the less he was able to move, slipping into a state of complete erotic relaxation, his body and mind separate, like oil and water. Allison stood up, slipped off her rose-pink underwear, pushed him back lengthwise onto the couch, and mounted him, moaning loudly.

He badly wanted to whisper, "Eliza."

It never occurred to him to summon images of Mariko, who stood for something very different in his mind.

"I'm gonna cum," Allison announced as she rocked back and forth.

Dan let forth a moan just to demonstrate that he was still linked to her, which, in a way he was.

"Can you cum with me?" she asked, letting slip a hint of vulnerability—an unfulfilled wish (replacing her ex). "Joseph—cum with me—"

Dan, self-enclosed, infinitely distant, was, in his solipsistic way, deeply turned on and ready to finish. Her fingers raked his chest; her hips dug into his hips.

"I'm cumming," he whispered, as he imagined ejaculating into Eliza. "I'm cumming."

Allison, completely unaware of what he was feeling, completely indifferent to it, completely hooked into her own physical needs (as was her right), slumped down, sweaty against his chest. "That was fun."

"Yeah," he said panting, opening his eyes, attempting to reconnect, "super fun."

"Well, I should go," she said, as she rolled off of him and gathered her clothing from the living room floor. "I've got stuff to do."

11

The sisters are whispering when Suzanne returns from the bathroom: they don't want her to hear what they're talking about.

"Suzanne, can you hold Olivia for a second? It's my turn to pee." Mariko stands up and hands the younger woman the child, who is two and giggly and generally pretty happy-seeming, but at the moment very, very sleepy.

Akari shoots her lover a look from the floor, where she is sitting in a relaxed pose, one leg curled in, the other straight out, like she is doing yoga or stretching. "I still can't believe I'm an aunt."

"Really?" Suzanne replies.

"I think I have a permanent case of arrested development."

"You'll adjust."

Akari looks great and she knows it; it's like she's growing younger. She's been doing so much yoga and whatever skin-care routine she's on is fucking amazing in Suzanne's opinion.

"My sister's getting fat," Akari whispers into Suzanne's ear. "I think she was waiting to get married to let go."

Suzanne giggles and holds her palms open to signal that she can make no further comment.

"She really is though. You should have seen her like when she was your age. She was so gorgeous. You would have fallen in love with her."

"I bet."

Suzanne thinks this is a strange thing to say.

Mariko returns from the bathroom and takes the cooing toddler from Suzanne's arms.

Olivia coos and giggles. Mariko kisses her forehead and whirls her around. "Wheee."

Akari and Suzanne exchange glances. The lovers were looking forward to their flight in the evening; they've been here for four days and the apartment is beginning to feel claustrophobic; plus, they've been sleeping on a pullout.

Akari says she should just start getting a hotel in New York and Suzanne agrees; Akari can afford it.

"Being trapped together is a family tradition," Akari told Suzanne before they left, and Suzanne is beginning to understand. The sisters do not seem to be able to distinguish between toxic and benign behaviors and communication styles.

Suzanne stands up and stretches and looks out the window. She likes Bedstuy (the neighborhood which Mariko and her new husband, Tim, have only recently adopted as their own).

All Suzanne can think about, watching Mariko play with little Olivia, is how ridiculously, stupidly ordinary, repeatable, universal, and human the scene is . . . how it's happened billions of times before, and will happen a billion times in the future. She wonders if this is not the most significant thing: the sameness of people.

She doesn't really want to think about it.

Mariko has been crying in the bathroom, but it couldn't have been for that long, but Suzanne can tell that tears have been shed. Apparently Mariko cries a lot now, and for good reason. Or just for reasons. Or just because.

Akari doesn't care though; Akari gives zero fucks. Suzanne thinks Akari is done with her sister, done with the whole saga, done with pity and routinized empathy.

All they do is pick at each other; it's so passive aggressive.

People learn this kind of behavior from their parents, Suzanne thinks. Akari and Mariko learned how to compromise, deflect, and suppress from their parents, and little Olivia will learn the same thing from her mother and her aunt; the little fragments of tragedy will pass through Olivia into the future.

The windows are open; it is a cool, bright day; dried leaves toss and crumble in the street.

Suzanne doesn't envy this family, which is barely a family, and more like a vague confederacy of unhappy, co-dependent people (with the possible exception of Tim, Mariko's husband).

Suzanne is uncomfortable with the idea that she fits into this: Akari's family. She doesn't want to resemble them, doesn't want to be like them.

"Should we order some food?" Mariko asks. "What do you want, Suzanne? My treat?"

"What do you have in mind?"

"Something yummy."

"That's helpful."

Olivia is getting rammy, so Mariko puts her down, and the baby crawls across the hardwood floor towards Akari.

"Such a cutie . . ." Akari says, beaming, picking up the gurgling child.

Does Akari imagine adopting kids? Or getting inseminated? Or asking a guy friend of hers to just fuck her (or Suzanne)? Is that in the back of her mind somewhere? Does she want to be one of those cool, queer, artsy moms? Does she want to raise a child with a twenty-six-year-old filmmaker who still sometimes gets acne? Who worries about money all the time? Who uses *TikTok*? Who doesn't read?

Suzanne has no relationship to this adult world of child-bearing, to the world of early middle age, to the time when you begin to admit that the best part of your own life is over.

Her story is just beginning.

She can't wait to get back to California and sleep in a bed with Akari again and to be able to fuck and be loud and in love again, to be sloppy together. Even though they've been sleeping on the same futon on this trip, Suzanne still feels like she misses Akari; it's like they're a thousand miles apart. Akari changes around her sister: she becomes competitive and cruel. She *wants* to embody everything that her sister is not. She wants to win.

Suzanne doesn't blame Akari, however, because she's the same way with her own brother, so she gets it.

"Have you been crying?" Akari asks Mariko, who looks away.

"Does it matter?"

"It matters to me."

"For the wrong reason—"

Akari looks at Suzanne. "What do *you* think, Suzanne? Doesn't Mariko just *feed* on other people's unhappiness?"

"Please don't include me . . ."

"Yeah, don't rope her into this—"

At this point Mariko starts crying openly. Akari moves to comfort her, but Mariko brushes her away. "Stop. Just let me be."

"What's wrong?"

Mariko doesn't even bother to respond to this question; she just raises her eyebrows, incredulously.

"I wish you would move on . . ."

"I can't . . ." Mariko glances at Olivia on the floor.

It's all super awkward.

"I can't—" Mariko repeats, "and you know why I can't . . . and again . . . I feel like you're just enjoying all of this so much; you're showing off in front of Su—"

"How the fuck—"

"You like acting like the older sibling, like—"

"Oh god, really? You really believe—"

"I mean you're proving it—"

"I'm not proving anything."

Suzanne can tell that Olivia can tell that something is wrong. It's amazing how adults pretend like children aren't there until they're old enough to articulate themselves in complete, cogent sentences.

Suzanne doesn't admire the way Akari has been behaving this week.

It can be so embarrassing, Suzanne reflects, to see someone you love · operating outside of the context in which you fell in love with them; the new context is usually unflattering. You see the beloved free of illusions, in raw, even harsh light—like an old house in the winter, when the trees are bare and the gardens and ivy have withered away.

Later in the day, Suzanne starts to feel a little sick: sore throat, running nose, a headache that makes her a little woozy. Akari takes her to a health food store to get elderberry and zinc, which helps her feel a little bit better. Her Covid test is negative. She is really ready to get the fuck out of New York.

Mariko keeps picking her cuticles, which are a bloody mess at this point. They'll probably never heal. She literally needs to keep the wounds open. It must keep her calm.

Suzanne knows very few women who haven't harmed their body in some way.

She doesn't really know anyone who hasn't harmed themselves.

"Mom is gonna fly out next week to take Olivia off our hands. Tim and I are gonna go upstate for a few days."

"And do what?"

"Just decompress. My friend has a little house that she's lending me."

"Who?"

"A friend from college. She and her husband bought a country spot. It's nice. I just—"

"Who?"

"Why does it matter?"

"I dunno, I just don't believe you."

"What's there not to believe?" Mariko asks, exasperated.

"I never get to meet any of your friends."

"I don't have that many."

"Let's order take out—"

"You need to tell me what you want? We can do *Seamless* or something—" Mariko pulls out her phone. "Here, just order whatever you want. It's on me."

"It's on your husband," Akari laughs.

"Actually, I booked a commercial recently. So, literally, my money. Enjoy."

"I'll try," Akari says flatly.

"I know, I know—you're the real working artist in the family—I'm just a pretender . . ."

"When did you start resenting me so much, huh? I don't remember."

"I couldn't tell you. Sometimes, you just wake up feeling a certain way."

"So you do—"

"Yep. For sure. There's some resentment." Mariko says this without emotion.

Suzanne can tell that her tone hurts Akari—but Akari never admits to being hurt.

The sisters used to be best friends until a few years ago. Now things are more strained, adversarial.

"Why don't we just do sushi?" Mariko asks.

Akari gags. "FUCK. No."

"Why not?"

"Because it won't be real sushi."

"Snob."

"I'm just saying."

"So what do you want?"

"Food is confusing. Something healthy."

"Salads?"

When Mariko finally places an order, Suzanne can see that Akari is a little thrown off by the idea that her sister is *suddenly* making decent money doing commercial acting; there's always an aura around making money from your "art" even if it's commercial work. It's so impressive to get that check.

Akari always slips in references to her payouts from shooting commercials—that's really how she pays the bills (serious films are a pittance). Suzanne doesn't think Akari likes the competition from her sister; she was beginning to take it for granted that she had *won*; she had assumed Mariko had simply settled on being a stay-at-home mom with a husband in finance.

Akari's slender back, floating in a delicate outline under the dress: Suzanne has the incredible urge to run her hands over it. *There she is*, she says to herself. *There is my lover.*

You can love someone even while you know all the things that are wrong with them, or perhaps because you know all the things that are wrong with them. Love isn't about goodness or purity or anything like that—just about acceptance.

People live by the capacity to forget quickly and completely and that's how they love too. You have to: you have to forget. You have to go to sleep a little bit, you can't be completely awake and remain with someone.

Akari is impulsive, greedy, shallow, needy—but also remarkably talented, intuitive, charming, smart. There's no separating the two sides of her; there's no idealizing Akari. Akari is just a person in her life—*the* person in her life. They're lucky to have each other, Suzanne thinks.

The next morning, Suzanne is in the kitchen making tea, before anyone else is up. Her throat is still a little sore, but *whatever*. Their flight is at one and Suzanne is neurotic about having all her shit together; she's always early; flying is one of the few things she's type A about.

The kitchen is small; there's just room for a little stool; the dining table is in the living room. The apartment gets good light in the morning though, and it's much prettier than the place they used to live in in Greenpoint, which Suzanne only visited once.

Suzanne likes early mornings; she's always been a morning person, even in high school because she was on the swim team. You can think when you're up before everybody else; it's the enchanted pause before the day becomes relentless.

In these moments Suzanne is a completely different person. She can sit still, not check her phone. Just be. Just relax. Breathe.

Akari says Suzanne carries a lot of tension and often gives her a neck and back massage before bed. Somehow, the tension never really goes away though.

Suzanne had to take a leave of absence her second year of college because she got so stressed; she was taking eighteen credits and literally didn't sleep (thanks to Adderall). She could go like five or six hours in a row without getting up to pee, which was a little bit dangerous, but also fun. Sometimes, her body would begin to involuntarily piss, and she'd have to run to the bathroom in a state of shock.

If Suzanne did sleep, it was in the middle of the afternoon, after classes were over. Her roommates would come home and find her passed out on the couch of their common room. She wouldn't even be able to make it to her bed.

Her grandparents sent her to hippie rehab that spring, during medical leave. It was in Colorado and lasted four weeks; it would have been longer, but the insurance only covered four.

In Colorado, Suzanne had a girlfriend and a boyfriend. She didn't tell them about each other, and they never guessed at each other's existence, and she never said anything to Akari.

She doesn't mention any of this—any of the things she's thinking about—when Mariko comes in to make coffee. Mariko is working a brunch shift at her restaurant, then she has an audition at four. There's a sitter on the way. Suzanne finds all this out relatively quickly.

Mariko looks groggy; she's wearing funny, frumpy pajamas.

Suzanne is already dressed, having woken up early and showered. Mariko seems surprised that Suzanne is a morning person; it seems to belie the rest of her personality.

Akari, on the other hand, will sleep to the very last minute and then order an *Uber* in a panic to get to the airport.

The kitchen is very peaceful. Mariko and Suzanne don't say anything for a while. There seems to be an understanding between the two women. They've both, in their own and very different ways, been through a lot the past few years.

If people could live every hour like it was dawn, they would be very happy, Suzanne thinks. It's hard to panic at dawn; it's hard to take things too seriously—you're in that perfect, half-awake state—half-awake, but completely receptive.

Mariko seems ready to have her apartment back. Akari and Suzanne have been a little messy (Akari almost on purpose—out of spite), and Akari has been high as shit most of the time.

If Akari and Suzanne break up at some point, which speaking rationally, is likely at some point—then Suzanne will never see Mariko again. The kitchen is silent because, in a sense, there is no rational incentive to talk. This is a transitory moment: Why ruin it with small talk beyond "good morning" and "would you like some coffee?"

"Hey Suzanne . . ." Mariko says softly, while she's looking out the window, towards the back garden, cultivated by the old couple that lives here, which is tangled with trees, bushes, and flowers. "I have a question."

"Shoot."

"I'm not sure I want to ask it."

"You should—"

"I just wonder what you think of us."

"Who? You and I—"

"Yeah yeah yeah. This house."

"I dunno," Suzanne says dumbly, "you're cool."

"That's not what I am asking."

"I dunno what else you want me to say. Like."

"I feel like you judge me."

"For what?"

"It's hard to say exactly, but."

"But . . ."

"Maybe I'm just projecting . . ."

"Yeah . . . maybe you are . . ." the younger woman mumbles.

Mariko seems to be lost in thought. She's pacing in small zigzags, as if she's tracing invisible lines on the floor. "I guess you don't know what it's like to live in a state of disgrace, do you?" she says, not making eye contact.

"Uh, nope. I do not. I don't think so . . ."

"It's really shitty, don't try it."

"I wasn't planning on it, no."

"It's strange . . . it's funny . . ." She's clearly been waiting to talk to someone. "I never knew why I was acting . . . I don't think I even knew how to act . . . until I gave up on quote 'serious' acting . . . and just like, accepted that my life kinda sucked. Which was recently actually, and . . . now, I'm beginning to understand what an artist's life *means* . . . like, literally, it's been coming to me in flashes. It means giving up this fucking bizarre American obsession with *happiness*. It means bathing in your own filth, your own bullshit—covering yourself head to toe with your own stink. It sounds absurd, but . . ." Suzanne is listening, Mariko's still pacing; she keeps talking. "Having a child changes everything; you immediately become less selfish, you immediately start to lose your obsession with yourself. Or you're clearly supposed to—which is why narcissistic parents are the worst. I guess my Dad was a little bit like that. My Dad was—*is*—a very vain person. Okay—and so is my mother. My parents are a little narcissistic—quietly so . . . And they um . . . I have to embrace what *they* did to *me*—just like I have to embrace what he . . . I have to really admit that there's this deep wound left by the lack of love in my upbringing. We said we loved each other and all that crap—but it wasn't true enough, you know? I got into the habit of believing that love really just was some crap you said before bed. 'Love you Mom, Love you Dad. Love you honey.' I don't want to raise my daughter just so that I have someone to talk to, you know?"

"Yeah, that makes sense."

"Does it?" Mariko asks, clearly anxious for her thoughts to be recognized as valid.

"Yep," Suzanne says, as if they were talking about nothing at all.

"Okay . . ." She's disappointed; she wants Suzanne to be more engaged—but what does she expect?

Suzanne is starting to feel a little guilty, however, because Mariko's clearly super lonely—and worse: completely lost.

"You don't have to feel sorry for me," Mariko adds, somewhat stating the obvious.

"I don't . . . I know . . ." Suzanne responds, which is true.

"I have a great life. There's been a lot of sadness, but, I'm still lucky . . . I have fragments of a life that could have been great, or at least, um. Fulfilling—and um . . . Like. There's nothing I want other than to wake up and feel—not happy, that would be lame—but like, determined. I want to point in one direction, not ten. I feel like I haven't started yet; that I've been looking for my start, like I'm looking for a lost penny. Something small, and almost worthless, but . . . not completely without value at the same time . . . like. Living is formless. And flat. Like living in the middle of a vast plain, with nothing but a few dead trees in every direction—it's hard to know . . . it's hard to know if you should stay put . . . and dig for water . . . or head out towards the horizon. It's deep space. There's no west or east or north or south. There's everywhere and it's all open . . . I think um. I mean, there's something seriously fucked up about me. I should be more diligent about therapy; I'm so self-undercutting—and I'm gonna pass that onto Olivia . . . I can see her going into acting or the arts just to compensate for me not entirely making it . . ." She bites her nails. "I don't know how to *not* burden my daughter with everything that I'm not."

"Hmm," Suzanne grunts, to indicate that she's still actively listening. "You've gone through something extremely difficult—"

"You know that feeling, when you're a little kid," Mariko starts up again, ignoring what Suzanne just said completely, "when you're sitting with your parents, maybe watching TV or something, and you can smell them, and they're so warm . . . and I guess like, it's a summer night, an evening—or maybe you're outside, having a picnic—not inside—and um, you *feel* that everything is perfect . . . ? You know that feeling? I've never gotten over losing it. I've never . . . I've never been able to compensate for the love that I had then—that feeling that earth itself *is* love. I've never forgiven the world for being a much scarier or darker place than I thought it was when I was five years old. Which makes me a coward."

"I don't think that's being fair to yourself, like . . ."

"It's more than fair, Suzanne . . ."

"I'm not entirely sure why you're telling me this, but . . ."

"It's so peaceful."

"Yeah." Suzanne looks down at the backyard, which is getting lighter and lighter. "It is."

Mariko brushes back her hair, which is black and shiny, and sighs, then brushes it back again, squares up, and looks Suzanne in her eye. "Do more than just survive, Suzanne, that's my advice."

"Why do you say that?"

"Because that's what I did. And even though I'm trying to change, the habit might be too strong for me."

"What's the alternative?"

"Risk everything, constantly."

"That's so romantic."

"Yeah, I'm saying: be romantic."

"I am romantic though—" Suzanne insists.

Suzanne is pretty hungry, so she opens the fridge and removes a half-eaten yogurt from the night before. It is one of those whole fat, grass-fed yogurts with a layer of cream on top. It's really good—but she ate the creamy part the night before and it's gotten a little watery.

Suzanne is taller than Mariko, and Suzanne can't help but make the gesture of eating her yogurt feel a little demeaning; Suzanne is basically looking right over the top of her head.

"How are things with—?"

"They're good," Suzanne answers right away, mouth full of yogurt. "We're happy."

"That's good . . ."

"What?" Suzanne wonders what she's thinking.

"Nothing . . ."

"You sure?"

"Olivia's gonna wake up soon."

"She wakes up this early?"

"Toddlers are random, like electrons."

"You've been a great hostess, by the way. I appreciate it."

"It's nothing. Thanks for watching Olivia when I've been at work. You didn't have to do that."

"It's nothing." Suzanne smiles at her.

At this point, she's just ready for Akari to wake up, to call a car, and to get out of here; she can't help but feel that it's dangerous to absorb too much more of *this*—to stay in this house much longer.

"I'm bothering you," Mariko says, as if she can read her mind.

"No, no . . . you're not; it's okay."

"I'm bothering you—I'll go—I should check on Olivia; she wakes up sometimes and if no one's there she gets upset—"

It sounds like Mariko's trying to talk herself into something.

Suzanne realizes that Mariko's never gonna open up about the suicide. She'll just keep indirectly alluding to it for the rest of her life. It will just permeate the room like too much perfume. It will linger. It will never go away.

Suzanne just wants to go home.

The urge to wake up Akari gets stronger and stronger.

She just wants to fall asleep on Akari's shoulder on the plane and forget about this. It's only been four days, but she hates being out of her routine. She's tired of being the buffer.

"What's up?" Mariko says, picking up on Suzanne's energy.

"What's an example of a truth that gets you to change your life?"

"That's what I'm trying to figure out."

"So what happens if you don't figure it out?"

"Then I think you disappear inside your own mistakes," Mariko says thoughtfully, "like a bird disappearing into a cloud."

Suzanne puts her phone on airplane mode. Akari plays *Candy Crush* next to her. The whole airplane hums with quiet busyness; people put their things away, settling in, tuning out, getting ready to fall asleep. That's all Suzanne can focus on: the plane getting airborne, and that gentle feeling that settles over airplanes once they're at altitude.

You just float along in your giant air pocket (almost like you're swimming with your eyes closed). The plane could begin to fall, and you might not even notice. The engines could shut off, altitude could suddenly drop, people could begin to scream, and it's possible that you could still be asleep. It just depends on how deep a sleep it is. If it's deep enough, nothing can harm you. There's no fear; there's no disturbance. You just have to keep your eyes closed, your earbuds in. It's not just biological sleep—it's a deeper, truer sleep than that: the sleep of the soul.

Less than one percent of one percent of one percent of what could happen, will happen, Suzanne thinks. Of the infinite universes that are possible, she's stuck in this one. Of the infinite thoughts she could have, she's having this one. For no good reason. Just because.

Suzanne keeps flashing to an image of Dan hanging from a ceiling fan (an event she was not present for, but which is nevertheless indelible in her memory).

"Did you bring any snacks?" Akari asks, nudging Suzanne.

"I brought some almonds, do you want me to get them?"

"No, that's okay, it's fine. I'll just eat later."

"Okay," Suzanne says, closing her eyes. "Wake me up when we land."